"Can books be better than television? You bet they can—when Lee Goldberg's writing them."
—Lee Child

Praise for the *Monk* Mysteries

Mr. Monk Goes to Germany

"The story flows so smoothly it's effortless to read."
—*CrimeSpree Magazine*

Mr. Monk in Outer Space

"You say you don't read tie-in novels? You should give the *Monk* books a try and find out what you've been missing. They're funny, they're well written, they're carefully plotted, and they're poignant."   —Bill Crider

Mr. Monk and the Two Assistants

"Even if you aren't familiar with the TV series *Monk*, this book is too funny to not be read."
—The Weekly Journal

Mr. Monk and the Blue Flu

"A must-read if you enjoy Monk's mysteries on the tube."   —Bookgasm

continued . . .

The Monk Series

Mr. Monk Goes to Germany

Mr. Monk in Outer Space

Mr. Monk and the Two Assistants

Mr. Monk and the Blue Flu

Mr. Monk Goes to Hawaii

Mr. Monk Goes to the Firehouse

MR. MONK
IS MISERABLE

A Novel by
Lee Goldberg

Based on the USA Network television series created by

Andy Breckman

AN OBSIDIAN MYSTERY

OBSIDIAN
Published by New American Library, a division of
Penguin Group (USA) Inc., 375 Hudson Street,
New York, New York 10014, USA
Penguin Group (Canada), 90 Eglinton Avenue East, Suite 700, Toronto,
Ontario M4P 2Y3, Canada (a division of Pearson Penguin Canada Inc.)
Penguin Books Ltd., 80 Strand, London WC2R 0RL, England
Penguin Ireland, 25 St. Stephen's Green, Dublin 2,
Ireland (a division of Penguin Books Ltd.)
Penguin Group (Australia), 250 Camberwell Road, Camberwell, Victoria 3124,
Australia (a division of Pearson Australia Group Pty. Ltd.)
Penguin Books India Pvt. Ltd., 11 Community Centre, Panchsheel Park,
New Delhi - 110 017, India
Penguin Group (NZ), 67 Apollo Drive, Rosedale, North Shore 0632,
New Zealand (a division of Pearson New Zealand Ltd.)
Penguin Books (South Africa) (Pty.) Ltd., 24 Sturdee Avenue,
Rosebank, Johannesburg 2196, South Africa

Penguin Books Ltd., Registered Offices:
80 Strand, London WC2R 0RL, England

Published by Obsidian, an imprint of New American Library, a division of Penguin Group (USA) Inc. Previously published in an Obsidian hardcover edition.

First Obsidian Mass Market Printing, June 2009
10 9 8 7 6 5 4 3 2 1

Copyright © 2008 *Monk* © USA Cable Entertainment LLC. All rights reserved

The Edgar® name is a registered service mark of the Mystery Writers of America, Inc.

OBSIDIAN and logo are trademarks of Penguin Group (USA) Inc.

Printed in the United States of America

To Philippe Bisson and Andrée Candela

ACKNOWLEDGMENTS
AND AUTHOR'S NOTE

My wife, Valerie, is French, so I have visited Paris often over the past twenty years. There are many places real and imagined in this book. I apologize, especially to all of my in-laws, for any geographical or historical liberties I have taken to suit my twisted creative needs.

The events in this story take place before the TV episode "Mr. Monk Is on the Run" and pick up where my book *Mr. Monk Goes to Germany* left off.

And, once again, I must thank the good and patient people of Lohr, Germany, and my friends Hermann Joha, Elke Schubert, Heiko Schmidt, Jasmine Steigler, Alexander Schust and the staff of the Franziskushohe Hotel for their help.

I would also like to thank Dr. D. P. Lyle, Cara Black, Lee Lofland, Alexia Barlier and forensic anthropologist Gwen Haugen for their technical advice, which I've probably misunderstood and used in all the wrong ways.

I found several books extremely helpful in my research, particularly *Paris Sewers and Sewermen* by Donald Reid, *Paris Souterrain* by Emmanuel Gaffard, *Paris Underground* by Caroline Archer and *Subterranean Cities* by David L. Pike.

As usual, this book would not have been possible without the enthusiasm and support of Andy Breckman, Kristen Weber, Kerry Donovan, Gina Maccoby, and Madison Goldberg. *Merci beaucoup!*

This book was written in Paris, Munich, New York, South Lake Tahoe, Pittsburgh and Los Angeles ... and in airplanes in between.

I look forward to hearing from you at www.leegoldberg.com.

1

Mr. Monk in Germany

If you think you have any control over your life, you are fooling yourself. You have no idea what is coming your way.

I'm not talking about those sudden, and often tragic, life-changing surprises like getting hit by a car, or the death of a loved one, or a hurricane wiping away your home.

I'm talking about the unexpected changes that make things a lot more interesting and put you in situations you never dreamed might happen.

For instance, if anybody had told me that I'd be spending a week in a picturesque village in Germany with Adrian Monk I never would have believed it.

In fact, I would have said it was impossible.

That's because it takes all of Monk's courage and will-power just to step outside his carefully organized and completely disinfected San Francisco apartment.

He's afraid of germs, splinters, coloring books, mixed nuts, lint, curly hair, milk, sleeveless T-shirts, balls of yarn, dust bunnies, Neil Diamond, bird droppings, untucked shirts, granola, Chia Pets, and so many other things that he's created a list of his phobias that spans several leather-bound volumes with footnotes, historical references, photographs, diagrams, and a detailed index.

Monk also believes that everything he sees, and everyone he meets, must adhere to his ridiculously arcane rules of order. Basically, he wants everything to be even, straight, balanced, symmetrical, organized, and consistent. And since nature and humanity generally refuse to comply, Monk finds the outside world to be a constant source of frustration and anxiety.

Nevertheless, his comfort zone has grown to include places beyond his Pine Street apartment and his shrink's office in Pacific Heights. But he gets twitchy if we cross the city limits, and he begins to hyperventilate if we dare to step into the next county. He doesn't like to travel across the Bay Bridge without a life vest, six months' worth of provisions, a priest, and a trailer containing all of his furniture, bedding, and dishes.

All of this makes life very hard for Monk, who copes with it by employing a full-time assistant to run interference for him. That poor soul happens to be me, Natalie Teeger. I have no formal training for this kind of thing, unless you count being the widowed, single mother of a young teenager.

It's not easy being his assistant, because not only do I have to head off a multitude of potential disasters just so he can function in society, but I also have to be his personal shopper, driver, secretary, and able-bodied investigative assistant.

Monk is a consultant to the San Francisco Police Department, where he worked as a homicide detective until his wife, Trudy, a journalist, was killed by a car bomb—a loss that left him crippled with grief and unable to control his phobias for years.

He still hasn't solved her murder, but since then he's closed hundreds of other puzzling cases that have stumped Captain Leland Stottlemeyer and his detectives. And I've been Monk's Dr. Watson, Kato, Rico Tubbs, and Boy Wonder all rolled into one.

Monk's obsessive need to put everything in order has given him this amazing ability to spot clues and inconsistencies that nobody else can see.

It's a gift and a curse, as he often says.

His investigative process, like everything else in his life, can be an arduous and exasperating experience even in the best of times, which was the period we were enjoying a week earlier.

Monk was happy more often than he was sad, was a lot less picky about things, and was solving puzzling murders at a brisk pace that astounded Stottlemeyer and Lieutenant Randy Disher, his right-hand man.

As grateful as Stottlemeyer was for Monk's assistance, his ego was getting bruised.

"I don't know why I even bother showing up anymore," Stottlemeyer said to me at one crime scene. "I could stand here for a month and not see what Monk does in five seconds."

"But you can pour yourself a bowl of Cap'n Crunch for breakfast," I said. "He fills his bowl one piece of cereal at a time to be sure they are perfectly square and that he has an even number of them."

"I'd trade my bowl of Cap'n Crunch for his detective instincts."

"He's afraid of wind."

"You mean like a tornado or a hurricane?"

"I mean any breeze at all," I said. "He has nightmares about being chased by tumbleweeds."

"But there aren't any tumbleweeds in San Francisco."

"Monk says it could happen," I said. "And when it does, we'll know our day of reckoning has come."

Stottlemeyer smiled, rubbed his bushy mustache, and seemed to feel better after that. He didn't have Monk's keen eye for detail, but at least he never had to worry about tumbleweeds.

So everybody was content. Things were good.

But then Monk's shrink, Dr. Kroger, announced at the end of one of their sessions that he was going to Lohr, Germany, to attend a psychiatric conference.

Monk had a complete mental and emotional meltdown. And that was just his immediate reaction. Things got even worse after Dr. Kroger left the country.

Monk was hysterical one moment, catatonic the next.

He forgot how to swallow. He forgot how to breathe. And he lost his ability to solve crimes.

So in an act of desperation and insanity that will probably go down in the annals of stalking history, Monk decided to follow his psychiatrist to Germany.

And I went with him.

I know what you're thinking—at least Monk had an excuse for his crazy behavior, but I should have known better. As a rational, intelligent, law-abiding woman, I should have talked Monk out of it or, failing that, found a way to have him locked up for his own good.

But it's my job to help Monk function, and he couldn't without psychiatrist appointments. So the obvious solution was to get him back together with his shrink, no matter what. I was simply acting in Monk's best interests.

I would be lying, though, if I didn't admit that I also had a few reasons of my own for not stopping Monk. I wanted to get even with Dr. Kroger for tacitly encouraging Monk to invite himself along on my Hawaiian vacation a few years ago.

A trip to Europe would atone for my ruined Hawaiian getaway, which I'd spent tagging along with Monk while he solved a murder instead of swimming in the ocean and sunning on the beach. I figured that once we got to Lohr, and Monk saw his shrink and got control of himself again, we could explore Germany in between his thrice-weekly psychiatrist appointments.

What I forgot was that Monk is Monk and that wherever he goes he inevitably stumbles over a corpse. It even happened at my brother's wedding, but that's another story and I'm getting ahead of myself.

I'm sure you're wondering how Monk flew all the way to Germany if he gets faint just thinking about driving across the San Francisco Bay. It's thanks to a miraculous little blue pill. And I'm not talking about Viagra.

He took Dioxynl, an experimental drug that obliterates Monk's anxieties and unlocks all his inhibitions for twelve hours. But it's like kryptonite on his powers of observation and radically alters his personality, making him unbearably obnoxious to be around until the drug wears off.

Once we got to Germany, we found Dr. Kroger, and Monk solved some bizarre murders, nearly getting us burned alive in the process.

The next morning, my hair still singed from my brush with flaming death—and no, I am not being overly dramatic about it—I decided I deserved some special consideration for what he'd put me through.

We were supposed to fly home out of Frankfurt

that afternoon, but since France was right next door, I thought we should take advantage of the opportunity and spend a few days in Paris. It would be good for both of us.

So I did what any trustworthy, dedicated assistant would do in my situation.

I blackmailed him.

I went to his room in our tiny bed-and-breakfast in Lohr and showed Monk a picture of him that was on my cell phone. I had taken the photo the previous night when Monk was, for reasons too complicated to explain now, high on Dioxynl, caked with mud, and eating an unwashed apple with his dirty hands.

He gasped with horror when he saw it, as I knew he would.

I threatened to send copies of the picture to everyone he knew unless he agreed to delay our departure for a few days and visit France on his dime.

I had him and he knew it.

He agreed to my terms with all the enthusiasm of a man being led to the guillotine.

Despite the victory, there were still major obstacles to overcome. We had to get to Paris, and we needed a place to stay once we got there.

That wouldn't be much of a problem for most people, but it is if you are traveling with Adrian Monk.

Driving there would take five hours, which is a long time to be in a car with Monk, and who knows what trouble he could get us into on the way? A car would also be more of a liability than a benefit in Paris, where we could get just about everywhere on foot or using public transportation. We could save money by not paying any more car-rental fees or parking charges.

Flying to Paris, on the other hand, wouldn't take

much more than an hour. But Monk was afraid to fly unless he was drugged, and then he would be an intolerable jerk for ten more hours (and that was assuming he was willing to take Dioxynl after the trouble it got him into the previous night). Without his drugs, Monk could freak out on the plane and get himself arrested when we landed. Then again, with Monk locked in the Bastille, I'd be free to roam around Paris on my own.

We could also travel by train, but it seemed to me like it combined the worst aspects of the two other options.

So I chose the flight.

Now all I needed to do was get on the Web to book our flights and hunt for accommodations.

We checked out of the bed-and-breakfast, left our bags with the owners, and headed across the town square. Lohr was built in the Middle Ages between the river Main and the hills of the Spessart forest. There were cobblestone streets, half-timbered houses, and a stone watchtower that rose over the steepled rooftops, the church spires, and the turrets of the castle where Snow White's evil stepmother had supposedly lived. It was like walking through a fairy tale. I expected to bump into a lovable elf or a bearded wizard at any moment.

But Monk was missing out on all the storybook ambience. He was watching his feet, carefully selecting each cobblestone that he stepped on as if he was walking across a minefield.

"How can people live like this?" Monk asked.

"The cobblestone streets have been here for centuries," I replied.

"And they still haven't had a chance to pave them?"

"I hope they never do," I said.

"Maybe they shouldn't have running water, electricity, and penicillin, either."

"That's different," I said. "These streets are one of the things that give Lohr its medieval charm."

"There's nothing charming about pestilence and death," Monk said. "Raw sewage once ran down these streets."

"You're missing the big picture, Mr. Monk. This isn't some amusement park or shopping center re-creation of a fairy tale village. This is the real thing. Take away the cars, and the people with their cell phones, and what you're seeing is pretty much the way things looked seven hundred years ago."

"That's exactly the problem. We aren't living in the Middle Ages anymore. Lohr should join the civilized world. These streets should be covered with a smooth, even coat of asphalt."

"Where's the charm in asphalt?"

"It's flat, it's smooth, and it's one color," Monk said. "It's uniformity in its purest sense. I could go on and on."

"Asphalt has no character. These cobblestone streets should be cherished and protected. We're walking on history here."

"We're walking on a giant toilet," Monk said. "I'm going to need a new pair of shoes."

We reached a one-story stone building that looked as if it would collapse if not for the half-timbered stores propping it up on either side. The doorway was short and square and only slightly larger than the front windows.

I was told back at the bed-and-breakfast that it had been a tavern for centuries but now it was an Internet café.

I peeked inside. It was dark. The floor was hardwood; the walls were exposed stone. The ceiling sagged against thick wooden beams.

There were three tourists in their twenties carrying backpacks huddled around one of the four flat-screen computers that were laid out on a long table carved from a tree trunk.

There was a young woman listening to her iPod behind the counter, which was another tree trunk with a coffee urn and a selection of pastries set out on top.

The electronic devices seemed totally out of place in that old tavern. It was as if there had been some rip in the time-space continuum and the future had inadvertently bled into the past. The visual incongruity had the same unsettling, emotional effect on me that looking at a bowl of Raisin Bran probably had on Monk.

I hoped that he wasn't rubbing off on me.

"You're not actually going in there, are you?" he asked.

"I need to go online to make our travel arrangements," I said. "I won't be long."

"You can't," he said. "The building isn't safe."

"It's been standing for hundreds of years."

"Which means it's long overdue for collapse."

"I'll take my chances," I said.

"At least wear a hard hat."

"I don't have a hard hat."

"You didn't pack one?" he asked.

"Did you?" I replied.

"I was on drugs. I have a valid excuse. What's yours?"

"I don't own a hard hat."

"Everybody owns a hard hat," Monk said.

"No, they don't," I said.

"I'm talking about in America," he said.

"So am I," I said. "And even if I did own one, why would I bring it with me?"

"In case you have to go into a condemned building."

"This isn't a condemned building."

"It's a mud hut," Monk said. "It's worse than a condemned building."

"I'm going in," I said. "Where will you be?"

"Standing right here," Monk said, "my life balanced precariously on these two cobblestones."

"You feel that way no matter where you're standing," I said. "Embrace the unknown. Open yourself up to new experiences. Live a little."

"That's not living," he said. "That's madness."

"And you think that stalking your shrink in Germany is a sign of mental stability?"

Monk's eyes went wide, and I realized I'd made a big mistake mentioning Dr. Kroger. I'd reminded him why we were there in the first place. I was hoping I wouldn't have to deal with that issue for another day or two.

"Dr. Kroger is coming with us to Paris, right?" Monk asked.

I shook my head. "He flew back to San Francisco this morning."

Monk stared at me in shock. "Without me?"

"That was the agreement."

"What kind of insane agreement is that?"

"One that saves you from having to find a new psychiatrist. Dr. Kroger is very angry with you. He needs some time to himself to cool off."

"How could he be so selfish?" Monk said. "What about my needs?"

"You can have your appointments over the phone while we are away."

"A phone call isn't the same."

"That was a major concession for Dr. Kroger to make, given the situation. You'll survive."

"I doubt it," he said.

That was in danger of becoming a self-fulfilling prophecy, because if he kept being stubborn, self-involved, and argumentative, I'd probably end up strangling him myself.

2

Mr. Monk Goes to the Airport

Booking the flight was easy, but finding a place to stay in Paris that fit Monk's unique requirements was considerably more difficult.

Monk was a man of modest means and a notorious cheapskate, so I knew that a four-star hotel was out of the question.

I also knew he'd never stay in a three-star hotel, not because he was a snob, but because it was one star short of an even number.

So I had to choose from the two-star hotels, which were probably more in his price range but less likely to meet his exacting standards of cleanliness and attention to detail.

On top of that, it seemed like every well-reviewed two-star hotel that I could find on the Web was fully booked. But I finally managed to locate a hotel on Avenue Carnot, less than a block from the Arc de Triomphe, that was relatively inexpensive, looked very symmetrical from the street, and had rooms that appeared to be very clean. I booked two single rooms, and we were good to go.

We picked up our bags and drove to the airport in Frankfurt. Although the speed limit was one hundred twenty kilometers per hour, Monk insisted that I keep the speedometer at eighty-six, which made no sense to me.

"That's thirty-four miles below the posted speed limit," I said.

"It's the equivalent of fifty-four miles per hour," Monk said. "That's the speed limit at home."

"No, the speed limit at home is fifty-five."

"Fifty-four is an even number."

"So is one hundred twenty."

"Not if you do the math," he said.

"What math?" I asked.

"One hundred and twenty kilometers is seventy-five miles."

"Okay, I'll go one hundred nineteen kilometers per hour."

"That's not an even number," he said.

"But it is in miles per hour," I said.

"I will still see the uneven number on the speedometer."

"So don't look at the speedometer."

"It's also twenty miles over the speed limit," he said.

"In America," I said. "We're in Germany."

"We're Americans," Monk said. "The law still applies wherever we go."

"No, it doesn't. We have to follow German law, and right now we are violating it by driving dangerously slow."

"That's an oxymoron," he said.

"What is?"

"Dangerously slow," he said. "Slow is never dangerous. It's always safer."

"Driving this slow makes us an obstacle. A car could slam right into us."

"Only if it's going too fast," Monk said.

I didn't have any Advil or Rolaids handy, so I decided to give up on arguing with him.

I kept the car in the right lane, and we puttered along at a steady eighty-six kilometers per hour.

Furious drivers leaned on their horns as they sped past us in a blur, their cars sounding like shrieking animals.

Luckily, I'd overestimated how long it would take us to get to the airport, so we arrived with plenty of time to spare. We even beat the flight crew to the gate.

The crew came in a group, walking in step with one another to an almost musical beat. It was as if they were modeling their uniforms for us rather than boarding the plane.

The pilots wore crisp, sharply tailored navy blue uniforms with stiff, shiny-brimmed hats and embroidered gold bands around their sleeves that made them look like military officers. There was no reason I knew why they had to dress that way, but I guess it was done to convey authority and imply that they'd been through rigorous training, were highly disciplined, and were men of honor.

By contrast, the stewardesses' tight-fitting knee-length dress uniforms had a kinky retro style that evoked the 1960s, martinis, Dean Martin, and the Playboy Club. It wasn't so much the dresses that gave it that feeling as it was the bright red berets, red leather gloves, and high-heeled shoes with sharp pointed toes. I was surprised the stewardesses didn't have bunny tails and whips, too.

The whole crew had matching rolling suitcases that were just the right size to fit in an overhead bin or under a seat. I admired how they could travel so light. It must be one of the benefits of wearing a uniform every day.

I knew Monk would be very happy if I wore a uniform, not because he was kinky, but because he liked uniformity.

Monk always wore the same thing.

His shirts were 100 percent cotton and off-white with exactly eight buttons and a size sixteen neck buttoned at the collar. His pants were pleated and cuffed and they had eight belt loops. His sport coats were brown and so were his Hush Puppies shoes.

His unofficial uniform was every bit as crisp and sharp as the crew's, and he wore his with the same sense of pride and authority.

He stepped in front of one of the pilots—the one with the most gold bars around his sleeves. The pilot was double chinned and slightly gray at the temples, and he had bags under his eyes that were big enough to check as luggage.

"Excuse me," Monk asked, "are you the captain of this aircraft?"

"Yes, I am," replied the captain.

The other crew members stopped to listen.

"Did you have a good night's sleep?"

"Yes, I did," the captain said with a polite smile. "Thank you for asking."

"Was it a full eight hours?"

"More or less."

"It either was or it wasn't. Are you always this confused?"

"I'm not confused."

"But you've lost track of time." Monk narrowed his eyes and sniffed. "Is that alcohol I smell on your breath?"

"It's mouthwash," the captain said.

"Would you be willing to take a Breathalyzer test to confirm that?"

"Who are you?"

"A concerned passenger," Monk said. "Very, very, very concerned."

I had to do something before things got ugly. I stepped up and flashed a big, cheerful American smile.

"Please forgive my friend, Captain. It's nothing personal. He's a little scared of flying."

"I understand," the captain said to me, then turned to Monk. "You can relax, sir. I assure you that I'm not impaired in any way. I have flown hundreds of flights in my career, and we haven't had an incident yet."

Monk held up a piece of paper with some writing on it and took several steps back from the captain. "Can you read what this says?"

"No," the captain said.

"And you still think you're fit to fly?"

"Have a pleasant trip." The captain tipped his hat and strode down the gateway to the plane.

"That's not what it says," Monk said, starting to go after him, but I blocked his path.

"Stop pestering the flight crew," I said. "You are going to get us in trouble."

"The pilot is a blind drunk," he said. "How much more trouble could we be in?"

"Lower your voice," I said, pulling him aside. "The flight will be over before you know it."

"That's what I'm afraid of," Monk said.

We heard the sound of a bell over the speaker system,

and then the gate agent, a man in a polo shirt with the airline's insignia on it, spoke for a minute in German, then announced in English that the plane would begin boarding from the rear of the aircraft, starting with rows twelve to twenty-four. While he was still making the announcement, people were already forming a line beside the ticket counter.

Monk approached the front of the line, where a man the size and shape of a refrigerator stood, his ticket in his huge hand.

"They are boarding from the rear of the plane," Monk said to him.

"I know," the big man said.

Monk motioned to the man's ticket. "You are in row seventeen. You're cutting."

"I was here first."

"That's irrelevant. You should be at least seven people back in line, forty-two if all the seats in the rows behind you are fully occupied. So please step aside while we get everyone in numerical order." Monk turned to face the line. "Let's see your tickets. Who is sitting in row twenty-four?"

Six people in various places in the line raised their hands and waved their tickets.

Monk ushered them forward. "You should all be up here in front. What were you thinking standing way back there?"

The big man growled. "Nobody is getting in front of me."

"If being first in line was so important to you, you should have bought a ticket in row twenty-four. But you didn't. You are in row seventeen. Live with it."

The gate agent stepped up to them. "What's the problem here?"

"This man is in row seventeen but insists on being first in line," Monk said.

"We're boarding from the rear of the plane, rows twelve to twenty-four," the gate agent said.

"Exactly," Monk said, turning the big man. "Now kindly move aside and let us get everyone organized."

The big man said something to the gate agent in German, and then the gate agent addressed Monk.

"Sir, this gentleman was here first. As long as he's in the last twelve rows, he can be in this line."

"I know that," Monk said. "He just can't be first."

"Yes, he can," the gate agent said.

"You said you were boarding from the rear of the plane," Monk said. "He's in row seventeen. Don't you know how to count? Or is it the counting backward that's throwing you?"

I grabbed Monk by the arm and pulled him aside like a misbehaving child. I was beginning to regret that we weren't driving to Paris.

"What is the matter with you?" I said.

"Me? It's them. They can't count."

"They aren't boarding in order from the rear of the plane. What they are doing is allowing anybody in rows twelve through twenty-four to board."

"That's not what they said."

"It's what they meant," I said.

"Then that's what they should have said."

"Maybe they did in German but it got lost in translation."

"But the insanity didn't," Monk said.

While the passengers in the rear of the plane were boarding, Monk began to organize the remaining passengers into reverse numerical order based on their ticket numbers.

I let him do it because it kept him occupied and out of the ticket agent's way. Perhaps the passengers let him do it because they, like me, had lost the will to fight with him.

When the rest of the passengers were called to board, Monk led them in a single-file line to the gateway.

Monk glowered at the ticket agent as we passed him. "See how much smoother this went? I hope you've learned from this experience."

The ticket agent was wise enough just to smile and say nothing. He was getting off easy. It was over for him. But not for me and the rest of the passengers.

This was already the flight from hell and we hadn't even left the airport yet.

3

Mr. Monk and the Unfriendly Skies

Once we were on the plane, we settled into our seats in row eight. I had the window, Monk had the middle, and nobody sat in the aisle seat.

I knew better than to ask Monk to move one seat over to give us more room. There was no way he'd sit in an odd-numbered seat (technically, it was a lettered and not a numbered seat, but I knew he counted them anyway).

The last people on the plane were a married couple, who sat in the row across from us. They were young, attractive, and well-to-do. They both wore Lacoste windbreakers, Nike shoes, and his and hers Ebel watches. Although they wore the same brands as each other, they weren't actually dressed alike, and I don't think they were intentionally matching to be cutesy. I've noticed that people who live together tend to shop together. My daughter and I wear a lot of the same brands, though she looks better in them than I do.

The man was carrying a bag with lots of torn baggage-claim tags on the handle. He opened his overhead bin, which was full, then turned and opened the one above us, which was empty. He began to slide in his bag when Monk spoke up.

"That's our bin," Monk said.

"It's empty," the man said. He was German and I knew Monk was about to make him hate American tourists.

"But it belongs to this row," Monk said. "You have to use your own overhead bin."

"Ours is full," the man said.

"I'm sorry, but those are the regulations. If you can't put it under your seat, you'll have to ask the crew to check it into the baggage compartment."

"I've logged tens of thousands of miles on this airline. I am very familiar with the regulations. I can put my bag in any bin I want, whether you like it or not."

The man shoved his bag into the bin, slammed the lid shut, and took his seat across from us.

Monk looked at me. "He's a troublemaker. Should we inform the captain?"

"I think he has enough on his mind."

"You're probably right," Monk said. "We should alert the stewardesses."

"They don't care," I said.

The head stewardess took a handset from the wall and introduced herself and the rest of the flight crew to the passengers.

Her name was Marise, and she began the usual pre-flight safety lecture. She did it first in German, then began again in English. Probably everybody in the plane, no matter what language they spoke, could recite the same speech from memory.

"In the event of a sudden loss of cabin pressure, an oxygen mask will automatically drop from a compartment above your seat. To start the flow of oxygen, pull the mask toward you, place it firmly over your nose and mouth, and breathe normally. Be sure to secure your mask first before helping others."

Monk raised his hand.

Marise seemed taken aback. It was probably the first time anybody had ever interrupted her speech with a question. Monk waved his arm to be sure she saw him.

"Yes, sir," she said.

"What would cause a sudden loss of cabin pressure?"

"Any number of things," she said. "But it's quite rare."

"When you say any number, can you be more specific?"

"No," Marise said and continued her speech. "A flotation device is located in a pouch under your seat. In the event of a water landing, open the vest and place it over your head—"

Monk raised his hand again. She ignored him as she put on a sample life vest.

"—like so. Pull the straps around your waist and snap them together. To inflate the vest, pull firmly on the red cord, but only do so when leaving the aircraft—"

Monk raised both his hands and waved them.

"Yes, sir," she said. "What is it?"

"Could you start from the beginning? I forgot to take notes."

"There's no need for notes," she said. "You can find complete safety instructions on the card in the seat pocket in front of you."

"Just a card?" Monk said. "Do you really think you can fit everything we need to know about airline safety on a card?"

"Yes," she said.

"You get more information with a model airplane."

I nudged Monk. "Would you please stop interrupting the stewardess?"

"She's only giving a three-minute talk," Monk said. "That can't possibly cover all the things that could go wrong with this aircraft."

"That's what the card is for."

Monk pulled out the card and showed it to me. "The card doesn't say anything more than she does. What if we hit another airplane? That's not mentioned. What if a window shatters? That's not mentioned. What if a fire breaks out? That's not mentioned. What if we fly into a twister? That's not mentioned. What if we crash-land on an uncharted island and have to form our own society? That's not mentioned."

"They can't possibly cover everything," I said.

"They could try," he said.

The stewardess had almost reached the end of her lecture.

"If you haven't already done so, please stow your carry-on luggage in the seat in front of you or in an over-head bin as we are about to taxi for takeoff."

Monk raised his hand. Marise barely hid her groan.

"Yes, the gentleman in row eight," she said. "Again."

Monk stood up and pointed to the man in the next row. "He put his bag in our overhead bin."

The other man stood up. "Our bin was full."

"Rule are rules," Monk said.

"You are an idiot," the man said.

"Heinrich," his wife said, tugging on his sleeve. "*Bitte.*"

I knew how she felt. I tugged at Monk's sleeve.

"Sit down," I said. "Please."

"Passengers may place their bags in any available overhead bin," Marise said.

Heinrich sneered at Monk and both men sat down.

"What kind of airline is this?" Monk asked me.

"One that is going to throw us off if you don't behave yourself."

"I'm the one following the rules," Monk said, then glared at Heinrich. "It's *him* they should throw off."

The stewardess continued her lecture. "At this time, you are required to turn off all cellular phones, pagers, and any wireless or remote-control devices for the duration of the flight as they may interfere with the navigational and communication equipment on this aircraft."

Monk raised his hand again. The stewardess pretended that she didn't notice. She wasn't much of an actress.

"You may use laptop computers, iPods, and other electronic devices once we reach our cruising altitude," she continued. "Please wait until you are notified by the crew that it is permissible to do so."

Monk waved both of his arms and whistled. Marise groaned, unable to ignore the obvious.

"Yes, sir?" she said.

He stood up. "If cellular phones and pagers and other wireless devices are so dangerous, why do you even allow them on the airplane?"

"As long as they are turned off while we are airborne, there's no problem."

"As long as a gun isn't fired, it's not a problem either," Monk said. "What if some suicidal lunatic tries to call home? I think you should confiscate the devices before we take off."

"That's not necessary," Marise said.

"I think it is," Monk said.

"You are an idiot," Heinrich said.

His wife nudged him. "Don't talk with the crazy person. You're just making things worse."

"I'm sorry, Gertrude," Heinrich said. "You're right."

I pulled Monk back down into his seat. "Please, Mr. Monk, try not to argue with the stewardess."

"They won't let us carry a bottle of water on board, but they'll let us carry devices that can cripple the plane's navigation system? A bottle of water never sent an airplane hurtling into a mountain. What are they thinking?"

"I don't know."

I didn't want to admit it, but Monk was making some sense.

"The other possibility is that they're lying about cell phones being dangerous," Monk said. "If it is a lie, we should sue for intentional infliction of emotional distress."

"What distress?"

"I can't stop thinking about all the cell phones on this plane. What if you didn't turn yours off? What if Julie calls us right now and sends our plane spiraling into doom?"

He was so busy complaining that he missed the remainder of the safety lecture. But he got me thinking about spiraling into doom. So I checked my phone just to be sure it was turned off. It was.

The flight crew took their seats and buckled up as the plane began to taxi toward the runway.

Monk leaned out into the aisle and waved his arm to get the stewardess' attention. But Marise ignored him. So he hit the call button a few times and then waved his arm again.

"What's the matter now?" I asked.

He ignored me and she continued to ignore him.

"Marise?" Monk called out. "Hello? Marise?"

She unbuckled her seat belt and shoulder strap and marched down to our row.

"We are about to take off," she said. "Can't it wait?"

"How come we're only wearing seat belts but you get a shoulder belt, too?"

"It's just a precaution," she said.

"Shouldn't we have the same precaution?"

"You are perfectly safe," she said.

"Fine. Then you can sit in my seat and I'll sit in yours."

"Do you want to be ejected from this plane?" she asked pointedly.

"No," Monk said. "That's why I'd like a shoulder belt."

I leaned across Monk to speak to Marise. "Please don't mind him. He's just having some preflight jitters. He'll be fine once we are in the air."

"I hope so," she said. "For his sake."

Marise glanced at Heinrich and Gertrude, who were holding hands on the armrest between them, and then returned to her seat.

I glared at Monk. "Do not say another word for the rest of this flight."

"You're right," Monk said. "I should save my voice for screaming as I plummet to my death."

Monk assumed the crash position, putting his head between his legs and clutching his knees, as we took off. He remained in that position until the food-and-beverage service started ten minutes later.

Marise and a stewardess named Diane came to us, offering soft drinks, juice, peanuts, and a light snack of a croissant and a slice of cheese.

I usually don't trust airplane food, but I glanced over at the croissant and cheese that Heinrich and his wife were eating and they looked pretty good, so I ordered the same thing.

Monk looked up, nudged me hard, and whispered, "Don't eat or drink anything from Marise. Only accept food from Diane."

"Don't you think you're being a little childish?"

"Marise uses her bare hands to put the food on the plate. The other stewardess uses tongs."

I looked up to see Marise wiping her hands on her pants and reaching for a pair of tongs to prepare my order. Monk had a point, but I wasn't going to say anything more to anger her. Besides, she wasn't using her hands to pick up my croissant.

Marise served me with a smile and moved on. Monk grimaced and resumed his crash position.

"Maybe I should put on my life vest now to save time."

"We aren't flying over water."

"But it might help me float if the plane breaks apart in midair."

"It's not a parachute, Mr. Monk."

Heinrich got up from his seat and hurried to the restroom near the cockpit.

"Where are the parachutes on this plane?" Monk asked.

"They don't have any," I replied.

"You're kidding."

"Nope."

"That's insane," he said. "That's like not having lifeboats on a cruise ship."

"You'd need to be a trained skydiver to use a parachute."

Monk regarded me in disbelief.

"When you are plunging to your death from twenty thousand feet in the air, it's usually better to have a parachute you may not know how to use than no parachute at all."

He had a point.

We heard some banging coming from the bathroom. We both sat up and peered over the top of the seats in front of us. The banging got louder and more forceful. It sounded as if Heinrich was having a fistfight in there.

Marise rushed up to the front of the plane. She bent down, pressed some hidden release button, and the door flew open, hitting her in the head. As she stumbled back, Heinrich burst out of the bathroom clutching his throat, his eyes bulging, his face a deep red. Someone screamed and then lots of people started screaming. I guess screaming is contagious. Even I was tempted to join in.

Heinrich staggered down the aisle, gurgling. His wife scrambled out of her seat just as he reached our row and collapsed with a heavy thud.

Gertrude knelt beside him and grabbed his shoulders, shaking him and frantically calling out his name.

Monk touched Heinrich's neck and looked into his wide, unblinking eyes. I didn't have to feel for the man's pulse to know what Monk was going to say.

"There's nothing you can do for him now," Monk said. "He's dead."

A hush fell over the plane. All we could hear for a moment was Gertrude's sobbing. Then the intercom began to buzz. Marise rose slowly to her feet, holding her bruised forehead, and picked up the handset. I could see her talking, and although I couldn't hear her words, I assumed she was telling the captain what had happened.

Monk snapped his fingers, breaking me out of my stunned daze. He gestured to me for a disinfectant wipe. I hurriedly dug one out of my purse and handed it to him.

I've seen a lot of corpses while working for Monk but I wasn't accustomed to seeing someone drop dead in front of me. It was a shock.

Diane approached from the back of the plane, put her arm around Gertrude, and tried to comfort her. Gertrude looked up at Monk with tear-filled eyes.

"How did this happen?" she asked him.

It was a rhetorical question—one he obviously wasn't meant to answer. But I could tell he was going to reply anyway. I prayed he wouldn't say that it had anything to do with Heinrich stowing his bag in the wrong overhead bin.

"It's obvious," Monk said, wiping off his hand and giving me the used wipe. "He was murdered."

4

Mr. Monk Makes His Case

It's always murder. Nobody dies of natural causes around Adrian Monk.

And there's no point in arguing with him about it. When it comes to homicide, Monk is never wrong, no matter how outlandish or impossible his declaration may seem at the time. I'd gradually accepted that. But what I couldn't get used to was the body count everywhere we went. Pretty soon, I'd have to start carrying body bags around with me.

It was so unfair.

Monk had already solved two murders in Germany—didn't that count for anything? Hadn't he met his cosmic quota of homicides for this trip?

"I can't take you anywhere," I said, feeling pretty grumpy.

"This isn't my fault," Monk said.

"Nobody ever drops dead around me when I'm alone."

"He didn't drop. He was pushed," Monk said and

turned to the grieving widow. "Your husband was allergic to nuts, wasn't he?"

"How did you know that?" Gertrude asked.

"When he came out of the lavatory, his face was flushed, his eyes were bulging, and he was clutching at his throat. It was because he couldn't breathe. He was in anaphylactic shock."

"But he didn't eat any nuts," she said. "He had the croissant and cheese."

That was when the captain's voice came over the loudspeaker. He spoke first in German, then in English.

"This is Captain Schubert speaking. One of our passengers has suffered a medical emergency."

That was an understatement.

"I ask that everyone remain calm and in their seats for the remainder of the flight," the Captain continued. "We will be landing shortly at Charles de Gaulle Airport. Thank you."

Marise approached us and glowered at Monk. "You heard the captain. Please sit back in your seat and mind your own affairs. We'll handle this."

"This entire plane is a crime scene," Monk said. "You and the rest of the crew need to remain in your seats to protect the evidence from being corrupted."

"I think we've heard more than enough from you on this trip," Marise said. "One more outburst and I'll have you arrested when we land for disrupting the flight."

"The police will be waiting, but it's not me they are going to arrest. It's you."

"I'm the senior member of this flight crew," she said. "Interfering with my duties is a criminal offense."

"Not when the duty you're performing is murder," Monk said. "You killed this man."

"That's absurd," she said.

It certainly seemed that way, but like I said before, I have come to trust Monk completely in these situations, so I do my best to support him, even if I have no idea what is going on.

When he solves a case, he enjoys a rare moment of complete confidence and pure contentment. I can hear it in his voice and see it in the way he carries himself. He has restored the natural balance, set right what was wrong, and put everything back where it belongs.

I wish he could always feel that way, even though it would probably mean I'd be out of a job.

"Why would the stewardess want to hurt Heinrich?" Gertrude said. "I've never seen this woman before."

"But your husband has," Monk said. "She and your husband were having an extramarital sex affair."

Gertrude stared at Monk wide-eyed. "That's not true!"

"Of course it's not," Marise said. "This man is mentally disturbed."

"The proof is irrefutable," Monk said.

"How can you have proof of something that never happened?" Marise said.

"There's a baggage claim stub from a hotel bellman on his carry-on bag. There's a matching one on your bag. The numbers are in sequential order. They were checked together."

"How could you possibly know what tags are on my suitcase or what is written on them?" Marise asked.

"I saw your tags when you boarded the plane and his when he stowed his suitcase in my overhead bin," Monk replied. "He really should have put it in his own bin, but he insisted, even though he was clearly in the wrong and—"

"Mr. Monk," I interrupted, "the man is dead. I don't think the bin issue really matters anymore."

Marise shook her head. "Do you really expect us to believe you were able to read the numbers on those tags and remember them?"

"I'm not blind," Monk said. "Unlike our pilot."

"This is a pointless argument," I said. "All it will take is one look at the tags to know whether Mr. Monk is right or not. And if he is, the police will be able to easily trace the tags back to the hotel where you both stayed."

"If we were at the same hotel, it's simply a coincidence," Marise said. "It's hardly evidence of an affair!"

"I think maybe I can explain what happened," said Diane, the stewardess who had her arm around Gertrude. "We usually fly the Frankfurt to Stansted route, but we got transferred to this flight at the last minute when the regular crew came down with food poisoning."

"Food poisoning," Monk repeated for my benefit. "Could you have picked a worse airline?"

"It was from the restaurant they went to last night," Marise said.

"Heinrich stays in Stansted when he does business in England," Gertrude said, her voice trembling. "He was there yesterday."

"It's not what it seems," Diane said, giving Gertrude's shoulder a reassuring squeeze.

"Then what is it?" Gertrude said.

"There is only one hotel adjacent to the Stansted airport. Many flight crews and lots of business travelers stay there," Diane said. "If you want to take the train into London, and your room isn't ready, the bellman will store your bags for you and give you a claim ticket. Marise and your husband probably just checked their bags in at the same time."

"Satisfied?" Marise said to Monk. "You should be

ashamed of yourself for adding to this woman's heart-ache with outrageous accusations."

"There's more," Monk said.

"Haven't you hurt her enough?" Marise said.

"There's the peanut oil on the croissant and the cheese."

"I suppose with your amazing eyesight you can also tell the ingredients of the sandwich just by looking at it?" Marise said.

Monk glanced at the corpse. "I can tell by looking at him."

Gertrude let out a sob. Monk wasn't the most sensitive person I'd ever met.

"I didn't make the sandwich or the cheese," Marise said. "They come to us prepackaged. If the food was exposed to peanut oil, it happened in the service company's kitchen."

"Your filthy habits say otherwise," Monk said.

"My *what*?" Marise said indignantly.

"You wipe your hands on your clothes," Monk said. "It proves you're a killer."

"You can find thousands of people who do the same absentminded thing, and they aren't killers," she said.

"But it's the first step on the road to moral degradation and total ruin," Monk said. "Before you know it, you're smoking marijuana cigarettes, dancing in strip clubs, and murdering your married lovers."

"I'm not a drug addict, a stripper, or a killer," she said. "You can't honestly be accusing me of being responsible for this man's death because I may have wiped my hands on myself."

"Here's what happened," Monk said. "You and Heinrich were having an extramarital sex affair. My guess is that he never told you that he was married. When you saw him on the plane with his wife, you were furious. You knew about his allergy from all the dinners you'd had together. So you opened a bag of peanuts into your hands and got them nice and greasy before handling the sandwich that you gave him. Afterward, you wiped your hands on your pants, as you always do. And that was your undoing."

He said those last few words with such disgust that I think he was more offended by her dirty habits than he was by the murder that she'd committed.

"This proves nothing," Marise said, but her voice wavered. She had to know now that she was finished. I certainly did. "If I had peanut oil on my hands and touched his sandwich, it was an accident."

I spoke up. "No, it wasn't. You handled his food with your bare hands but you used tongs to serve everyone else. Mr. Monk saw it and so did I."

"You're with him," Marise said. "Of course you are backing up his insane story."

"I saw it, too," Gertrude said quietly, her lower lip trembling.

"You only think you did," Marise said. "He's putting the image into your head."

"The luggage tags, the sandwich, the peanut oil on your pants, the open bag of peanuts with your fingerprints on it, and the loose nuts in the galley trash will be enough for the police to hold you," Monk said. "It shouldn't take long for them to backtrack your movements and find witnesses who saw you both together at other hotels."

Diane gave Marise a cold, hard stare. "You'd better sit down until we land."

"Don't listen to him, Diane. It's not true."

"The police can sort that out," Diane said. "Until then, I'm keeping my eye on you."

Diane didn't have to bother. Everyone on the plane had watched the drama unfold in rapt, silent attention. And now all of them were staring at Marise as she backed up and sat down in her seat.

Monk sighed. "It's so sad."

"Yes, it is," I said.

"If only someone had taught her to wipe her hands with a napkin, her life would have followed a different path and this tragedy would never have happened."

"What about him?" I whispered. "He's the one who was cheating on his wife with a stewardess and living a lie. Isn't he partly responsible for his own horrible fate?"

"Undoubtedly. He knowingly put his bag in the wrong overhead bin," Monk whispered back to me. "Only a man with a callous disregard for human life behaves that way. Something like this was bound to happen to him."

5

Mr. Monk Goes to Another Airport

As it turned out, it would have taken us far less time to drive to France than it ended up taking us to fly there, but I stupidly hadn't factored a homicide into the equation when I was weighing our travel options.

There was a squad of police cars and other official-looking vehicles waiting for our plane as we arrived at the terminal. We were told by the captain to stay in our seats until we were instructed otherwise by the authorities, who would be boarding the aircraft.

Heinrich's body hadn't been moved and Monk wouldn't let the stewardesses cover him with a blanket because it would contaminate the crime scene.

I knew that he was right, but it was painful for Gertrude and awkward for everyone else to have a corpse in the aisle for the last hour of the flight. The only one who seemed to be completely relaxed with it all was Monk. He reclined in his seat, crossed his legs, and browsed through the *International Herald Tribune*.

Solving a murder seemed to have eased all his anxieties about flying. It was more effective than Dioxynl and didn't have the unpleasant side effects, though I'm not sure Heinrich would agree with that.

Monk would probably travel a lot more if he could be guaranteed a murder to distract him on every flight.

Diane opened the hatch and two uniformed police officers entered the plane. They were followed by a man in his forties who wore a bow tie, suspenders, and a long tan overcoat that was open to free his round belly. He had a wisp of a mustache that looked as if it had been drawn on his face with a pencil.

"Bienvenue à Paris," the man said, addressing the passengers. "I am Chief Inspector Philippe Le Roux and this is my assistant, Inspector Guy Gadois."

He motioned to Gadois, who bounded onto the aircraft like a puppy, a big, happy smile on his face. At least he didn't have a tennis ball in his mouth.

Le Roux sighed wearily and faced us again. "I regret to inform you that this aircraft is the scene of a crime and must be properly secured."

"I told you so," Monk said to no one in particular.

Le Roux looked at him. "You must be the American detective, Monsieur Monk."

"You've heard of me?" Monk said.

"I've spoken with Hauptkriminalkommissar Stoffmacher in Lohr and Captain Stottlemeyer of the San Francisco Police."

"That was fast," I said.

"We are professionals, Mademoiselle Teeger, are we not?" Le Roux said.

"Vous l'êtes mais je ne le suis pas."

I told him that he was, but I wasn't. And in doing so, I got to show off the incredible affinity for foreign languages that earned me a C- in my high school French class.

"Et vous êtes?" Le Roux asked.

"Sous-payée, surchargée, et prête pour les vacances."

He asked me what I was, and I told him the truth: underpaid, overworked, and ready for a break.

"Moi, aussi," Gadois said.

Le Roux glared at him.

"The stewardess sitting behind you murdered this passenger," Monk said to Le Roux. "They were having an extramarital sex affair."

"Qui n'en a pas en France?" Gadois asked and winked at me, which earned him another glare from his boss. Roughly translated, what he said was "Who isn't in France?"

Le Roux turned back to Monk. "It is my understanding that you believe the murder weapon was a peanut."

"You could say that," Monk said.

The chief inspector nodded and faced the rest of the passengers again.

"Alors. Please do not move from your seats. We will be photographing the interior of the aircraft and wish to document exactly where everybody is. When you are instructed to exit the aircraft, you will leave all your personal belongings behind. They will be returned to you after they are examined. You will be escorted into the terminal, where we will take your formal statements. I apologize for the inconvenience."

And with that, Le Roux and Gadois escorted Marise, the captain, and the cockpit crew off the plane.

Monk looked at me. "I didn't know you spoke French."

"There's a lot you don't know about me, Mr. Monk. I'm a woman of mystery and intrigue."

It took another hour for the officers to photograph the passengers and for Heinrich's body to be removed before we were allowed to file out, row by row, one by one.

Monk loved that part. He even offered to help.

The passengers were held in a roped-off area in the terminal, where a dozen detectives were waiting to interview them. But the two of us were escorted into a separate, windowless room that must have been used for interrogations and strip searches.

There was a metal table with three matching chairs on one side and one on the other. It was furniture straight from the prison decor catalog. There was nothing in the room that would have indicated to me that we were in France.

I sat down in the chair that was by itself while Monk rearranged the three others so that there were two on each side of the table, equally spaced apart.

"You need to get up," Monk said.

"I'm fine," I said.

"But your chair isn't."

"It's fine, too."

I knew he wanted to move my chair a few inches to the left so that it was even with the one across the table, but I didn't feel like giving him the satisfaction or peace of mind.

"Please," Monk said.

"No."

"Why are you being such a sourpuss?"

I looked at him in disbelief. "We haven't been in Paris one minute and already we're involved in a homicide."

"It's been solved. I don't see what you have to be upset about."

"You just got done investigating two murders in Germany," I said. "Just once I'd like to go somewhere with you without seeing a butchered corpse."

"Heinrich wasn't butchered," Monk said. "He wasn't even scratched."

"You're missing the point."

"You haven't made one."

"People go their entire lives without seeing a murder but you see them almost daily."

"It's my job," he said.

"You're on vacation!"

"You don't stop being who you are just because you are somewhere else," Monk said, and as if to prove it, he yanked the chair out from under me.

I fell onto the floor with an involuntary yelp—more from the surprise than from pain.

"That was rude," I said.

"You gave me no choice," Monk said. "You'll thank me later."

"Why would I thank you for knocking me down onto the hard floor?"

"It was for your own good. I am creating a restful environment for you," Monk said, "so you can relax."

"I suppose that was what you were doing on the plane, too."

"You noticed," Monk said with a smile. "I was beginning to think you were insensitive."

I climbed back on the seat, put my elbows on the table, and covered my face with my hands. My vacation to Paris was off to a marvelous start.

Then again, maybe it was. Maybe this was fate taking pity on me and getting the obligatory homicide out of the way quickly so our next few days would be murder-free.

What I wondered, though, was whether we were technically still in German airspace when the murder occurred. If so, would the investigation count in the ledgers of Fate as Monk's France murder or would it go on the German tally? But if Heinrich's murder was counted in the German total, hadn't we exceeded any reasonable quota there and earned a pass in France?

Ledgers of Fate. Murder Quotas.

I was losing my mind. I chalked it up to post-traumatic stress from last night's near-death experience and not to my long-term exposure to Adrian Monk.

At least, I hoped that was what it was.

The door opened and I looked up to see Chief Inspector Le Roux and Inspector Gadois as they came in.

"I am so sorry for keeping you both waiting, but it was unavoidable under the circumstances," Le Roux said. "We have arrested Marise Lambert for murder."

"We've confirmed almost everything that you guessed," Gadois said.

"I wasn't guessing," Monk said.

"Heinrich Wilke and Marise Lambert have been lovers for months," Gadois said. "The credit card statements show that they've stayed at the same hotels at the same times in several European locations."

"The medical examiner believes you are correct about the cause of death," Le Roux said. "The victim had a rash and tiny blisters on his skin that are typical signs of anaphylaxis."

"We've found her fingerprints on the peanut wrapper in the plane," Gadois said. "We've sent her uniform in for analysis."

I still had one unanswered question about the murder. "Why were Heinrich and his wife coming to France so soon after he returned from a business trip?"

"To celebrate their twentieth wedding anniversary," Gadois said. "How ironic is that?"

"It's sad," I said.

"Murder usually is," Le Roux said and shifted his attention to Monk. "I am very impressed, Monsieur Monk. If I was in your place on that flight, I doubt I would have performed as admirably. You are a genius."

"That's what they tell me," Monk said.

"It is also the opinion of my predecessor, Chief Inspector Dupres," Le Roux said. "I had no idea that you were the same American detective who solved the infamous Madame Beaudreau murder."

"You must be mistaken," I said. "Mr. Monk has never been to France before."

"It's a case I read about in the newspaper a few years ago," Monk said.

"Madame Beaudreau and her husband were in the prison museum at the Bastille," Le Roux said. "She was found strangled with both of her hands cut off."

"My God," I said.

"We found the hands a few meters away from the body," Le Roux said. "The case was unsolved until Monsieur Monk read a small item about it in the newspaper and called Chief Inspector Dupres."

"It was obvious what happened," Monk said. "Madame Beaudreau was killed by her husband, who restrained her with antique handcuffs from the prison museum collection. But he lost the key. If he left the cuffs on her, they would have led right back to him. So he cut off her hands."

"Monsieur Monk deduced the solution to the crime from nine thousand miles away," Le Roux said, "without ever seeing the body or visiting the scene."

"*Incroyable,*" Gadois said.

"We'll take your statements, and then it will be our pleasure to drive you to your hotel," Le Roux said. "Perhaps you will allow us to take you both to dinner tonight."

"We'll accept the ride," I said, "but I'm afraid we have to pass on the dinner invitation."

"We do?" Monk said.

"We're on vacation, and no offense intended, we want to stay as far away from homicide and police work as we can."

"You don't seem to be having much success," Le Roux said with a friendly smile.

"I know," I replied.

"Ce n'est pas grave. Je comprends parfaitement," Le Roux said. *"Ma femme déteste quand je parle des affaires pendant nos vacances. Peut-être pourrions nous vous voir avant votre départ?"*

He understood how I felt and suggested that maybe we could get together before the end of our trip. But I wasn't ready to commit to anything yet.

"Peut-être. Nous verrons comment les choses tournent," I said.

"D'accord," he said.

Le Roux didn't take it personally. He and Gadois sat down across from us, took out their notebooks, and asked us to tell them everything that happened on the flight.

Unfortunately, that was exactly what Monk did, without sparing a single detail, focusing more on the safety lecture and the overhead-bin debate than the murder.

By the time Monk was done telling his version of events, I think Le Roux might have been relieved that we didn't accept his dinner invitation after all.

6

Mr. Monk Checks In

We didn't talk much during the drive to our hotel. I was lost in my thoughts, my face pressed against the window, looking at the Basilique du Sacré-Coeur lit up against the night sky atop Montmartre.

I was remembering the last time I was in Paris, which was nearly twenty years ago. I found it hard to believe (and more than a little terrifying) that I'd aged enough to have memories that old already. I'd eloped to Europe with Mitch. We'd traveled all over the place before ending up in Paris, nearly broke and desperate to put off returning home to the realities of married life, the anger of my parents, and his active duty as a navy pilot. Neither of us knew that we were on borrowed time, that he would be shot down over Kosovo.

Paris was the most beautiful place on earth to me back then. But I was so much in love that anywhere we were together was the most beautiful place on earth to me, simply because I was there and he was with me.

I thought every day would feel the same way for the

rest of my life, and because of that, I would have the strength and confidence to overcome whatever obstacles lay ahead of us.

I didn't have a career or even an idea of what I wanted to do but that was okay because I was absolutely sure that I was meant to be with him, and that was all that mattered.

Love is like that. Or so I remember.

It's not that I haven't loved, or been loved, since then. But I haven't experienced anything that felt like what I had with Mitch during those precious weeks.

I was beginning to sense a very slight tingle of those feelings, the emotional equivalent of hearing the faintest echo of distant thunder, as we drove into the heart of Paris.

I guess that was why I wanted to return to Paris so badly, to bring him alive again in some way. But as we got deeper into the city, it was as if Paris was a lake I was sinking into, and I was afraid I might drown. I was tempted to ask Le Roux to turn around and take us back to the airport.

And yet my fear was matched by my eagerness to do exactly what frightened me, to get out into the street, to immerse myself in it all. I knew from before that Paris is like love: You have to surrender yourself to it, no matter what happens.

We drove around the Arc de Triomphe, veered off onto one of the streets that radiated from la Place de l'Étoile, and pulled up in front of our hotel, La Reine Étoile.

We got out. Le Roux and Gadois took our suitcases from the trunk while Monk and I breathed in Paris. On one end of the tree-lined Avenue Carnot was the Arc de Triomphe and, on the other, several *patisseries* and cafés.

Monk stood on the sidewalk, regarding the front of the hotel, and nodding his head in approval. It was a beautiful, late-nineteenth-century building with decorative corbels and elaborate, wrought-iron balconies.

"Twenty-four Avenue Carnot. One of my favorite even numbers. Six floors, each with six windows, very symmetrical," Monk said. "We've returned to civilization."

"I thought you'd like it," I said and turned to Le Roux. "Thank you for the ride, Chief Inspector."

"De rien," Le Roux said, studying me with undisguised curiosity, as if trying to figure out something about me. "If there is anything I can do to make your stay more enjoyable, please do not hesitate to call."

Le Roux handed me his card.

"Me, too," Gadois said, handing me his card as well, his back to Le Roux so his boss couldn't see the wink he gave me.

That was two winks I'd received from Gadois already. He probably thought we'd already begun a torrid affair.

"At the very least," Le Roux said, "I hope you will allow me to give you a ride to the airport when you're ready to go home."

"I'm sure that you have more important things to do than be our airport taxi service," I said.

"It's pure selfishness on my part," Le Roux said. "I would like to learn more about Monsieur Monk's methods of deduction."

"I don't have a method," Monk said. "I just pay attention to things."

"But it is what you choose to see that is interesting to me," Le Roux said. "Like your observation about the hotel. I would never have looked at the building that way."

"It's the only way to look at it," Monk said.

Le Roux smiled. "And that, my friend, is your method."

The two detectives got into their Peugeot and drove off. We went into the hotel.

The lobby was ornate and elegant with sconces, travertine floors, Empire-style mahogany chairs and settees, and an overmantle with a white marble medallion of huntsmen on horseback. It looked nice, but I didn't find the room very inviting. It was like the living room in my parents' house, which was for guests only, a space more for show than actual use.

The mahogany reception desk was crescent shaped and topped with marble; it doubled on the opposite end as the two-stool bar of a tiny cocktail lounge. Both the desk and the cocktail lounge were simultaneously staffed by a young woman who was so pale, she could have been mistaken for a ghost haunting the hotel.

She greeted us in French, and I did her the courtesy of conversing in the same language. It wasn't a very difficult conversation, even for someone with my rudimentary French skills.

She gave us the keys for rooms 204 and 206 on the second floor. Since Monk got claustrophobic in elevators, we took the stairs, which wasn't as easy as you might think. The stairway was narrow and curving, wrapping around an elevator that was probably added at least a century after the hotel was built.

We trudged along, dragging our heavy suitcases behind us, when Monk came to an abrupt stop at the next floor. He stared at a bronze plaque on the wall with the number one etched on it.

"What does this mean?" he asked.

Could this be the same man whose incredible deductive skills had so impressed Chief Inspector Le Roux only moments ago?

"We're on the first floor," I said. "Hence, the number one."

"But this isn't the first floor. It's the second."

"Not in France," I said. "They don't count the lobby as the first floor."

"They're delusional," Monk said.

"It's just their way," I said.

"If you stand outside and look at the building, it clearly has six stories."

"Right," I said. "The lobby and five floors."

"You're playing word games."

"You aren't in America now," I said. "The French have a different culture. You have to respect it."

"The laws of nature and gravity still apply, regardless of where you are."

"What do nature and gravity have to with this?"

"You can call a tree a rock or you can say the world is flat or you can call the second floor the first floor, but it doesn't change the fact that a tree is a tree, the world is round, and the second floor is the second floor."

"It's a matter of culture and perception."

"When we were in the lobby, what were we standing on?"

"The floor," I said.

"Therefore, it counts as a floor," Monk said. "That's common sense, not to mention an immutable law of nature."

"What about the basement?"

"What about it?"

"Doesn't it count?"

"It's not on street level," Monk said. "So it's not a legitimate floor."

"Says who?"

"It's the way it is," Monk said.

"If you were standing in the basement," I said, "what would you be standing on?"

"I don't know," Monk said. "I haven't seen the basement."

"You would be standing on something, and it would be the floor."

"Or the ground, though, technically, you are belowground, so you would be standing on dirt."

I didn't see why that wouldn't count as a floor, even using his bizarre logic, but I decided not to pursue that specific issue.

"My point is, Mr. Monk, that you come from a culture that doesn't count the basement as a floor. Perhaps there are cultures that do."

"Name one."

"It doesn't matter if there really is one or not."

"There isn't," he said, "because nobody is that stupid."

"I'm illustrating how the culture we come from shapes our perceptions of the world."

"You're illustrating how a culture based on ignorance would shape the perceptions of an idiot," Monk said. "You might as well be talking about Martians, but there is no such thing as Martians, so you're basically talking gibberish. I am not staying on the third floor, no matter what they call it here."

I knew this wasn't an argument I could win. The truth was, I knew that before I began arguing but I couldn't stop myself. It's only when I feel a headache coming on, or a pain in my stomach, that I finally give up. I was feeling both.

We went back downstairs and I approached the woman at the front desk.

"Let me handle this," I said to Monk. "I speak her language."

"Maybe you can teach her how to count," Monk said. "You could change France forever."

"I'd rather just change our rooms for now."

I was sure she probably spoke English, but I didn't want Monk to understand what we were saying and complicate things by interjecting his opinions about floor counting.

She asked if there was a problem, and I told her that my friend didn't want to stay on the second floor. I asked if they had any vacancies on the third or fifth floors. All she had left besides the two rooms she'd offered to us was a double on the fifth floor with two king-sized beds and a balcony with a partial view of the Arc de Triomphe.

I asked her how much it would be for one of the two single rooms on the second floor and the double on the fifth. The cost was nearly twice as much as the two singles. There was no way Monk could afford that, so I tried to bargain her down, but with the hotel nearly sold out, and no vacancies at any of the decent two-star places, I didn't have much leverage.

So I took the double room instead of the two singles. I knew Monk would have a problem with us sharing the room but we were both adults, and he would just have to act like one for a change.

I didn't want to have that argument with him at that moment. I was already exhausted by the floor-numbering debate, and I was eager to see the city. So I asked the desk clerk to hold our bags and our keys and we'd come back later. She was glad to do it.

I turned to Monk. "Problem solved. We are staying on the sixth floor in room five-oh-six."

"That makes no sense," Monk said. "It should be six-oh-six."

"You can write a letter to the management when we get back to San Francisco," I said. "In the meantime, let's go explore Paris."

"Aren't we going to check out the room first?"

"Go ahead," I said. "But I'm going for a walk and don't know when I'll be back. I've been cooped up long enough."

He surrendered with a sigh. "Where are we going to go?"

"Wherever our whims take us," I replied.

"We're in a foreign land," Monk said. "That could be dangerous."

"There was a murder on our airplane," I said. "How much more dangerous could the streets of Paris be?"

I walked outside without waiting for his reply.

I went to my left, toward la Place de l'Étoile and the Arc de Triomphe, passing a row of two dozen identical bicycles, locked in place beside a kiosk that looked like a stand-alone ATM machine.

Curious, I read the instructions on the kiosk. The bikes were available for rent and could be ridden to one of many other kiosks throughout Paris for a small fee. It sounded like fun.

I turned to Monk, who lagged behind me, touching each bike he passed. He often did that with rows of identical objects, like parking meters and streetlamps, despite his fear of germs. Don't ask me why because I don't know. I gave up long ago trying to figure out how all his Monkish behaviors fit together. I just cope with what comes.

"How would you feel about renting a bike one day?" I asked.

"It depends."

"On what?"

"On whether I have to choose between that and being gored by a wild bull."

"I doubt you'll ever have to make that choice."

"Then no, I don't feel like riding a bike," he said.

I turned to admire the Arc de Triomphe but I was immediately distracted by the Eiffel Tower in the distance. The tower was decorated with blinking multicolored lights like an enormous Christmas tree.

How could the Parisians have let that happen?

It was one thing to accentuate the power of a structure with dramatic lighting, as they had done with the Arc de Triomphe. But wrapping the Eiffel Tower in blinking lights made it look cheap, crass, and gaudy—a commercial come-on rather than a powerful icon and historical landmark.

It was like seeing an elegant, refined, and educated woman of mystery and natural beauty wearing a low-cut dress and short skirt to show off her horrible breast implants.

What other horrors awaited me? The Paris Opera building covered in neon that blinked and pulsed to the beat of Michael Crawford singing "Music of the Night" from hidden speakers? Enormous TV screens affixed to Notre Dame cathedral showing scenes from *Shrek*? The statues on Pont Alexandre, the most beautiful bridge in Paris, replaced with animatronic robots that sang and danced every hour to the boats on the Seine?

"This gives me hope for the French," Monk said.

"The Eiffel Tower in lights?"

"The twelve streets radiating off of this roundabout," Monk said. "It's a model of sensible urban planning."

From la Place de l'Étoile, we had a clear view down the grand Champs-Élysées to la Place de la Concorde, which, to my horror, was dominated by a huge Ferris wheel adorned with lights.

Between the Ferris wheel on one end and the Eiffel Tower on the other, it was like I was visiting an amusement park re-creation of Paris rather than the great city itself. All that was missing was a roller coaster and maybe an erupting volcano.

This was Paris Disneyfied, commercialized, and franchised. It wasn't the Paris I'd been to before, the one I longed to see again.

That Paris had to be here somewhere. I wanted to stroll through the Jardin des Tuileries. I wanted to stand in front of Basilique du Sacré-Coeur and look out over the city. I wanted to browse among the booksellers' stalls along the Seine. I wanted to absorb Paris completely into my being and bring it home with me.

I wanted Mitch back.

I broke into a run. I was only vaguely aware of Monk chasing after me, of the people I collided with on the sidewalk, of the rain on my face.

But it wasn't rain. It was my own tears.

I stopped and leaned against a *colonne Morris*, one of those uniquely French advertising pillars that say *spectacles* across the top and are crowned with an onion-shaped dome. I was breathing hard, unable to catch my breath between my sobs.

Why was I crying? What was happening to me? I got

ahold of myself and became aware of Monk with his back to me, hiding my irrational outburst from the passersby and protecting my privacy. It was sweet. I sniffled and wiped my eyes.

"Would you like a disinfectant wipe?" he asked without looking at me. Emotional displays, especially mine, made him uncomfortable.

"No, thank you," I replied. "There are some things a wipe can't cure."

"I'm sorry."

"It's not your fault, Mr. Monk."

"I know," he said. "It's Mitch."

His comment caught me off guard. He could be so irritating and out of touch with what was going on around him, and yet at times he could also be astonishingly perceptive. I guess that was one of the things that made him a great detective.

"Then why did you apologize?"

"I'd forgotten until now what this place must mean to you," Monk said, daring a glance over his shoulder at me. "I suppose that it's changed since you were here with him."

"It's a stupid thing to cry about. Everything changes."

"My life has changed a lot since Trudy was killed, and so has the world around me, but my feelings about her will always be the same."

No wonder he hated change so much.

"So what do you do about it?" I asked.

"I see things the same way I always have."

That was probably one of the reasons for his stubborn refusal to accept anything that clashed with his worldview and to impose his own order on everything.

"But they aren't the same," I said.

"It's not what you see that's important. It's how you perceive it. Julie changes every day, but she will always be your little girl."

I felt the tears welling up in my eyes again. "I could hug you."

"Take a wipe instead," Monk said, offering me one. "It will do you more good."

7

Mr. Monk and the Croque Monsieur

I cleaned my hands with the wipe for Monk's benefit and dropped the used tissue into a nearby trash can.

I was embarrassed and confused. Between Monk and me, I'm supposed to be the rational, stable, dependable one. But I had no idea what provoked my mad dash down the Champs-Élysées.

Was I running toward something or fleeing from it?

Maybe it was just a reaction to the combined stress of escaping from a fire the previous night, witnessing a murder that afternoon, and returning to a place filled with cherished memories.

Any one of those things would make a reasonable, normal person crack just a little bit, right? So was it really any surprise that I'd lost my head for a moment? That was how I tried to rationalize my inexplicable behavior to myself.

So I took a deep breath, let it out slowly, and decided to pretend that it had never happened. I looked around and got my bearings, emotionally and physically.

I was smack in the middle of the Champs-Élysées. It hadn't changed much since the last time I'd been there. It was still a provocative mix of class and crass, elegance and decadence.

The Champs-Élysées was perhaps the only street on earth where you could find Cartier, McDonald's, Louis Vuitton, the Virgin Megastore, Lancel, Pizza Hut and a Peugeot car dealership all lined up side by side.

Yet the eclectic mix of high-end designers, cheap souvenir shops, global chain stores, and fast-food franchises couldn't erase the *haute bourgeoisie* aura that lingered from the days when the boulevard was an enclave for the rich and powerful, nor could it diminish its status as the symbolic heart of the city.

It was on the Champs-Élysées that Parisians gathered to celebrate their triumphs, express their outrage, and honor their past. And it was there that invading armies marched to claim victory and demonstrate their domination, and it was there where the triumphant liberators paraded to symbolize the return of freedom.

It would take more than a Kentucky Fried Chicken outlet to knock the Champs-Élysées from the place it held in French culture. But it was enough to drive me away.

I dashed into the Virgin Megastore to buy some Paris guidebooks while Monk waited for me outside. He stood there, watching the people on the street suspiciously, as if he expected one of them to suddenly attack him with a dagger or, worse, unwashed hands.

Books in hand, I led the two of us away from the Champs-Élysées onto the nearest side street, and headed north, in the general direction of the neighborhood known as the seventeenth arrondissement.

Within a block or two, I felt myself relax. The streets

were narrow, the buildings were old, and there wasn't a familiar chain store or fast-food franchise in sight.

We passed tailors and jewelers, bakeries and restaurants, galleries and law offices, shoe stores and hairdressers. There was something intimate and warm about this warren of streets and the tiny shops and the rich, comforting aroma of food being cooked and coffee being brewed in cafés and apartments.

Monk walked with his arms close to his sides, trying hard not to brush against anyone or anything. He looked very ill at ease, as if he was moving among a herd of restless buffalo instead of a few polite pedestrians.

It wasn't all that different from the way he walked down a street at home.

"How do you like Paris so far?" I asked him.

"They have sidewalks," he replied. "That's a plus."

He was obviously still reeling from his encounter with the cobblestone streets of Lohr.

We passed a restaurant where I could see diners eating tiny potatoes and *jambon* that they pinched together with a morsel of fresh bread and then dipped in hot cheese shaved off of a sizzling hot half a round known as a *raclette*.

I remembered enjoying *raclette* with Mitch in an ancient bar in Troyes, a medieval French village that we'd stumbled across on our way to Paris. It was a fun, tasty, and cheap meal unlike any dining experience we'd ever had at home.

I would have gone in to try the *raclette* again if I wasn't with Monk. He liked simple foods, nothing that dripped, or had to be dipped, or that couldn't be divvied up in distinct, symmetrical, geometrical, or quantifiable portions on the plate.

But the thought of the tangy cheese, dried meat, and

tender potato made my stomach growl loud enough to
startle small animals.

I didn't realize until that moment that I was starving.
I could add low blood sugar to the list of reasons (or
rationalizations) why I'd freaked out before.

"Are you hungry?" I asked Monk.

"Yes and no."

"This isn't a choice between eating and being gored
by a wild bull. You either are or you aren't."

"Then yes, I'm hungry," he said, "but I think I'll wait
to eat until we get home."

"There isn't a restaurant in our hotel."

"I was referring to my apartment in San Francisco."

"That could be a week from now," I said.

"I might just make it," Monk said.

"French food is wonderful," I said. "It won't hurt
you."

"That's not what all the signs say."

"What signs?"

Monk pointed to a *boulangerie* two doors down from
us that had a mouthwatering display of breads and pastries in the window.

"Right there, in big letters, all over the awning," Monk
said. "Pain. Pain. Pain."

"It's the French word for bread," I explained.

"If bread is so strongly associated with illness here
that pain has become the common name for it, why
would anyone sell the stuff, much less eat it?" Monk
said. "They should try Wonder Bread instead."

"It's spelled the same as *pain* but it's pronounced *pan*
and doesn't have the same meaning."

"And the number two here means the number three,"
Monk said. "What a country."

"No, two is two."

"Not in our hotel," he said. "So what is the word for *pain* in French?"

"Monk," I said, and then gestured to a café across the street with several tables out on the sidewalk. "Let's eat there."

I started across the street before he could argue with me about it and sat down at one of the small round tables on the sidewalk.

"Is this safe?" Monk said.

"What could possibly be dangerous about this?"

"We could be trampled."

"People will walk around us," I said.

"What if there is a stampede?"

"I'll take that chance." I picked up a menu. They offered a small selection of sandwiches and cakes. Everything sounded delicious, and since we were in Paris, it probably was.

Monk pulled out the chair beside me and looked both ways, as if he was about to cross a busy street, before he took a seat.

"Would you like me to translate the items on the menu for you?" I asked.

"I don't eat anything called *pain*, *agony*, *pestilence*, or *feculence*, no matter how those words are pronounced or what they might mean in French," Monk said. "That's a big rule of mine."

"Since when?"

"Five seconds ago but it's already etched in stone," Monk said. "What is the French word for *toast*?"

"You're not going to have toast for your first French dinner."

"I don't want it to be my last meal."

"It won't be," I said. "I know what to order. Trust me."

"I do," he said.

"Really?"

"More than just about anyone."

I was touched. I mean it. I gave his arm a tender squeeze. "That's the nicest thing you've ever said to me, Mr. Monk."

"I trust you out of necessity," he added.

"Don't go and ruin the moment by qualifying your remark," I said. "It was sweet. I wish you'd keep it that way."

"I don't want you getting the wrong idea."

"What would that be, Mr. Monk?"

I couldn't resist teasing him just a little.

He was saved from answering by the arrival of the waiter at our table. I ordered in French two croque monsieurs with the crusts cut off and a glass of the house wine for myself.

We were in Paris, after all.

"What would you like to drink?" I asked Monk. "Evian or Perrier?"

He glanced at the waiter. "Do you have Sierra Springs?"

"Perrier is French for Sierra Springs," I said.

"No, it is not," the waiter answered in heavily accented English. It sounded like he was speaking through his nose.

I could have killed him.

"But they are the same thing," I said firmly, hoping he'd get the message. *"L'eau est de l'eau."*

"They are very different," the waiter said.

"Obviously," Monk said to me.

"Sierra Springs is the finest bottled table water in the United States," the waiter said. "Of course we have it."

"You do?" I was astonished.

"We have water from all over the world—Italy, Switzerland, Germany, to name a few places. The only water we don't have is Belgian, because it is piss." The waiter mimed spitting, then turned to Monk. "Would you like your Sierra Springs served chilled or at room temperature, in the bottle or in a glass?"

"Chilled in the bottle, please," Monk said, beaming with delight.

The waiter nodded and went off to fill our order.

"Things are looking up," Monk said.

Indeed they were. Since he was warming up to France a bit, I thought it would be a good time to start thinking about how we'd spend our next few days. I pulled out the guidebooks that I'd purchased and handed one to Monk.

"You should flip through this," I said. "Maybe you'll find something in Paris that you'd like to see."

"I only have one thing on my list," he said.

"You have a list?"

"I have a list for everything."

Of course he did. That was a dumb question.

"So what's on it? The Louvre? Notre Dame? Maybe a stroll along the Seine?"

"The sewer," he said.

I stared at Monk in disbelief. "It's the filthiest and most disgusting place you could possibly go. Sewers are number one on your list of places to avoid, even if it's a matter of life and death. In fact, you have a footnote that says that you'd prefer death."

"The Paris sewer is different."

"I can assure you that sewage is just as awful here as it is anywhere else."

"It is the first sewer of its kind anywhere in the world. It is the sewer that all other sewers are measured against," Monk said. "I've wanted to visit the sewer museum since I was a child. Then again, who doesn't?"

"There's a museum for the sewer?"

"What kind of education did you have? That's like asking if there's a Smithsonian in Washington, D.C."

Monk passed the book to me and pointed to the open page. It described the Musée des Égouts de Paris, which was located underground on the left bank of the Seine near the Pont de l'Alma, a bridge that was walking distance from our hotel.

"In the late nineteenth century, the Paris sewers were the most popular tourist attraction in the city," Monk said. "People came from all over the world to see this marvel of technology and sanitation."

"What's so amazing about it?"

"Its vital role as an instigator of social, political, and sanitary change in Paris and, eventually, the world."

"How could a sewer do that?"

"In the early eighteen hundreds, tens of thousands of Parisians died of cholera because of the filth in their drinking water. And those who survived often fainted on the streets from the unbearable stench of decaying waste. The sewers changed all that, making the city a cleaner, healthier place to live. The healthier people are, the more content and productive they will be. Happy people don't riot in the streets or overthrow governments. So thanks to the sewer system, Paris became known as the City of Light, renowned throughout the world as a beacon of sanitation and sparkling cleanliness."

I'd heard Monk make speeches about cleanliness before, but never anything with even a hint of social or political commentary.

It was obvious to me that the history of the Paris sewers, or at least his interpretation of it, imbued his outrageous rules of sanitary living with a broader social significance and gave him a moral justification for trying to impose them on everybody else.

It wouldn't surprise me if it was his crazy mother who'd made him read up on the Paris sewers to instill in him an almost religious devotion to cleanliness.

I'm not a shrink, but the more I heard about her from Monk, the clearer it became to me that she was responsible for most of the psychological problems that Monk and his agoraphobic brother Ambrose suffered from.

I wondered how much I was screwing up my daughter without knowing it. But I shrugged off that thought and addressed Monk's speech instead.

"That's all very interesting, Mr. Monk. But Paris isn't known as the City of Light for its sewers."

"Of course it is."

"Don't you think it has to do with the city being the inspiration for timeless works of art, literature, and architecture?"

"Painters don't find much inspiration in streets thick with human waste and poets have a hard time being creative when they are choking on their own vomit."

"I hadn't thought of it that way."

And I didn't want to think about it now, right before dinner.

I still couldn't imagine Monk, with his claustrophobia and fear of germs, slogging through a tunnel full of effluent, no matter how much reverence he had for this particular sewer's place in the history of sanitation.

"You're just going to stroll through all the feculence as if it was the Louvre?"

I'd never used the word *feculence* before—I'd only heard it for the first time when Monk said it a few minutes earlier—but it sounded almost as disgusting as what it described. It was a fun word, and I was glad to have a chance to use it.

"I'm sure it's the cleanest sewer museum there is," Monk replied. "But I'll have protection."

"Do you think that rubber gloves and disinfectant wipes will be enough?"

"Hell no," Monk said. "You're going to get us hazardous-materials suits."

I didn't know how he expected me to do that.

The waiter brought our meals. The croque monsieurs were perfect square sandwiches of French ham and Swiss Gruyère that were grilled in a press that left a wafflelike impression in the melted cheese on the top. They looked a lot better than the grilled-cheese sandwiches my grandmother used to wrap in aluminum foil and then press with her iron.

Monk looked at his croque monsieur with something akin to wonder.

"So this is gourmet food."

"I wouldn't say that," I said. "It's just a typical French sandwich. Every bistro has it."

"Does it taste as good as it looks?"

"Try it and find out."

Monk cut a piece of the sandwich with his knife and fork and put it in his mouth. He smiled as he chewed, then washed it down with a sip of Sierra Springs.

"This is living," he said.

A bottle of water, a grilled-cheese sandwich, and the promise of a trip to a sewer—what more could any man want?

8

Mr. Monk Goes to Bed

While we were waiting for our dinner check, I called Chief Inspector Le Roux and asked him for a favor. I wanted to know if he could get Monk one of the outfits that forensic investigators wear to prevent contaminating crime scenes and to protect themselves from toxic materials.

"I would be glad to," Le Roux said. "Are you expecting to encounter a violent crime or is this just a precaution?"

"Neither," I said. "We're just doing some sightseeing."

"In a full forensic outfit."

"He is, not me," I said and gave him Monk's measurements from memory.

"Will he need the goggles, boots, and a gas mask?"

"Absolutely," I said.

"You should know that the jumpsuit is bright yellow," Le Roux said. "Monsieur Monk will attract attention wherever he goes."

"We're used to it."

"The suit will be waiting for you at the front desk in the morning," he said. "He can take it home as a souvenir with our compliments."

"That's a very thoughtful gesture," I said. "But he'd appreciate it if you had it burned after he's worn it."

"Burned," he repeated.

"It's nothing personal," I said.

Le Roux offered to show us the sites of Paris himself, perhaps thinking that being driven in his car might limit my embarrassment, but I graciously declined. I already felt bad having to contact him again only a few hours after we'd parted.

After we paid our check, Monk and I took our time walking back to the hotel, avoiding the Champs-Élysées and sticking to the less commercialized streets.

I looked at everything, trying to see all the details that were different from home. The architecture. The cars. The way the people walked. The names of businesses. The advertisements on every *colonne Morris*.

I eavesdropped on people speaking in French and listened for snippets of Gallic music and the uniquely European wail of the sirens on police cars, fire trucks, and ambulances.

I sniffed the air for traces of strong cheese, Gauloises cigarettes, freshly baked bread, and the breeze wafting off the Seine. Anything that smelled French.

And I touched the buildings, lampposts, and trees to ground myself in the place and to connect on a visceral level with the history it was steeped in.

This made Monk very uncomfortable.

He touched each lamppost that he passed. Sometimes my hand would brush his as we reached out simultaneously for the same lamppost. When that happened, he'd yank his hand away as if he'd been shocked.

I didn't care about his discomfort. I wanted to immerse myself in Paris, to soak it into my bones and my being.

To me, Paris wasn't a place that you visited, it was something that you experienced. I was trying to speed up the process.

By the time we reached our hotel, I was exhausted from all that looking, listening, sniffing, and touching, as well as from the stressful events of the day.

Monk looked pretty tired, too. It takes a lot of energy just to deal with life when you are neurotic and obsessive-compulsive. Now imagine what it takes when you're in a totally foreign environment and solving a murder, too.

He had my sympathy and understanding, even if he'd depleted most of my patience.

I went up to the front desk, got our key from the ghost at the counter, and started up the winding staircase. Monk followed along.

When we got to our room, I unlocked the door and opened it for him. He stepped inside.

The room was elegant but inviting, more so than the lobby was. The two beds, the writing desk, the tall armoire, and the reading chair were all crafted in the Louis XVI style. The small flat-screen TV mounted on the wall looked totally out of place with the other decor. It was like seeing a trash compactor in an adobe hut.

The bathroom was to our left, with a free-standing tub, a handheld showerhead, and a chain-pull toilet with the tank mounted up high on the wall. It was quaint.

In front of us was a set of curtained French doors that

opened onto a very narrow wrought-iron balcony, which looked more decorative than practical.

I was wondering why French doors were called French doors when Monk spoke up.

"Whose room is this?" he asked. "Yours or mine?"

"Ours," I replied.

"I don't understand."

I think he understood perfectly but didn't want to face the horrifying implications. A man with his incredible eye for detail must have immediately noticed that our suitcases were beside the armoire.

"We're sharing the room, Mr. Monk."

"We can't," he said.

"There are no vacant single rooms on even-numbered floors, and you can't afford this room for yourself and another single room for me."

"There are other hotels."

"Not any two-star hotels that are within your price range, meet your standards of cleanliness, and have vacancies. This is it. This is where we are staying."

"It's not right," he said.

"People share rooms all the time," I said. "That's why they come furnished with two large beds."

"I can't," Monk said.

"We spend hours alone in your apartment together in a space not much bigger than this almost every day. What's the difference?"

"We don't sleep and bathe in the same room," Monk said with a shudder.

"You slept at my house for a few days while your building was being fumigated. All three of us shared a bathroom. This is the same thing."

"But we slept in separate rooms. With the doors closed. And locked."

"My door wasn't locked," I said. "Neither was Julie's."

"You weren't in jeopardy."

"And you were?"

Monk rolled his shoulders and tipped his head from side to side. "This is so wrong."

"I thought you said you trusted me."

"I do," he said.

"Then what is the problem?"

"There isn't a problem."

"Good," I said.

"There are a *thousand* problems," Monk said. "I don't know where to begin."

"You can think about it while I get ready for bed." I picked up my suitcase and unzipped it.

"You're not going to do that in here, are you?"

"I'm going into the bathroom."

I removed my toiletries and a nightgown from my suitcase, and he immediately turned his head away, embarrassed by my girlie things.

"This one?" he asked.

"What other bathroom is there?"

"One not in this room."

"If you want to use a different bathroom, Mr. Monk, be my guest. I am using this one. I would offer to let you use it before me, but I don't think I can hold my bladder for the three hours it will take you to clean it first."

Monk winced. "Don't use the *B word* in public."

"We aren't in public," I said. "We are in the privacy of our hotel room."

"You still shouldn't talk like a sailor."

"Do sailors say *bladder* a lot?"

Monk winced again. "And don't say *our hotel room*."

"What should I say?"

"The place where I am sleeping in ill repute."

"Ill repute?"

"I am an employer spending the night in a hotel room with a vivacious employee of the opposite sex. How will it look to the others?"

"What others?"

"Others who might look," he said.

"We could hang a bedsheet across the middle of the room," I said. "Like *It Happened One Night*."

"What happened?"

"Nothing happened. It's the title of a movie with Clark Gable and Claudette Colbert."

"It won't work."

"Why not?"

"The room isn't symmetrical," he said. "One half would have a balcony and the other the facilities."

"Then you'll just have to live with it."

I smiled vivaciously and went into the bathroom, closing the door behind me.

Monk immediately turned on the TV for fear, I assume, of hearing things that he didn't want to hear and that shouldn't be allowed to happen.

I used the toilet, took off my makeup, brushed my teeth, and had a quick shower before slipping into what Julie called my *grandmother* nightgown and emerging from the bathroom.

Monk sat on the edge of the bed nearest the window and pretended to watch a French-dubbed version of *CSI: Miami* that made David Caruso sound like a stylishly dressed Inspector Clouseau.

"It's all yours," I said and gestured to the bathroom.

"I'm fine," he said without looking at me.

"Aren't you going to get ready for bed?"

"I am ready," Monk said.

"You're fully dressed."

"This is how I go to bed in hotels."

"You can look at me, Mr. Monk," I said.

"I am," he said, staring at the TV.

"I'm not naked. I'm wearing a nightgown. You have seen me wearing a lot less."

"I have not."

"I wore a bikini when we were in Hawaii."

"I didn't notice."

"Okay, fine, avert your gaze," I said. "But you, of all people, should know better than to wear those clothes to bed."

"They are comfortable."

"They are filthy. You've had them on for sixteen hours. You wore them on the airplane, where you were in a seat that hundreds of other people sat in before you. You wore them in a police car, which has carried God knows how many criminals, rapists, drug dealers, prostitutes, and drunks. And you wore them out there, on the street, where you brushed against countless strangers. Do you really want to sleep in those clothes and dirty your sheets with them?"

I knew I had him with that argument.

Monk took a deep breath, rolled his shoulders, then picked up his suitcase and carried it to the bathroom, still making an effort not to look at me. He slammed the door.

And locked it.

I guessed I'd have to control the urge to barge in and watch him floss.

I took the bed near the window, left the TV on for his peace of mind, and then got into bed and snuggled up with some of the Paris guidebooks.

There was so much to see and do, but I wanted to

avoid the things I had done, and the places I had gone, with Mitch.

Then again, wasn't that why I was here, to experience some aspect of that joy again, even if it was tinged with deep sadness and loss?

I didn't know. I was a mystery to myself, and I'm betting to Adrian Monk, too, and he's a great detective, so that should give you a hint how mysterious I am. Not to mention vivacious.

I read up a bit on the Musée des Égouts de Paris, and though I'd never admit it to Monk, the Paris sewers actually sounded fascinating and every bit as historically relevant as he'd made them seem.

When Victor Hugo immortalized the sewer in *Les Misérables,* he described it as a "trench of truth" and "the conscience of the city," because in those putrid tunnels, "there are shadows, but there are no longer any secrets."

It was the sewers where Hugo had his tragic hero Jean Valjean flee, carrying a wounded man on his shoulders. It was also where Gaston Leroux's doomed and dangerously romantic Phantom of the Opera fled with his captive lover to meet his heartbreaking end.

If Hugo and Leroux could find all that romanticism, adventure, and social significance in the sewers, then I figured I might get something worthwhile out of a visit, too.

While I was reading about that, I stumbled across the catacombs—another underground historical site that sparked my curiosity and that I thought Monk might enjoy. I marked the page by bending down a corner and browsed some more.

After an hour, I could barely keep my eyes open. Monk was still in the bathroom, and there was no point waiting up for him. We had nothing left to say to each other except, perhaps, *sweet dreams*.

So I put the books on the nightstand, turned off my reading light, and was asleep before I put my head back on my pillow.

9

Mr. Monk Takes a Walk

I awoke around seven with my pillow over my face to shield me from the sunlight that was blasting through the thin drapes. My sheets were twisted around my body like a boa constrictor squeezing its prey.

I freed myself from the sheets, rolled over, and glanced across what might as well have been a bottomless chasm between my bed and Monk's.

At first, I thought he'd made his bed and left the room. But then I sat up on one elbow and saw his head poking out from under the tightly tucked sheets. He was lying on his back, his eyes wide, staring at the ceiling.

I don't know how he managed to get into the bed without untucking anything or how he'd deflated his body so that he barely made a ripple on the bedspread. It was like a magic trick.

"Good morning, Mr. Monk."

"Good morning," he said.

"Did you sleep well?"

"As well as could be expected," he said.

"Which was?"

"Not at all."

"You didn't sleep?"

"I counted sheep," Monk said. "I'm up to 29,280."

"That's a lot of sheep."

"I can't get them to go away," Monk said. "I can still see them, jumping over the bed."

"You're hallucinating," I said. "Or you're delirious."

"What should I do?"

"Close your eyes," I said and got out of bed, which forced him to do what I recommended.

I padded across the room, took some clothes out of my suitcase, and went into the bathroom. I showered, brushed my teeth, put on some light makeup, and got dressed.

Monk was asleep when I came out, and we weren't on any kind of schedule, so I quietly left the room to let him rest, and went downstairs.

There was a different desk clerk on duty, a middle-aged man with cheeks that were so round, I thought he might be holding two tennis balls in his mouth. He wore what looked like a sweater hand-knitted by someone who didn't know how to knit.

I smiled at him and said a cheery *bonjour*. He ignored me. That was more like the France I remembered.

I went outside and strolled down the street to a *presse*, a small newsstand inside of a large *colonne Morris*, where I bought the latest issue of *Le Monde*. Then I found a small café. I bought myself a hot, buttery croissant, a strawberry tart, and a cup of coffee and settled down at a table outside to read the paper.

The croissant was incredibly light, flaky, and delicious, nothing like the crescent-shaped things we dare to call croissants at home. But the truth is, I could have been eating dry dog food, and it would have tasted delicious to me, because I was sitting outside having breakfast at a café in Paris.

I opened up my copy of *Le Monde* and, feeling very Parisian and not the least bit touristy, read up on the world news. All I needed was a scarf and a poodle, and I would have blended in perfectly with the Frenchwomen around me.

Reading the paper wasn't easy, and I had flashbacks to high school French class that made me sweat. But even with my bad French, I found a small article about the murder in the airplane, and it even mentioned Monk.

I was proud of him, even though I'd found the whole situation on the plane aggravating at the time. It was easier to be impressed by him now that the investigation hadn't ended up sabotaging our trip. I was also pleased to see Monk getting acknowledged for his brilliance half a world away from home.

I folded up the paper and stuck it in my purse for him. What could possibly be a better, or more appropriate, souvenir for Monk than that article? The clipping might even help him get a raise when it was time to renegotiate his consulting contract with the SFPD. World-renowned detectives ought to be paid more than a mere local deductive genius, don't you think?

I sat for a while and people-watched, picking very slowly at my incredible tart to justify occupying my seat for so long. It was nine a.m. when I finally got up, bought Monk a croissant, and headed back to the hotel.

The first thing I noticed when I walked in was the distressed look on the desk clerk's face, and the horrified expressions on some of the guests as they emerged from the elevator. They were all reacting to something in the sitting room portion of the lobby.

It was Monk, of course, in his bright yellow hazmat suit. He was wearing the whole thing—the hood, the goggles, the gas mask, the gloves, and the boots. A hotel claim check tag hung from a belt loop.

I marched up to him. "What are you doing in that suit?"

"I'm ready to go to the sewer museum," he said.

"We aren't there yet," I said. "You don't need to wear the suit now."

"It can't hurt."

"You're freaking out the guests, and you're going to scare off anybody who comes through the door. You make it look like the hotel is contaminated and is being quarantined."

Monk took off the hood, the goggles, and the gas mask. He looked like an astronaut who'd just returned to Earth.

"The French are so touchy," he said.

I hustled him out the door and handed him the bag from the café. "I got you a croissant for breakfast."

"I was planning on a croque monsieur."

"But that's what you had for dinner," I said.

"And I survived the night," Monk said. "Why take a risk on anything else?"

"Because it might be as good, or even better, than the croque monsieur."

"The café also has my water."

I could see that if Monk had his way, we would be eating all of our meals at the same café. There were worse things that could happen, so I decided to count my blessings, one of which was the fact that I got to eat his croissant.

So we walked back to the café where we had dinner, using the backstreets and avoiding the Champs-

Élysées. Along the way, I devoured the croissant, and Monk got fewer stares from people than I thought he would. Most people seemed to take it in stride, which I thought was odd. When Monk wore a gas mask on the streets of Los Angeles, he was such a distraction that he nearly caused a few car accidents.

The same waiter who'd served us the previous night was there again. I'd heard that the French didn't like personal questions, so I didn't ask why he worked such long hours. If he was shocked by Monk's attire, he didn't show it.

I ordered Monk *la même chose* as the night before and a cup of coffee for myself.

The waiter walked away and I heard Monk gasp.

I followed his gaze to see a woman at the next table feeding pieces of bread to a Jack Russell terrier in her lap. The woman was probably in her sixties and dressed elegantly, as if she was on her way to some high-society event.

"Tell her she can't do that," Monk said.

"Here you can," I said.

"It's unsanitary to bring dogs into a restaurant."

"We aren't in the restaurant. We are outside. Besides, it's not like the dog is eating from the table."

"Look again," he said.

I did. The dog was now eating from the same plate that the woman was.

"It's not our place to criticize," I said.

"I don't want this wonderful restaurant closed down by health inspectors because of one woman's savagery."

Before I could say anything, Monk got up and marched over to her table.

The dog started yapping immediately and scrambled to get at him. If the woman wasn't clutching the animal to her enormous bosom, it might have leaped for Monk's throat.

"You can't bring your dog to a restaurant and let it eat off your plate," Monk said. "Do you have some kind of death wish?"

"How dare you talk to me that way?" the woman said firmly in perfect, if slightly accented, English.

"It's about time someone did," Monk said. "I can understand your dog behaving that way, but you are a human being. Start acting like one."

"Do you know who I am, you impudent little trash collector?"

Her comment made me realize why Monk wasn't getting many stares. He looked like a French garbageman.

Her little beast barked incessantly and struggled wildly to get out of her arms.

"I know that you are filthy and disgusting and an extreme danger to public health," Monk said. "If you and your dog don't leave this restaurant immediately, I will have you arrested for attempted murder."

Her face turned such a deep shade of red that I feared she'd suffered a stroke. She opened her mouth to speak, but instead she let out a surprised, horrified shriek and released her dog.

Now I could see that her outfit was wet. The animal was so excited that he'd peed all over her.

Monk jerked away as if he'd been shot, repulsed by the dog and the urine staining the woman's clothes.

The dog scrambled after him, but was snapped back by the short length of the leash the woman was holding.

The woman was in tears, crying both with rage and humiliation. I was surprised she didn't let her dog attack Monk.

She grabbed her purse and hurried away, dragging the

barking animal after her on his leash, his nails scraping on the ground like chalk on a blackboard.

The way she'd talked to Monk, she was obviously someone of power and authority, or perhaps married to someone who was, and was used to deference and respect.

I half expected her to return with Nicolas Sarkozy in tow, pulled along behind her like her terrier.

Monk returned to his seat. "That table is going to have to be incinerated. You should inform the waiter."

"I'll do that," I said.

The rest of our breakfast passed uneventfully, and afterward we set off on foot for the sewer museum.

Our walk took us across the Champs-Élysées and down Avenue Georges V in the direction of the Seine and the Eiffel Tower. The avenue was lined with the kind of fancy shops where a sock cost more than my car and I would have to take a second mortgage on my house to buy a handbag.

We neared an elegant nineteenth-century building at 39 Avenue Georges V that looked as if it was melting in the morning sun. But as we got closer, I could see that it was an illusion. It was actually a painting on a canvas that covered the scaffolding around a building undergoing renovation.

The painting was a startlingly realistic, distorted image of what the finished building would look like if it was reflected in a fun house mirror or, perhaps, as seen through the eyes of Salvador Dalí.

There was a placard on the canvas that described it as a work of *urban surrealism*. I was wowed by it. They'd even added polystyrene cornices and ravens to the canvas, giving the illusion even more realism than just the painter's tricks of light, shadow, and forced perspective.

The fact that anyone had gone to such an effort to make something meaningful and memorable out of a construction site was, to me, indicative of what made Paris so special. I took a picture of the building with my cell phone camera.

Monk was appalled, of course, by the illusion of the melting facade. To him, it was offensive, a nuisance, and a safety hazard.

You're probably as tired of his tirades against nonconformity by now as I was that morning, so I won't bore you with the speech that he made. Besides, I couldn't share it with you if I wanted to because I didn't listen to him. I was too busy admiring the sly and engaging work of art.

As we continued on our way, we stumbled on another piece of urban art—one that had the added dimension of doubling as biting social commentary, though I was certain that this *objet d'art* was created unintentionally by people with nothing but practicality and function in mind.

But I knew that Monk would love it.

I'm talking, of course, about the *sanisette* directly across the street from the *très exclusif* and *très cher* Four Seasons Georges V Hotel.

The *sanisette* is a public toilet, but it's far removed technologically from the stinky *pissoirs* you can still find in some corners of Paris or any bathroom that you've ever been in.

The cylindrical hut was made of corrugated concrete and stainless steel that gave it a futuristic look, less like a toilet and more like a time machine. Only the sign above it that said *Toilettes gratuites* and the icons of a man and woman gave away its true function.

I found the juxtaposition of the *sanisette* and the five-star hotel compelling, whimsical and worth capturing in a photo with my cell phone camera.

"What kind of restroom is that?" Monk asked.

"It's a unisex, totally automated, flushless, self-cleaning toilet," I said. "After every use, the entire interior is chemically washed down, scrubbed, cleaned, and disinfected. They're free and can be found all over Paris."

I assumed this one had been installed in the neighborhood so tourists and vagrants wouldn't go into the exclusive shops or Four Seasons anymore looking for a toilet or, worse, resorting to relieving themselves on the street.

"I have to see this," Monk said. "Stand back."

I don't know what kind of danger he thought I was in, but I humored him and took a step back.

Monk put on his gas mask and goggles, hit the button to open the toilet's sliding stainless steel door and stepped into the brightly lit, all-white plastic interior.

The door closed and locked automatically behind him. A moment later he came out and took off his gas mask and goggles.

"Incredible," Monk said.

The door slid shut automatically and we listened as the *toilette* washed itself inside. We could hear gears and the low hum of spraying cleaning fluid.

"What did you do in there?" I asked.

"Not that," he said.

I shrugged. "It's what it's for."

"I spit on it," Monk said.

"That's not a crime."

"Not if the evidence is thoroughly cleaned up," he said. "We shall see. If it's not, I can always use a wipe."

"That's a relief," I said.

After a few minutes, the control panel light glowed green, and Monk pressed the entry button again. The door slid open, and he stepped into the open *toilette* without bothering to put on his gas mask this time, a truly courageous act on his part.

Monk sniffed the air inside and looked at the gleaming surfaces in wonder as the door automatically slid shut.

I half expected the *sanisette* to lift off and carry Monk away to whatever planet Mr. Clean came from—a germ-free place where every surface sparkles. Of course, the price people pay on that planet for all that cleanliness is shocking-white eyebrows and total baldness. That look may work for Mr. Clean, especially when you add that stylish earring, but I think most people, if given the choice, would gladly live with a few dirty counters and some germs, if they could keep their hair and matching eyebrows.

When Monk came out again, having finished his inspection, he declared: "I wish I could live in here."

"In a public toilet?"

"It's a little piece of heaven. Imagine if they could build homes like this, places that completely cleaned and disinfected themselves after every use. It would be paradise."

"It sounds nightmarish to me."

Monk studied the exterior of the *sanisette.* "I wonder if I could get one of these installed in my house."

"I doubt it," I said.

"It could fit."

"I don't think that's the issue. You'd have to get the approval of the planning commission, your neighbors, and your landlord. And assuming you got all of that, how would you afford the purchase, shipping, and construction costs of installing the unit?"

"I would sell everything I have," he said. "It might also mean a slight reduction in your salary."

"You don't have anything," I said. "And if my salary were reduced any further, I would be working for nothing."

"Would you do that?"

"No, Mr. Monk, I wouldn't."

"You don't think that's a little selfish?"

"I have a daughter to raise," I said.

"What about after? She's got to leave home eventually."

"I'll still need a roof over my head and food to eat," I said.

Monk rolled his shoulders. "You're certain about that?"

"Yes, Mr. Monk, I am."

"Your father is a very wealthy man," Monk said. "I'm sure that he wouldn't let you go hungry."

"I respect you, I care about you, and your happiness is very important to me, but I won't work for you for free so you can afford to purchase a *sanisette*. You can just drop that whole idea."

He nodded and sighed. "Do you think there is one of these near our hotel?"

"Are you thinking of using it instead of our bathroom?"

"I was thinking that you could."

"Think again," I said and marched on.

10

Mr. Monk in the Sewer

If you weren't looking for the Musée des Égouts de Paris, and didn't already know where it was, you could easily mistake the museum's small blue-and-white ticket booth on the park above the banks of the Seine for a snack shack or a newsstand.

I'd expected something whimsical or clever to mark the entrance to the sewer museum, if for no other reason than to draw visitors. Or if not something lighthearted, I figured they'd go the opposite way and have some kind of monumental structure that projected authority, permanence, and reverence so people would take the sewer museum seriously.

I didn't expect some mundane little hut.

But when I saw the prime waterfront apartments that lined the street behind the museum, the utterly unremarkable design choice made sense to me. Whoever lived in those expensive apartments along Quai d'Orsay didn't want people to know they were located next to the entrance to the sewer.

It was stupid, of course, since every apartment in Paris is located above the sewer, but it's easy to forget that. A noticeable museum would, on other hand, draw attention to the fact.

The sewer museum wasn't exactly drawing a Louvre-sized crowd. There were only a half dozen people in line in front of us. They got their tickets and then descended the steps of a large square manhole.

Monk watched them go and shook his head.

"I'm surprised that none of them is wearing protective clothing," he said.

"Why should they?"

"Because they are going *in the sewer*." Monk looked at me. "You should have some protection, too."

"In the late eighteen hundreds, the rich and famous would tour the sewers in their finery, riding in elegant gaslit gondolas on rivers of waste."

Even to me, it sounded like I was describing a ride at the Disneyland in hell.

"How do you know?" Monk asked.

"I did some reading about the museum last night in our guidebook."

"What they don't tell you," Monk said, "is that those visitors died immediately afterward of the plague."

"I thought you said this was the cleanest sewer on earth."

"It is," Monk said. "But it is still a sewer."

"Well, you are wearing your finery, and I am wearing mine."

Monk gave me a disapproving look and then put on his goggles, gas mask, and gloves.

I paid for the tickets and got the brochure for the self-guided tour. Then we descended into the depths.

I braced myself to be assaulted by the pungent odor

from the feculent rivers of raw sewage—a foul smell a thousand times worse than any outhouse or portable toilet you could ever imagine.

But to my surprise, and great relief, the smell in the wide tunnel wasn't bad at all. I'd walked past freshly fertilized lawns that had a much more powerful stench. All I smelled was a slightly sour dankness, exactly what you'd expect from an underground cavern with water running through it.

I didn't see any water yet, but I could hear the muffled sound of it, rushing by somewhere beyond the walls of the tunnel we were comfortably standing in. It had vaulted ceilings, was brightly lit, and was easily wide enough to fit an SUV.

There were large placards on the walls that explained and illustrated the evolution of the Paris sewer. The text was written in French and I tried to summarize what it said for Monk as we went along.

The most interesting tidbit was that until 1859 the prefecture of police, in addition to maintaining order, was in charge of public health and hygiene, which meant keeping the streets and the sewers clean.

"It was a perfect world," Monk said.

I knew he'd like that.

He'd love to be patrolling the streets of San Francisco today, armed with a bottle of Fantastik, a scrub brush, and a wash rag, citing people for improper hygiene.

There were some pictures from the late eighteen hundreds of people taking the sewer tour. According to the caption, they were impressed how everything around them was clean except the water. You could walk the sewers for miles and emerge without a single speck of dirt on your clothes.

The women in the pictures wore bonnets and high heels, as if going to a Sunday picnic. The men wore top

hats, ties, and long coats. Uniformed sewer men pulled
the boatloads of *la bourgeoise* through the canals of
human waste. But if the sewer men felt demeaned at
being treated like horses, you wouldn't know it from the
proud smiles on their faces.

Monk studied the pictures, tilting his head from side
to side, and getting as close to some of them as his gas
mask would allow. I didn't know what he was looking
for and I didn't ask.

We walked past several mannequins dressed as sewer
workers and posed beside their dredging equipment.

The tools of the sewer trade hadn't changed significantly over the past century or so, despite huge techno-
logical advances in just about every other field of human
endeavor. Workers still used sluice boats and huge, man-
ually powered plowlike contraptions to move the waste
along because of the explosive danger of using electric
devices in the sewers.

There were thirteen hundred miles of sewer tunnels
under Paris, each one a subterranean reflection of the
street above. The tunnels even had the same blue-and-
white enamel street signs as the avenues they were
under. The addresses of the buildings above could also
be found etched in, or painted on, the walls.

Here's what Victor Hugo wrote about it:

> Paris has another Paris under herself, a Paris of
> sewers that has its streets, its crossings, its squares,
> its blind alleys, its arteries, and its circulation, which
> is slime minus the human form.

I thought it was cool, so I gave my French a workout
translating it for Monk and his reaction was worth the
effort.

"Wow," he said, bowing his head with almost religious reverence. Either that or the weight of the gas mask was hurting his neck.

A man in his thirties with a belly purse around his waist stuffed with maps and holding a palm-sized camcorder tapped Monk on the shoulder.

"Excusez-moi, monsieur. Où est la toilette?" he asked haltingly as he stumbled for the correct French words. He was an American.

"He doesn't work here," I said.

"Then why is he dressed like that?"

"Because I want to live," Monk said.

The man looked at me. "Do you know where the bathrooms are?"

"No, I'm afraid not."

"But you're a woman," he said.

"What does that have to do with anything?"

"Women always know where the bathrooms are," he said. "It's the first thing they look for."

"Not me," I said.

He shrugged and moved on.

I turned my attention back to the placards and learned that the sewers weren't the only tunnels under Paris.

The city was built from the gypsum and limestone that was mined from underneath it. The miners left behind their quarries, nearly two hundred miles of passageways and immense underground chambers that were intertwined with the sewers and subways.

With so many tunnels under Paris, I was surprised the city hadn't collapsed. But maybe it was one reason there weren't many tall buildings.

We followed the sewer tunnels into a vast gallery with more displays, historical photos, and a five-ton flushing boat. There was a grate on the floor that ran the length of the gallery and covered a fast-moving flow of waste water in the darkness ten feet below. A sign on the wall read Rue Cognacq-Jay.

Monk avoided the grate, not even hazarding a glance at it. I couldn't resist a peek, but from our height, all I saw was a dark stream.

While Monk studied the flushing boat, I studied him.

I've seen Monk throw a hissy fit over a couple of crumbs on a tabletop, but there he was, walking in a sewer tunnel, only an iron grate away from a rushing stream of human waste, and he wasn't complaining.

This was not how I imagined Monk reacting in a sewer.

Granted, he was protected by his suit, but I don't think that explained his reaction. Or, rather, his lack of one.

I couldn't see his face behind the goggles and gas mask to judge his expression; all I had to go on was his silence and his body language, but I think it was veneration. He was humbled by the respect he felt for the achievements represented by the museum displays.

I became aware of the sound of dribbling water nearby. Monk whirled around and I followed his gaze.

The American tourist we'd met before was urinating into the grate to the river below.

"Stop!" Monk yelled. "In the name of the law."

But the man kept going. Monk shoved him from behind.

"Hey, watch it. You're ruining my aim," the man said. "I almost got some on my shoes."

Monk staggered back, making little choking sounds. The man finished and zipped up his pants.

"How could you?" Monk said.

The man shrugged. "I couldn't find the bathroom."

"So you thought it would be a good idea to just urinate on the floor of the museum?" Monk said, his voice cracking with exasperation.

"It's the sewer," the man said. "This is where it's going to end up anyway. I took the direct route."

He was a disgusting jerk but he had a good point.

"You are the ugly American," Monk said, pointing a gloved finger at him. "You are the tourist they all talk about."

"I'm not the one wearing a hazmat suit," the man said.

"It's a good thing I am," Monk said. "You could have killed someone."

"With pee?" the man said.

"That's what it does," Monk said. "Pee kills."

The man shook his head and walked away. "You're a loon."

"You're a disgrace to our country," Monk yelled. "They should revoke your passport."

Other people were staring now—people who hadn't seen the offense the man committed.

"Mr. Monk, you should lower your voice," I said.

"I'm sending a full report to U.S. Customs. You're going down, Mr. Pee," Monk yelled after him. "I will see you in hell."

"Ssssh," I said. "It's over."

Monk looked at me. "He can't be allowed to go all over the world, peeing in every country he visits. He's got to be stopped. You need to call Chief Inspector Le Roux and have him alert Interpol to watch the borders."

"That really isn't necessary," I said. "He won't do it again."

"How do you know?"

"You've put the fear of God into him."

"You think so?"

"Oh, yeah," I said. "He was quivering when he walked away."

"Really?"

"Definitely. I think he may even have been sobbing with shame. That's why he turned his back to you and hurried off. You broke him, Mr. Monk."

"It had to be done," Monk said.

"I understand," I said.

"Now we have to clean it up."

"Clean what up?"

"What he did," Monk said. "We can't leave it there in the middle of the museum."

I motioned to the grate. "He peed into a stream of raw sewage. Where do you suggest we start cleaning?"

Monk stared at the grate and shook his head.

"He's an ugly, ugly American," he said.

"Yes, he is." I put my arm around him and gently steered him back to the tour.

We walked over more grates, read more displays, and looked at more pictures detailing the history of sanitation in Paris. I wanted to get his mind off the ugly American as quickly as I could, so I read just about everything to him.

Monk seemed particularly interested when I translated the story of Eugène Poubelle, the prefect of the Seine, who made it illegal to toss dirty water from windows and imposed strict laws on trash disposal and collection.

"I know all about him," Monk said. "He's the Abraham Lincoln of France."

"Abraham Lincoln held our country together and freed the slaves," I said. "I don't see how Poubelle compares."

"He freed the Parisians from the shackles of filth. The French revere him."

"I'm not so sure about that," I said.

"He's a legend," Monk said. "The man every French boy aspires to be."

"You know what they call garbage cans in France?" I said. "Poubelles."

Monk nodded. "It's a great honor to the man and the ideals that he represented."

Until that day, I'd always assumed the word *poubelle* had something to do with a smell that wasn't pretty. It never occurred to me it was someone's name.

"I don't think that's how it was intended," I said.

"What other meaning could there be?"

"Maybe they resented him for making them clean up after themselves."

Monk waved off my suggestion. "Don't be ridiculous. Who doesn't love to clean?"

We reached the end of the tour and came upon a huge, sand-filled wooden ball that looked like the prop from the opening scene of *Raiders of the Lost Ark*. It was a *boule de curage*, which they rolled down the tunnel to flatten waste and improve water flow.

"Would you like me to take your picture next to the ball?" I asked Monk.

"That would be nice." Monk stood next to the ball and I took out my cell phone camera.

"You might want to take off your goggles and gas mask for a moment so I can see your face."

"Why would I do that?" Monk said.

"So we know it's you," I said.

"Who else would it be?"

"It could be anyone under that mask."

"Like who?"

He had a point. I took the picture. We walked through the museum shop and then up the steps back to the street.

Monk took off his gas mask and goggles. "That was unforgettable."

"It was interesting," I said. "But it's not the Louvre."

"You're so right," Monk said. "The Louvre can't touch this."

"The Louvre has the *Mona Lisa*," I said. "This has a big wooden ball for crushing crap."

"It's no contest," Monk said, nodding in agreement. I don't think he realized that we didn't agree at all.

"There's another underground attraction I think you might like and it's close by, only a five-minute subway ride away at Denfert-Rochereau."

"You want to go on a subway train?" Monk said.

"It's how people get around," I said.

"Then it's a good thing I have this suit," Monk said. "Where are we going?"

"The catacombs," I said.

11

Mr. Monk in the Catacombs

Paris had grown fast in the late seventeen hundreds. Revolutions, executions, foreign wars, devastating epidemics, and generally poor sanitation had left tens of thousands of people dead, their bodies dumped on cemetery grounds and churchyards. The rotting corpses were piled ten feet above the mass graves at the *Cimetière des Innocents*.

Not only were the decomposing corpses creating a horrific odor and a health hazard but the property that the cemeteries occupied was far too valuable to be wasted on the dead.

So the government came up with the perfect sanitary solution to both their public health and real estate development problems. The bodies were cleared out of the church grounds, disinterred from graveyards, and stuffed into the vast labyrinth of empty quarries underneath Paris.

Over the next eighty years, more than six million corpses—including the bodies of Louis XVI, Marie Antoinette, and Robespierre—were sent to the catacombs as more people died and cemeteries were plowed under for grand boulevards and buildings made from the stone mined from beneath the city.

Like the sewer, another place once viewed with fear and revulsion, the subterranean ossuary was turned into a popular, if morbid, tourist attraction in 1804. Two hundred four years later, it was still an attraction but to a much smaller degree, both in terms of attendance and the size of the tour. Now only a minuscule portion of the labyrinth of bones was open to the public.

They stopped adding bones to the catacombs over a century ago, but even today there are twice as many dead people interred beneath Paris than there are living ones walking the streets above.

The entrance to *les catacombes* was on the Boulevard Raspail at Place Denfert-Rochereau, the intersection of several avenues dominated at the center by the Lion of Belfort, a sandstone copy of a statue designed by the architect of the Statue of Liberty.

The nineteenth-century art nouvelle entrance to *les catacombes* was more prominent than the one to the Musée des Égouts de Paris, and a much larger line of people was waiting to get in. Apparently, no one was deterred by the declaration above the doors of *les catacombes*: *Barrière d'enfer*.

The Gateway to Hell.

I didn't bother translating that for Monk. Besides, it didn't really apply to him. His idea of the gateway to hell was the front door of Hometown Buffet.

We weren't even inside yet, but already the catacombs struck me as less a somber, sacred resting place for six million souls than it was an elaborate haunted house attraction.

Monk wasn't wearing the gas mask and goggles

anymore—they were hooked to his belt. He'd also taken his hood down, so he didn't stand out quite so much. Even so, Monk got a few curious, sideways glances from the tourists, the ticket agent, and the security guard at the turnstile.

We followed the single-file line of tourists down the eighty-three winding steps to the narrow, gravel-floored passageway that led to the crypts.

Our visit almost ended for us right then because Monk wanted to go back up to the ticket window to complain about the missing step.

There should have been eighty-four steps, of course, because in Monk's opinion an odd number is a clear danger to public safety. People could stumble and break their necks. An extra step, or even one less, would make all the difference.

I told Monk that rather than complain now, he should make a list of all the public safety problems he discovered in Paris, and at the end of the trip, we could give the report to Chief Inspector Le Roux to forward to the proper authorities.

Monk liked that idea. Anytime he could make a list, he was happy.

We walked for twenty minutes in the dimly lit tunnel, the gravel moist and crunchy under our feet, before we came to an archway with a warning etched across the top: *Arrête! C'est ici l'empire de la mort.*

"What does that say?" Monk asked.

"It says you ought to stop and take a look at this arch. It was designed by Mort."

"Who is Mort?"

"A famous designer of French arches and tombstones," I said and hurried on. "You'll see his name a lot down here."

I was pretty certain that if I'd translated the inscription accurately, Monk would have heeded the warning: Stop, this is the empire of death.

I didn't take it seriously. The words struck me as cheap theatrics, no different from the warnings scrawled on any haunted house attraction. Call me cynical, but I wondered if the inscription even existed before the tours began.

I figured it must have taken some showmanship to attract crowds to the dark, damp caves full of bones—mere curiosity wouldn't have been enough of a draw for long.

We walked under the arch, and I heard the shocked gasps of the people ahead of us as they got their first look at what the catacombs contained.

I gasped, too. I'd never seen nor imagined anything so macabre before.

On either side of the passageway, in the deep caverns that stretched into darkness, were immense piles of densely packed human bones. The piles were held in place by retaining walls constructed of meticulously stacked femurs inset with an almost decorative ribbon of skulls.

It was a ghoulish sight, but it was also orderly in its own, morbid way.

I took the decorative arrangement of the femoral walls as an attempt to turn death into art, and even whimsy, without being entirely sacrilegious.

I'm not sure they succeeded.

But that was just one retaining wall, one pile of bones.

There were many, many more.

The passageway we were in branched off into others, which split off into still more of them, every crevice, cranny, and cavern stuffed to the top with thousands of bones. The scale of it was staggering.

I noticed that the femoral or cranial retaining wall of each ossuary cavern had a distinctive design. For instance, one was made of skull caps, broken at even intervals by skull faces and lined along the top with a row of thigh bones laid out tightly side by side, knob side out.

Another was composed of femurs, the facade crisscrossed with a stripe of skulls that alternated between faces and smooth craniums.

There were countless variations on the theme, mixing femoral bones with skulls.

Some of the retaining walls were also inlaid with crosses or stone tablets that explained where the bones were gathered from, like: *Ossements du cimetière de Saint-Étienne déposé en Mai 1787* and *D.M. Combat à la manufacture de Reveillon, Faubourg Saint-Antoine, le 28 Avril 1789.* Bones from a cemetery and bodies from a battle.

Other markers were less explanatory and more pithy, like bumper stickers for the dead inscribed with comments such as: *Où est-elle? La mort toujours future au passée à peine est-elle présent que déjà elle n'est plus.*

Which, translated, goes something like this: "Where is death? Always in the future or in the past. As soon as she is present, she is no more."

Not the catchiest thing I've ever read, but I guess it was in keeping with the spirit of the place, no pun intended.

Another one read: *Insensé que vous êtes pourquoi vous promettez vous de vivre longtemps, vous que ne pouvez compter sur un seul jour.* In other words, you're crazy if you think you're going to live a long time when you can't be sure you'll even last the day.

I don't know when that was written, but clearly it wasn't the most optimistic of times in Paris.

The inscription that struck a nerve with me, though, came from Homer's *Odyssey*: "To insult the dead is unjust."

I found Homer's comment ironic given the context, surrounded by bones used as raw material for decorative walls, as if they were just rocks of different shapes and sizes.

At first, seeing all those bones creeped me out bigtime. Each bone represented a human being, someone who loved and was loved. It was someone's Mitch, someone's Trudy.

It could have been me.

But the deeper I got into the catacombs, the sheer enormity of it overwhelmed me, the bones ceased to be bones, and their emotional power over me wore off. I stopped relating what I saw in those piles with what was inside of me, to my own mortality and to my ultimate insignificance in the march of time.

It was only once that happened that I remembered I wasn't alone down there with all those bones. Monk was with me.

I turned to look for him. He was just a few steps behind me, moving along the passageway with the lumbering gait of a sleepwalker. I put my arm around him.

"Are you okay, Mr. Monk?"

"We have to do something about this," he said.

"About what?"

"The skeletons have been taken apart, their bones are all mixed up," he said. "You can't tell who is who."

"You are not seriously suggesting that we reassemble each skeleton, are you?"

"Someone has to," he said.

I felt stupid for not anticipating that this might be Monk's reaction to the catacombs. Then again, what little I read in the guidebook hadn't prepared me for what I'd seen.

"Do you know how many bones are in the human body?" I asked him.

"Two hundred and six," he replied. "A little more than half of them, one hundred and six, are in the hands and feet."

"Now multiply that by six million."

"One billion two hundred thirty-six million," he answered almost instantly. I would have needed a calculator.

"That's how many bones are in here," I said. "Even if each of those one billion two-hundred thirty-six million bones was labeled with the name of the deceased, which they are *not*, it would take us decades to put all the skeletons back together."

"I know," he said with a sigh. "I guess the sooner we get started the better." Monk picked up a femur from the top of a wall and shoved it into my hands. "Hold this while I look for the matching tibia."

"You aren't allowed to touch the bones."

"I'm wearing gloves," he said.

I wasn't. *Yuck.*

I tossed the bone back onto the pile and wiped my hands on my jeans.

"That's not the point," I said. "You are disrespecting the dead."

Monk motioned to the pile. "And this isn't?"

"If you think the skeletons need to be reassembled, you can make it one of the recommendations in your letter to the Paris authorities," I said. "It's not your responsibility or mine to do the work."

"It would be fun," Monk said.

"Fine," I said, "You do it. I'll come visit you in ten years and see how it's going."

I marched away. After a few moments of indecision, Monk followed after me.

"It's going to be a scathing letter," he said.

"I'm sure it will be."

We passed several passageways that were roped off from the public, but the bones in the many caverns on the other side were lit for dramatic effect anyway.

You know how it looks when someone holds a flashlight under their face in the dark? Okay, now imagine that with a few thousand skulls.

Creepy, huh?

Monk stopped at the rope and peered at a cavern that was near one of the dim lights.

He cocked his head from one shoulder to the other.

"What is it?" I said.

Monk stepped over the rope and headed straight toward a wall of bones: rows of femurs with an enormous crucifix made of skulls in the middle.

"What are you doing?" I demanded in the loudest whisper I could manage. "You aren't allowed back there!"

"I want to look at a skull," he said.

"There are plenty of them over here."

Monk climbed up on the wall, sending a bunch of thigh bones on the top spilling over and clattering to the floor. It sounded like tumbling bricks and echoed down every passageway.

"Get down," I said.

But Monk was scrambling over the top, amid the loose bones, knocking even more to the floor as he reached for the skull and brought it back down. Tourists began to gather behind me and mutter to themselves. I heard words like *crazy man* and *nutcase* in two languages I understood and many that I didn't.

I looked to one side and saw two security guards heading our way. Terrific.

"Mr. Monk, security is coming."

He was holding the skull and regarding it like he was Hamlet.

"Good," Monk said. "Have them secure the crime scene."

"Don't tell me this about the bones being scattered."

"This is about homicide," Monk said.

"Oh, God," I said, feeling a dull ache beginning in my chest. "Don't tell me that, either."

Monk brought the skull under the light and examined it from every angle. "This man was murdered."

"Two hundred fourteen years ago, Mr. Monk." I pointed to a marker inset in one of the cavern walls. "Those bones came from the prisoners who were guillotined during Robespierre's Reign of Terror."

"This man's head wasn't cut off," Monk said. "And he was killed within the last twelve months."

"How do you know?"

"The color of the skull," Monk said.

"We're practically in the dark," I said. "It's probably just a trick of the light."

"You may be right," Monk said.

"Thank you," I replied, relieved.

"But that doesn't explain this." Monk pointed to the skull's teeth. "These fillings in the back are amalgam, a mixture of silver, tin, copper, and mercury that was invented in France and has been common in dentistry worldwide since the early eighteen hundreds. But these up front are composite-resin ionomers colored to match his teeth."

I felt my face flushing with anger. "When were those invented?"

"The nineteen sixties," Monk said. "But these particular fillings are from the last decade."

"Of course they are," I said.

The guards pushed through the crowd and reached me, demanding in outraged but firm French that Monk drop the skull and step over the rope.

I didn't bother translating what they said or explaining what Monk was doing. I just handed Chief Inspector Le Roux's card to one of the guards.

"Tell him Adrian Monk has uncovered a murder," I said and glared at my boss. *"Again."*

12

Mr. Monk Finds the Needle in the Haystack

I was leaning against one of the few walls not made of bones and trying to keep my anger down to a dull simmer when Chief Inspector Le Roux showed up.

He walked with a little bounce in his step and an amused grin on his face. It was easy for Le Roux to be happy; his vacation wasn't ruined. He'd brought Inspector Gadois and a team of forensic techs outfitted just like Monk along with him.

"Mademoiselle Teeger," Le Roux said, "this is a surprise."

"I wish it was," I said.

"I guess the forensic suit came in handy after all," Le Roux said. "Where is the body?"

"There is no body," I said.

"There isn't?"

"Only bones," I said.

I gestured farther down the passageway, where a small crowd and the two guards were gathered at the rope to watch Monk as if he was an animal on display at the zoo.

Several even took pictures of him carefully laying bones down on the floor in a rough approximation of where they would be in a human body.

Le Roux had the guards disperse the crowd and lead them away. Then he and Gadois approached the rope to see Monk surveying his work.

"Monsieur Monk," Le Roux said, "I understand you have a murder to report."

Monk picked up a skull that he'd placed off to one side from the other bones and brought it over to Le Roux and Gadois.

"This man," he said, holding the skull up for them to see.

"What makes you think it's a man?" Gadois said.

"The face is less rounded and the teeth are larger than a woman's," Monk said. "A man also has more pronounced superciliary ridges and mastoid processes and a larger glabella."

"*Ah, oui*, the glabella," Gadois said, nodding. "It's much bigger. I hadn't noticed that."

"Because you don't know what a glabella is," Le Roux said.

"Not in English," Gadois said. "But I do in French."

Le Roux stared at him for a long moment, and I felt a strange sense of déjà vu. When had I experienced this exchange or something like it before?

"The victim was in his forties, smoked a pipe, and he lost his second premolar several years before his murder," Monk continued, pointing to a gap in the upper-left row of teeth.

"How could you possibly know that?" Gadois asked.

If I had a dollar for every time someone asked Monk that, myself included, I wouldn't have to work anymore and would never have another vacation ruined by a murder investigation.

"You can see polishing on the teeth where he held the pipe and the void has healed where the premolar was," Monk said. "You'll also notice that the victim had a mix of amalgam and composite-resin dental fillings. The materials establish a time line that gives us his age."

"No offense, Monsieur Monk, but I'm sure there were a lot of forty-year-old pipe smokers with bad teeth who went to the guillotine," Le Roux said. "Why should his death be of any concern to us now?"

"Because these particular resin ionomer fillings didn't exist in the seventeen hundreds," Monk said. "Or even twenty years ago."

"*Mon Dieu.*" Le Roux turned to Gadois. "This is a homicide crime scene. I want the tour sealed and the employees assembled for questioning."

Gadois nodded and set off on his mission. Le Roux shifted his attention back to Monk and the skull that he held.

"What is your opinion of this wound?" Le Roux pointed to cracks radiating from a strange honeycomb impression in the bone.

"It's the imprint of whatever killed him," Monk said. "But I don't know what the weapon was."

"We will find out." Le Roux snapped his fingers at one of the forensic techs, who stepped forward, carefully took the skull from Monk, and placed it in a plastic evidence bag.

"I think he was killed somewhere else," Monk said. "His skeleton was scattered here later in an attempt to make sure it was never found."

"What better place to hide bones than amid millions

of others? It's like hiding a grain of sand on a beach." Le Roux gestured to the bones Monk had arranged on the floor. "And what about those other bones?"

"What about them?" he asked.

"Do they also belong to the victim?"

"No, these belong to other people," Monk replied.

"Were they also murdered recently?"

Monk shook his head. "These bones are hundreds of years old."

"Then what are you doing with them?"

"He's trying to reassemble their skeletons," I said.

Le Roux raised his eyebrows. *"Pourquoi?"*

"Because they need to be," I said.

"They do?"

"Look around," Monk said to Le Roux. "The bones are all mixed up willy-nilly. It's a mess in here."

Le Roux stared at him, baffled. I think the chief inspector was finally getting a glimpse of Monk as something more than a detective genius.

"Don't worry about that," Le Roux said. "We will take over now and search the immediate area for any of the victim's other bones. They were probably scattered on top of nearby piles."

"What about the rest?"

"The rest?" Le Roux said.

"Of these bones," Monk said, waving to the piles all around him. "Aren't you going to put them back together?"

Le Roux was at a complete loss for words. He looked to me for guidance.

I told him in French to tell Monk what he wanted to hear or Monk would never leave. Le Roux replied in French that what Monk was suggesting was crazy.

"Bienvenue à ma vie," I said. Welcome to my life.

Le Roux looked back to Monk. "What you are asking us to do will take an enormous amount of time and money."

"It has to be done," Monk said.

"Yes, of course," Le Roux said. "We will get right on it."

"You'll thank me later," Monk said and stepped over the rope. "Let us know the moment you've identified the victim."

"Please don't," I said to Le Roux and pulled Monk off to one side for a private conversation, though I'm sure everyone could hear us.

"Why do you want him to notify you?" I demanded.

"We can't find the killer if we don't know who the victim is," Monk replied in a patronizing tone of voice.

"But we aren't going to be the ones looking for the killer." I pointed at Le Roux, who was conferring with his forensic team. "They will."

"So will we," Monk said.

"Why would we do that?"

"It's what we do," Monk said.

"In San Francisco. This is Paris. You're on vacation now."

"This will be like a vacation," Monk said.

"How?"

"Like the vacations we had in Hawaii and Germany."

"We spent all of our time solving murders," I said, loud enough that they probably heard us up on Boulevard Raspail.

"Yes," Monk said, "like that kind of vacation."

"That isn't a vacation," I said.

"It is for me," he said.

"Good for you," I said. "But it's something I would rather not repeat."

"How's that going?" he asked.

My hands involuntarily balled into fists at my sides. I wanted to deck him.

"If you want to help Chief Inspector Le Roux with his investigation, go right ahead," I said. "But you will be doing it alone. I've had enough."

"You're quitting?"

"No, Mr. Monk, I'm on vacation. I want to discover Paris."

"Do you really think you can discover Paris by taking walks, eating in restaurants, visiting museums, going to theaters, and seeing all the historical sites?"

"Yes, I do."

"There's no better way to discover Paris, its culture, and its people than through a murder investigation. You'll see the city and its people laid bare. You'll go where the tourists never go. You'll see what life here is really like."

"It's a shame everybody can't enjoy a good murder when they come to Paris."

"We're the lucky ones," Monk said.

Obviously, my sarcasm was lost on him. It always was. But that rarely stopped me.

"It was bad enough when this happened in Hawaii and in Germany. I won't be a part of it again," I said. "You'll have to do this investigation without an assistant."

"But I can't," Monk said. "I don't even speak the language."

"That's not my problem," I said. "There's more of Paris that I'd like to see today. Are you staying here or coming with me?"

Monk looked from me to Le Roux, then back to me.

"Let's compromise," Monk said. "I'll investigate the murder and you can be my assistant."

"That's what I already do."

"Great. So that will make it easy," Monk said. "I'm so glad we worked that out."

I turned my back on him and marched down the long corridor of bones.

13

Mr. Monk Sees the Sights

I was so mad by the time I got back up to the street that I was tempted not to wait for Monk, who I knew would show up at any moment.

I hadn't given him any choice but to give in to my demands. He could barely function on his own at home without me, so here he wouldn't have a chance.

He knew it and I knew it.

That gave me a lot of leverage with Monk. I'd never used that leverage before, so I didn't feel any guilt about using it now.

He was completely ignoring my feelings.

Sure, I was his employee, but I was also his friend. I helped him get to Europe so he could find Dr. Kroger and put his life back together again. And doing it almost cost me my life.

All I wanted in return was a little break, a murder-free vacation to decompress from that adventure and all the others that had preceded it.

Hadn't I made that clear to him at the airport yesterday? Didn't he care at all about how I felt? Why did everything always have to revolve around his needs?

But I wasn't doing it just for selfish reasons. We'd solved enough murders in the past week or so as it was. I needed a break, and whether he wanted to admit it or not, he probably did, too.

I'd forgotten what it was like to go a week without seeing a dead body or questioning people about where they were at the time of the murder and what their relationship was to the victim. I bet he had, too.

There was actually a time in my life when death wasn't following me around wherever I went. That time ended when I met Adrian Monk.

Solving the murder on the plane was unavoidable. We'd witnessed the crime, and the guy had dropped dead at Monk's feet. And it wasn't like there was anywhere else we could go. We were trapped in midair.

But this was different. Discovering the skull didn't obligate Monk to find the killer, too. That was what the police were for. It wasn't our problem.

Monk finally emerged from the catacombs. He'd left his hazmat suit behind, and I was surprised to see that he'd been wearing his jacket, shirt, pants, and shiny brown Hush Puppies shoes underneath it the whole time. Even more amazing was that he'd done it without wrinkling his clothes or breaking a sweat.

He winced at the sunlight and, shielding his eyes with a hand over his brow, looked at me with a sad face.

"It won't hurt you to let the police investigate a murder on their own," I said. "You don't have to look so mopey."

"This is my natural expression," Monk said. "The happy-go-lucky, devil-may-care expression you see on my face every day is an act."

"I've never noticed it," I said.

"I'm a good actor."

"I meant the happy-go-lucky, devil-may-care expression," I said.

"It was there."

"I guess what threw me off is that happy-go-lucky usually involves a smile for most people."

"That would be overacting," Monk said. "What I do is a more subtle performance."

"So why aren't you doing it now?"

"Because I'm not in the mood," Monk said.

"You're mopey," I said.

"I'm me," Monk said.

Without a murder to solve, Monk was a man without purpose, a man without direction or distraction. There was nothing to occupy his brilliant mind or to distract him from the thousands of little messes all around him.

I understood that.

And I didn't give a damn.

We spent the rest of the afternoon sightseeing and barely speaking to each other.

That was fine by me.

He was sullen and sulky, just like my teenage daughter was with me whenever she didn't get her way. So I was used to it.

Besides, I had plenty of other things to occupy me.

After we left the catacombs, we had some lunch at an outdoor café. Monk ordered Sierra Springs water and plain toast while I indulged in some crepes, a glass of wine, and a pastry.

He also rearranged some chairs, shooed away a couple who wanted to eat at a table with their dogs, and got very upset with a man who parallel-parked his little

Mercedes by repeatedly bumping into the cars that he was squeezing in between.

The driver didn't speak English, so Monk's tirade was wasted on him, and I pretended not to notice the argument.

With some food in my stomach and alcohol in my veins, I was feeling much more relaxed and ready to roam. We took the subway to the Jardin du Luxembourg in the heart of the Latin Quarter and roamed the same garden paths and cobbled streets as Jean-Paul Sartre and Simone de Beauvoir. I could pretend I was a French intellectual or struggling poet.

I stopped to admire Saint-Sulpice church, which my guidebook said took one hundred thirty-four years and six architects to build, starting in the mid-sixteen hundreds. Not that it was ever really finished. There were still some uncut masonry blocks sticking out of the shorter, uncompleted south tower that had never been sculpted, as Monk was quick to point out. That wasn't the only thing that bothered him about the place.

"You'd think one of those six architects would have noticed that the two towers don't match at all," Monk said.

"Make a note of that," I said. "It can be one more recommendation for your report."

We continued our walk. I peeked into the bookstores and shops and wandered in no particular direction, which I am sure drove Monk crazy. I didn't care. I wanted to get lost in those streets and we did.

We eventually ended up on Quai Saint-Michel in front of the Shakespeare and Co. Bookshop, looking across the Seine at Notre Dame Cathedral. I didn't want to cross the bridge to the Île de la Cité to take a closer look. The police department was across from Notre

Dame, and I didn't want Monk to be tempted to stop in for a visit with the chief inspector.

Instead, I headed west along the quai to Pont Neuf, the oldest surviving stone bridge in the city.

Pont Neuf crossed the tip of the Île de la Cité. Tour boats glided under its twelve graceful arches over the Seine. The bridge was lined with stone faces that seemed to be scowling in distaste or howling in pain. I don't know if they were supposed to scare away birds, taggers, or the elements, but it seemed like an odd design choice to me.

When Pont Neuf was completed in the early sixteen hundreds, it was remarkable for being the first bridge not to have houses built on it. Bridge homes were sought-after places to live at the time because of their indoor toilets, which were basically holes in the floor to the river below.

I didn't share that fact with Monk.

Maybe that was what those stone faces were so upset about—all the yucky stuff they had to see falling from those other bridges.

I stood for a while and watched the boats go by. Monk stood beside me and watched them, too.

He wasn't any less sullen-looking, but at least he wasn't complaining about anything. The bridge had twelve arches. What more could he want?

The sun was setting over Paris, and we were in a great spot to appreciate it. As the skies darkened, we walked across the bridge to the right bank. We strolled west on Rue Rivoli, past all the souvenir shops and restaurants that were strategically situated across from the Louvre to entice the tourists.

We headed northwest, toward the Place de la Concorde and the Champs-Élysées. My feet were sore by

the time we got to the restaurant where we'd had breakfast that morning and dinner the night before. I didn't
want to go there, but I did it anyway as a concession to
Monk, not that he'd asked.

Monk seemed to enjoy his Sierra Springs water and
croque monsieur.

I ordered an *entrecôte avec des frites*. The food tasted
great, particularly the fries. I found several fries of equal
length, separated them from the others on my plate with
my fork, and offered them to Monk.

Much to my surprise, he ate them right off my plate.

One small step for mankind, one giant leap for
Monk.

The second night in our hotel room was a lot like the
first. But we were both so exhausted that the debate
over the situation didn't last long.

Monk was up and dressed when I awoke the next
morning, sitting on the edge of his bed and staring at the
TV, which wasn't on. He was deep in thought and I had
a pretty good idea what about.

The skull he'd found.

So I didn't ask what he was doing. I threw back the
sheets and got out of bed. He immediately left the room,
leaving me alone to shower and dress.

I found him waiting for me in the lobby.

"We should probably check in with the chief inspector and see how he's doing," Monk said.

"Why would we do that?" I said.

"I'm curious," Monk said.

"I'm sure you are," I said. "We can call him later."

"Today?"

I shook my head. "I was thinking we could do it from
the airport on our way home."

"If we wait that long," Monk said, "I won't be able to give him much help."

I gave him a look. "That's the idea."

"It's a bad idea," Monk said.

"You can go and see him right now. I'm sure the man at the front desk can get you a taxi to the police station."

"What about you?"

"I'll be just fine," I said. "Don't worry about me."

"I'm not worried about you," Monk said. "I'm worried about me."

"That's a change," I said.

I know how surly I must sound to you. You're probably siding with Monk right now. But imagine how you'd feel if you were me, if you'd investigated fifty or sixty murders in a row at the side of an obsessive-compulsive detective, and you never had a vacation. My irritability only proved how much I needed a rest.

"I don't want you to be unhappy," I said. "You do what you want. I'm having breakfast."

I went outside and stopped by the newsstand again. Every French newspaper had a different picture of Monk holding the skull in the catacombs. The pictures must have been taken by the tourists and sold to the papers.

Terrific.

I walked on as Monk joined me. If he saw the newspapers, he didn't say anything about them.

We had breakfast at the same place I went to the previous morning and I thought about our schedule for the day. I quickly scratched the Louvre off my mental list. I could just imagine Monk making a scene over the missing arms on the Venus de Milo and demanding that it be repaired immediately.

So I ruled out all museums and decided we'd just take a walking tour.

I won't bore you with a travelogue, or with all the irregular, uneven, and unsanitary things that disturbed Monk along the way. Suffice to say that it was a beautiful day, we had a wonderful walk, and best of all, we didn't come across a single dead body.

I considered the day a big success, though. Monk was no more difficult than usual, even if he was sulking, and Paris was spectacular, which compensated for everything.

It was truly a vacation day.

I wanted to celebrate with a special dinner, but I had to be careful where I took Monk if I wanted a peaceful meal. So I made reservations for us at a unique place that I'd read about recently in the *San Francisco Chronicle*.

The restaurant was called Toujours Nuit, and what made it special was that you ate in total darkness, unable to see a thing, and were served by blind waiters.

I figured that if Monk couldn't see the decor, the table settings, the other patrons, or what he was eating, there wouldn't be much left for him to find fault with.

Toujours Nuit billed itself as more than just a place to eat—the restaurant promised an unforgettable experience. I had no idea at the time how true that would turn out to be.

14

Mr. Monk Is in the Dark

We rode the subway to the Left Bank neighborhood where Toujours Nuit was located.

Monk took a seat on the train and tried very hard not to touch anything with his hands, which he tucked into the sleeves of his jacket for extra protection.

He also closed his eyes and gritted his teeth.

It's not easy to scream with gritted teeth, but he tried. He sounded like he was choking on something, or gargling.

When we emerged on to the street, Monk sucked in the air and clutched his chest as if he'd nearly suffocated.

Toujours Nuit was on a narrow cobblestone street on the Left Bank that was tightly packed with restaurants, cafés, and bars catering mostly to tourists.

The entire facade of the restaurant was black, except for the name of the place, which was written in white in very small letters above the door.

I hadn't told Monk anything about the restaurant yet.

I was waiting until the last possible moment so it would be harder for him to back out.

Monk hesitated at the door. "This looks scary."

"Don't be afraid just because it's painted black," I said.

"That's not what scares me."

"Then what's frightening about it?"

"It's a restaurant," Monk said.

"So it's no scarier than, say, the Chinese one next door."

"The Chinese restaurant is much scarier."

"Why?" I asked.

"They have sweet-and-sour pork."

"What's wrong with sweet-and-sour pork?"

"It's sweet," Monk said. "And sour."

He cringed from head to toe.

"Then you can be thankful that you are eating here." I opened the door to the restaurant and waved him inside.

We found ourselves in a small cocktail lounge. There were about two dozen people milling about, having drinks and leaning on the bar, which ran the length of the back wall. To our left was a set of heavy black curtains and, to our right, a bank of lockers at the base of some stairs that, according to a sign on the wall, led down to the restrooms.

The goateed bartender motioned us to the bar, where he handed us each a colorful tropical drink with his compliments and asked in French for my name so he could check us off on his reservation ledger.

I replied in French, but the moment I spoke it must have been clear to him that I was American because after that he began speaking to us in English.

"My name is Stephan, and I welcome you to Toujours Nuit. Have you been with us before?"

"No," I replied.

Stephan looked like a beatnik poet, which was the romanticized image I had when I was a kid of what sexy, young French intellectuals should look like, though I'm not sure there ever was such a thing.

"Please put your coats, purses, cell phones, pagers, and anything that might emit light or glow in the dark into one of the lockers and take the key," Stephan said.

Monk looked puzzled. "Why should we do that?"

I took a big sip of my very sweet drink to fortify myself for the struggle to come and let the bartender field the question for me.

"To keep the dining room completely dark and to make sure that there's nothing for our servers to trip over."

"Completely dark?" Monk said. "What don't you want us to see?"

"Anything, of course," Stephan said.

I set my drink down, tugged Monk by the sleeve, and led him over to the lockers.

"This is a very special restaurant, Mr. Monk. The dining room is pitch-black, and you are served by blind waiters."

"You're joking," Monk said.

I opened a locker, stuffed my coat and purse inside, and closed the locker, pocketing the key.

"I'm being completely serious," I said. "You won't be able to see a thing."

"Is this how the French eat?"

"No, this restaurant is unique," I said. "The idea is to make dining a more sensual experience."

"You've brought me to an orgy?" Monk shrieked.

People turned and stared at us. I shushed him and pulled into a corner out of earshot of the others.

"Of course not, Mr. Monk. Why would you say something like that?"

"Because we are in France and you said this was going to be a sensual experience."

"What I meant is you will have to rely on your senses of smell, touch, and taste to discover what you are eating."

"I don't want to discover what I am eating," Monk said. "I need to know before I put it in my mouth. I hear these people eat snails and frogs. They could feed me a slug or a caterpillar."

"That's not going to happen."

"How do you know?" Monk said. "What if the chefs are blind, too?"

"They aren't," I said. "Only the waiters are."

"That's supposed to make me feel better?"

"This could be a wonderful experience for you."

"I don't see how," Monk said.

"No pun intended," I said.

"What pun?"

"The one you just made," I said.

"I didn't make one," Monk said.

"That's what I said."

"You shouldn't have had that drink," Monk said. "It has gone right to your head. You're completely drunk."

I sighed. "You aren't considering the positive side of this situation."

"Because there's never a positive side."

"A couple of years ago, a guy threw solvent in your eyes and blinded you. You didn't know for days if you'd ever see again."

"That's the positive side?" Monk said. "I get to be blind again?"

"Yes, it is. You felt sorry for yourself at first, but then you loved being blind. You were freed from all your anxieties. For the first time in your life, you didn't care whether things were clean and orderly or not. You were so happy."

"For a little while, but it never lasts," Monk said. "I realized all the good things I wouldn't see again, like pictures of Trudy."

"I thought you might like to experience that happiness again, and that freedom from your anxieties, only this time without the fear of losing anything," I said. "Tonight you're going to be in the perfect dining room, where everything is the way you think it should be."

"How will I know?" Monk said. "I won't be able to see anything."

"Exactly," I said. "Because you are in total darkness, the dining room can be whatever you want it to be. Use your imagination."

"I'm not sure I have one," Monk said.

"Now is your chance to find out," I said.

The bartender rang a little bell and motioned everyone up toward the black curtain.

Stephan told us that we'd be walking into the restaurant single file behind our waitress, our hands on the shoulders of the person in front of us like in a conga line.

The waitress would introduce herself, lead us to our table, and show us to our chairs. The guests were not allowed to move around the dining room on their own. If we needed anything, or had to be escorted to the bathroom, all we had to do was call out to our waitress by name, and she would come see to our needs.

A woman raised her hand and asked if the bathrooms were in the dark, too.

Everyone laughed. I was sure the bartender got that question a lot.

He said the bathrooms were lit and were located down the stairs, beside the lockers. He suggested that people use them now, since the dinner service would last approximately an hour and a half.

Stephan then asked if anyone had any special dietary requirements or food allergies that the chef needed to know about.

Monk raised his hand. "Milk."

"You are allergic to dairy products?" Stephan asked.

"I don't drink bodily fluids," Monk said.

"Very well," Stephan said. "Anyone else?"

Monk raised his hand. "Sausages."

"You are allergic to sausages?"

"I don't eat anything that has come in contact with an intestine," Monk said.

"I understand," the bartender said. "Anyone else?"

Monk raised his hand. "Tossed salad."

"You're allergic to salad?" Stephan asked.

"I don't eat anything that has been tossed."

"We'll make sure your salad isn't tossed." Stephan's irritation was beginning to show. "If that's all—"

Monk raised his hand. I yanked his arm down.

"He's done," I said to the bartender.

"There's more," Monk said to me.

"I know," I said. "An entire volume. We don't have time for it. We'll still be standing here next Tuesday."

"But what if I am served something I can't eat?"

"Don't eat it," I said.

"How will I know what it is if I can't see it?"

"You'll have to rely on your heightened senses," I said.

"I forgot about my heightened senses," he said.

Waiters and waitresses stepped out from behind the curtain and began to lead people into the dining room. I got in front of Monk.

"You can put your hands on my shoulders," I said.

"I'd rather rely on my heightened senses," he said.

"It's the rules, Mr. Monk."

He put his hands on me very gently, as if he was afraid he'd get burned.

"Just so we're clear," he said, "this is not one of the sensual experiences."

"Definitely not," I said.

The waitress came out.

"My name is Gayle," she said. "I will be your host tonight. May I get your names?"

"I'm Natalie," I said.

"I'm Adrian," Monk said. "I don't drink milk."

"So I've heard," she said, and led us through the curtain.

We made some lefts and rights, and I felt curtains on either side of us. I think we were walking through some kind of curtained buffer zone designed to make sure no light at all came into the dining room. What it succeeded in doing was completely disorienting me.

My eyes were wide-open but I saw nothing except the deepest, darkest blackness of my life. Almost immediately, my heart began to race, and I found my eyes straining to pick up any light at all.

But there was none.

All I could hear was people talking excitedly and some awful New Age harpsichord music coming from speakers. If they didn't turn off the music, I might fall asleep before dinner arrived.

Gayle came to a stop.

"You are at a table for four," she said. "You will be

sharing it with others. Adrian, your chair is to your left. You can let go of Natalie's shoulders now, pull out the chair, and sit down. She will be seated across from you."

I could hear the sound of Monk pulling out his chair. I kept my hands on Gayle's shoulders as she led me around the table to my seat.

"There is a table setting in front of you," she said. "There is a bottle of wine between you and a basket of bread. Your first course will be out in a moment."

"Gayle," Monk said, "there's a big problem."

"What is it, Adrian?"

"My plate is chipped," Monk said. "On the rim."

"That happens," she said. "But I can assure you the plates are clean."

"That doesn't matter. You can't expect people to eat off a chipped plate. It has to be thrown out." Monk reached out and touched my plate. I only know because he brushed my hand by mistake. "Her plate is chipped on the rim, too."

"But they are perfectly good plates," she said.

"If it's chipped, it's far from perfect, and it's certainly not good. Promise me you'll throw it away so no one will get hurt."

"A chipped plate can't hurt you," I said.

"One chip leads to more chips," he said. "Before long, it's like eating off a saw blade."

"The plates will go right in the trash," Gayle said, taking our plates. "I'll bring you a new plate with your appetizers."

I reached out and felt my silverware, a sharp steak knife, my glass, the bread basket, and the bottle of wine. I felt along the tabletop and discovered the edge was to my right.

"My heightened senses are awakening," Monk said.

"What are you sensing?"

"There are nineteen patrons who have been seated. There are six waiters, two of whom have gone out a curtained exit five yards behind you, while the other two have gone out the exit behind me and to my left to bring in the remaining guests."

"Can you smell how fresh the bread is?"

"Yes, of course."

"Why don't you have some?" I asked. "You can be the first one at the table to tear off a piece."

I heard the fabric of his jacket move against his sleeve as he reached for the basket, and then I heard the crack of the crust as he tore off a piece of bread for himself. The smell of fresh bread was even stronger once the heat was released from the loaf.

I could almost taste the bread myself from the aroma alone, which taught me something about how our sense of smell influences our perception of taste.

I reached out to tear off a piece for myself to confirm my theory.

The bread tasted great, but I wondered if that had more to do with the sensory deprivation, and the chance to actually experience something in that darkness.

I could hear people walking in behind Monk and nearing our table.

"Adrian, Natalie, this is Sandrine," Gayle said. "She's dining on her own tonight and will be joining you."

"Bonsoir, Sandrine," I said to the darkness.

"Bonsoir," Sandrine whispered, and I heard her pull out a chair beside Monk and sit down.

"Le pain est excellent," I said to Sandrine, just to be sociable.

I felt the displacement of air as she reached for the basket and helped herself to the remainder of the loaf.

I imagined that she had a slender arm and delicate hands, though I have no idea why I thought so. Perhaps I was reacting on pure instinct, based on factors I'd unconsciously picked up from the way she moved or the sound she made, or didn't make, when she sat down in her chair.

"All the patrons are in the dining room now," Monk said.

"Good to know," I said.

I felt for my glass with one hand and the wine with the other. I carefully filled my glass, keeping one finger on the rim so I'd know if the wine was about to spill over.

"That's odd," Monk said. "There's one more person in the room than there was when we were escorted in."

"You can't know that," I said.

"All the patrons are sitting," Monk said.

"It's probably a waiter, Mr. Monk."

"There are six waiters, and this person isn't waiting or sitting," Monk said. "He's lurking."

"You can hear him lurking?"

"Can't you?"

"What does lurking sound like?" I asked.

"Like the man approaching us slowly and methodically from the wall, approximately two tables away to my right."

I concentrated on the sounds around me. I heard the clatter of silverware and dishes, the footsteps of waiters, people talking in French, and that awful New Age music, but nothing I could identify as lurking, slinking, or slithering.

The darkness was so thick that it seemed to have a

physical presence. I could feel it pressing all around me. It was like being in a sleeping bag that was zipped up over my head.

Then I heard heavy footsteps, followed by Gayle's cheery voice.

"I have your first course," she said. "I am going to lean down and place the plates in front of you."

I heard the dishes being placed in front of Monk and Sandrine, and then a moment later, Gayle came up behind me.

I was aware of the warmth of her body and the smell of her shampoo as she leaned past me to set down my plate. She touched my shoulder.

"I'll be back in a few minutes with your entrée," she said. "Enjoy."

I leaned down over my plate. I smelled some kind of smoked fish and a hint of garlic. I felt around on the plate and could make out lettuce, mushrooms, and cucumbers. There was also something that felt like sliced meat. But was it ham? Roast beef? I would have to taste it to find out.

"How am I going to cut my food?" Monk asked.

"With a knife and fork," I said.

"I won't know if I am cutting perfect squares," he said.

"You will have to trust your heightened senses," I said. "Or just not worry about it."

And then I heard Sandrine whisper something. "Monsieur Monk, I can help you."

"I appreciate the offer," Monk said. "But I don't let strangers cut my food."

"I know who you found," she said softly.

I could tell from her voice that she was a young woman, at least no older than me. I could also tell from the quaver in her voice that she was frightened. Perhaps she was afraid of the dark.

"I'm sorry but I don't understand what you're trying to say," Monk said. "Maybe it's your English. You can speak in French to Natalie, if you like."

I heard a strange, mushy sound, a sigh, and then I felt the displacement of air as someone passed me, leaving behind a musty, damp smell in his wake. There was a dull *thunk* from Monk's side of the table as something hit the floor.

"Natalie," Monk said carefully.

"Yes, Mr. Monk?"

"Don't panic," he said.

"Why would I?"

"Because there's a killer in the room, and he's just murdered the woman who was sitting beside me."

I grimaced and felt my body tense up with anger.

The odds of stumbling on three murders in three days were astronomical, even for Monk. I was tempted to toss the wine bottle at him for even suggesting it but I was afraid I'd miss him in the dark.

"That's impossible. You've got murder on the brain. You're incapable of going two days without investigating a homicide," I said and turned in Sandrine's direction, not that she could see me. "I know this sounds silly, Sandrine, but could you please tell Mr. Monk that you're alive so we can go on with our meal?"

That was when I heard a surprised yelp to my left and the crash of dishes hitting the floor.

"That's the sound of a blind waiter tripping over a corpse," Monk said.

Suddenly the lights in the room seemed to burst on. I reflexively squeezed my eyes shut against the unexpected brightness and the stinging pain that came with it.

When I opened my eyes, I had to blink hard several times to adjust to the light, which was actually pretty dim but a harsh contrast to the total darkness we'd been in before.

Through my watery eyes, I could see the black walls and ceiling, the black tables and chairs, and the stunned, watery-eyed patrons blinking hard just like me.

Gayle was on the floor in the aisle between two tables, surrounded by broken dishes, keeping her hands raised and staying very still, probably out of fear of cutting herself on broken glass.

That was when I realized that Monk and I were the only ones seated at our table. He was looking down at the floor beside him.

I stood up and leaned over the table to see what he was staring at.

There was a young red-haired woman on the floor. Her skin was very pale and she wore a flowery dress. She was as delicate as I'd imagined her to be.

Her eyes were wide-open and unblinking.

And there was a steak knife buried to the hilt in her blood-soaked chest.

It was a brutal, bloody sight, the second murder committed in front of me in the last three days. I started to tremble.

Someone screamed, and the horror moved like a breeze through the room, even among people who had yet to see the corpse. I guess the scream was enough, or on some instinctive level, they picked up on the iron ore scent of fresh blood.

The bartender burst through the curtains from the lounge holding a shotgun. He looked at the body, then at the table, and then leveled his weapon at Monk.

"Don't move," Stephan said.

"I haven't done anything," Monk said.

"Then how did your steak knife get in that woman's chest?"

Monk and I glanced at the tabletop at the same time. The only knife missing was from his table setting.

"Good question," Monk said and raised his hands.

15

Mr. Monk and the Locked Room

"Everyone stay right where you are," Monk said. "That includes the service staff."

Stephan jabbed Monk with his shotgun. "You are in no position to be giving orders."

"He didn't kill that woman," I said. "But whether you believe that or not, this is a crime scene, and it's essential that no one disturb the evidence."

"Are you some kind of cop?" Stephan asked me.

"I'm not." I tipped my head toward Monk. "But he is."

Stephan glanced at the body. "He's got a funny way of showing it."

I wasn't happy about the situation, but I was stuck with it, and I didn't like someone pointing a gun at Monk. I saw a cell phone clipped to Stephan's belt.

"If you give me your phone, I'll call the police."

The bartender tossed his cell to me. I still had Chief Inspector Le Roux's card in my pocket. He was going to be sorry he ever gave it to me.

I got Le Roux on the second ring.

"How was your day?" he asked jovially.

"We visited Montmartre, window-shopped along Rue Saint-Honoré, the usual tourist things," I said. "But that's not why I called. We're having dinner now at Toujours Nuit, not far from you, and we'd like you to join us."

"I appreciate the invitation, but I'm afraid I must decline," he said. "I'm very busy."

"A woman has just been murdered in the dining room."

"Ce n'est pas possible!" he exclaimed.

"I wish," I said sadly.

"When did this happen?"

"About thirty seconds ago," I said. "The victim was sitting right next to Mr. Monk."

"Are you sure it was murder and not natural causes?"

"She was stabbed in the heart with a steak knife."

"Who did it?"

"I don't know," I said.

"But you just said you were at the same table as the victim," Le Roux said.

"In this restaurant, you eat in the dark and the waiters are blind."

"Incroyable," he said and hung up.

The restaurant was on a side street off of Boulevard Saint-Germain, only a few blocks away from the police headquarters, so I'd barely set the phone down on the table when I heard sirens approaching.

The room was eerily silent. Nobody moved. Everyone was waiting for something to happen.

After a moment or two Chief Inspector Le Roux pushed through the black curtains into the room, followed by Inspector Gadois and several uniformed officers.

Le Roux stopped beside the woman's body. He shook his head and shifted his gaze to Monk. The chief inspector didn't seem nearly so amused this time and I took some pleasure in that.

He turned to Stephan. *"Vous pouvez poser l'arme maintenant. On va s'en charger."*

The bartender lowered his shotgun and motioned to Monk. *"Vous connaissez cet homme?"*

"Oui," Le Roux replied with a weary sigh. "Is it possible, Monsieur Monk, for you to go anywhere without encountering a homicide?"

"This wasn't a chance occurrence," Monk said. "Sandrine was killed to keep her from talking to me."

Everyone stared at him.

"Sandrine?" Gadois kneeled beside the body. "Did you know her?"

"No," I said. "The waitress introduced us by our first names."

"C'est vrai," Gayle said to Le Roux as Stephan helped her to her feet.

"But she knew me," Monk said. "She came in late so she would be seated with us. She called me Monsieur Monk."

"Because she heard me use your name," I said.

"She wanted to help me," Monk said.

"To cut your food," I said.

"What she said was *I know who you found,*" Monk said. "I think she was referring to the skull I found in the catacombs yesterday. I think she wanted to talk to me about the murder but also wanted to remain anonymous."

Le Roux stepped up to Monk's seat at the table. "You were sitting here?"

Monk nodded.

"And she was sitting to your right?" Le Roux continued.

"Yes," Monk said. "The killer came up to her from behind."

Le Roux glanced down at the body, then back to the table. "Are you sure he came from behind?"

"Yes," Monk said. "I heard him lurking."

"What does lurking sound like?" Gadois asked.

"It's a slow creep," Monk said. "Almost undetectable unless you have heightened senses."

"You have heightened senses," Le Roux said skeptically.

"It's a gift," Monk said. "And a curse."

"Did you notice anything else?" Le Roux asked.

"He smelled like mildew, and he was ticking."

"Ticking?"

"Like a clock," Monk said. "I heard it briefly when he leaned over her."

"I smelled him, too," I said, "as he went past me."

"Toward the back curtain," Le Roux said.

"I guess," I said. "I was disoriented."

Le Roux nodded and turned to the bartender.

"Did you see anyone come in after the diners were seated?"

"This poor woman was the last person to come in," Stephan replied.

"Are you absolutely certain?"

"I didn't leave the bar until I heard the crash. If anyone came in, I would have seen him."

"Could he have snuck in the back door?" Gadois asked.

The bartender shook his head. "The door is locked, and there is a security camera outside. The monitor is under the bar. Even if someone did come in the back door without me seeing them on the monitor, they would have had to walk right through the middle of the kitchen."

"Past the blind chefs," Gadois said. "How hard could that be?"

"The chefs aren't blind," Gayle said.

"So the killer must be someone in this room," Gadois said, narrowing his eyes and shifting his gaze from person to person.

Monk began his slow detective dance, moving around the dining room and doing little pirouettes and crouches, bending and twisting, as things caught his eye. We were all watching him, except for the blind waiters, of course.

"You are forgetting something," Monk said. "It was pitch-black in here. The killer had to know where she was, make his way to this table, and kill her in total darkness. How did he do that?"

"So the killer must be one of the blind waiters," Gadois said, shifting his scrutiny to the service staff, who were standing along the back wall.

"I am troubled by something, Monsieur Monk," Le Roux said. "According to you, the killer leaned over her, grabbed your knife, and stabbed her in the heart with it. That's an odd and cumbersome way to kill someone from behind. Why not stab her in the back or slit her throat?"

I didn't like what he was implying and wanted to call him on it. "Are you suggesting that Mr. Monk murdered her?"

"There was no way in or out of the room without being seen. It was pitch-black in here. How did the killer get in, find his victim, and escape again? I would be remiss not to consider the obvious explanation."

"That Mr. Monk murdered the total stranger who

was sitting next to him?" I said. "It's preposterous. Why would he do that?"

Le Roux shrugged. "Perhaps he has a pathological need for attention that he gets only when he's solving a murder."

I looked at Monk, waiting for him to defend himself, but he was busy peering under and over tables and examining every object and person. It was going to be up to me.

"Mr. Monk is an experienced homicide investigator, perhaps the best on earth. If he wanted to kill someone, he'd do it in a way that was so clever, so cunningly brilliant, that it wouldn't even occur to you that he was involved in the crime, if you could even figure out that a murder had been committed at all."

"Aha!" Gadois said. "That's exactly what makes this murder so diabolically clever."

"That doesn't make any sense," I said.

I noticed that the diners no longer seemed tense or frightened. A few had even gone back to eating their appetizers. It was as if they were watching a dinner-theater performance instead of sitting at the scene of a murder.

"It's so simple that it's complex," Gadois said. "Nobody would ever think he'd do something as simple as stabbing the person sitting next to him. His fingerprints are probably all over the knife, too, just to throw us off the trail."

"I don't understand your thinking at all," I said to Gadois.

"Reverse psychology. Only an imbecile would murder the woman beside him with his own knife and leave his fingerprints on the murder weapon, which would further throw suspicion away from a man as brilliant as Monsieur Monk."

Gadois smiled, very satisfied with himself. Le Roux nodded thoughtfully.

"You've convinced me, Gadois," Le Roux said.

Gadois puffed out his chest. "I have, sir?"

"Monsieur Monk didn't do this," Le Roux said.

"You're falling for his fiendish ploy," Gadois said.

"Perhaps," Le Roux said. "Check the victim for her locker key and retrieve her purse. Maybe we can learn something about her."

Gadois nodded and slipped out of the room.

Monk shrieked and stepped away from something, holding his arms out at his sides as if keeping a crowd at bay.

"Everyone stand back," Monk said.

There was no one around him, but I didn't see any point in mentioning that to him.

"What is it?" I asked as Le Roux and I rushed over to him.

"Horse droppings," Monk said.

I looked at the black carpeted floor and didn't see anything. Apparently, neither did Le Roux. He reached into his pocket, took out a tiny flashlight, and aimed it at the floor.

We both crouched and I could see a tiny brown fleck illuminated.

"How do you know that's horse manure?" Le Roux asked.

"Isn't it obvious?"

"Not to me," Le Roux said, clicking off his light. "Are you suggesting the killer rode in here on horseback?"

"It's evidence," Monk said. "Of what, I don't know."

"Of course you are right," Le Roux said. "I'll have it collected and examined by our forensics team."

"This entire restaurant will have to be quarantined," Monk said. "And the neighboring buildings evacuated."

"Over a speck of horse manure?" Stephan said.

"A speck of plutonium could kill everyone in this room," Monk said.

"But it's not plutonium," Stephan said.

"E. coli poisoning kills more people every year than plutonium and your floors are covered with manure," Monk said. "No wonder you keep the lights out."

Stephan opened his mouth to protest but Le Roux quieted him with a wave of his hand and a shake of his head.

Monk kept his distance from the speck and, watching carefully where he stepped, went through the back curtain. I followed him and so did Le Roux, who motioned Stephan to join us.

It wasn't just a curtain, but actually a series of them arranged to create two L-shaped passages to securely block out the light.

We emerged into a lit corridor that led to the swinging doors of a kitchen. There was a buffet table against one wall with dishes, silverware, glasses, and napkins laid out on top of it in sections. Beside the buffet was an empty trash can.

There were two doors off the corridor. One was ajar and led into what appeared to be an employee changing room. The other door was closed.

Monk motioned to the closed door. "Where does this lead?"

"To the basement storage area and laundry room," Stephan said.

Monk nodded, peered into the trash can, then led us back into the dining room.

Gadois was waiting for us, holding a purse in his gloved hands.

"Her name is not Sandrine," Gadois said. "According to her *carte d'identité*, it's Aimee Dupon."

Le Roux sighed. "So we have a woman murdered while she was sitting beside a legendary homicide detective in a dark dining room full of people and a staff of blind servers. And there was no way for the killer to enter or leave the room without being seen by either the cooks in the kitchen or the bartender in the lobby. It seems we have a very perplexing case, Monsieur Monk."

"*We* don't have a case," I said to Le Roux. "You do."

"The woman was killed trying to talk to me," Monk said. "I have to investigate her murder."

"You don't know that's why she was killed," I said.

"It doesn't matter," Monk said. "I'll find her killer anyway."

"Chief Inspector Le Roux is capable of investigating this homicide on his own," I said. "You don't have to get yourself involved."

"I already am," Monk said. "So are you. We're witnesses."

"We didn't see anything," I said.

"But we heard it all," Monk said.

"I agree with both of you," Le Roux said. "I agree with Mademoiselle Teeger that we can investigate this crime without your assistance, but I agree with Monsieur Monk that you are both witnesses to a homicide. You were the last two people to see her alive."

"We didn't see her," I said. "We hardly even spoke to her."

"I suggest that you both go now and get some rest," Le Roux said. "There's no need for you to stay. We have a long night ahead of us, interviewing every guest and employee and gathering forensic evidence. You can come to my office tomorrow morning and give us your official statements then."

"We don't want to leave," Monk said.

"Yes, we do," I said, leading Monk to the curtain.

"What could we possibly have to do tonight that's better than investigating a murder?"

"Anything," I said.

"But we're on vacation."

"That's my point," I said. "You don't investigate murders on vacation."

"I do," Monk said.

We emerged from the other side of the curtains into the bar, where a uniformed officer was posted. I headed straight for the lockers.

"Go ahead," I said to Monk, "without me."

"Maybe I will," Monk said.

I opened the locker, took out my things, and walked out of the restaurant. By the time I reached the corner of Boulevard Saint-Germain, Monk was sulking at my side.

"One of these days," Monk said, "that threat isn't going to work."

"I hope you're right," I said.

"Why?"

"Because that will mean you won't need an assistant anymore."

"I thought you liked working for me," Monk said.

"I do," I said. "Very much."

"Then why are you looking forward to the day you can leave me?"

I looked at him. "Because I'm your friend, and the

day you don't need me anymore is the day you can get your badge back. I know how much that means to you and I want you to be happy."

"If that was true," Monk said, "you'd help me investigate this murder. And the murder in the catacombs. And any other murder that comes along while we are here."

"You're expecting more of them?" I asked in disbelief.

"I'm on a lucky streak," he said.

"Tell that to the dead people," I said and headed for the Métro station.

16

Mr. Monk Meets an Old Friend

I found something for Monk to enjoy that didn't involve solving a murder. I got him on the phone with his shrink. It was just about time for his appointment with Dr. Kroger anyway, give or take an hour or two. So when we got back to our hotel room, I called Dr. Kroger, gave Monk my phone, and went for a walk.

I had at least an hour to myself, so I took one of the avenues off the Étoile at the Arc de Triomphe and walked down to Place de l'Alma at the Seine, then strolled along the quai toward the Grand Palais, its huge, illuminated glass roof glowing against the night sky.

It was a beautiful night but that was true of any night in Paris, regardless of the weather, at least if you're an American tourist.

The long tour boats, known as *bateaux-mouches*, chugged up and down the Seine, casting their mounted spotlights on the bridges and historic buildings that they passed.

I was glad to get away for a little while from Monk, his

anxieties, and the ever-present specter of violent death that seemed to follow him around.

I know it was wrong of me to blame Monk for all the corpses we were stumbling across, but I couldn't help it. All I wanted was a vacation, and it felt like he was trying his best to keep me from having one.

It was probably foolish of me to think that a vacation was even possible with Monk at my side. But what choice did I have? He'd followed me to Hawaii the last time I tried to get away and I knew he'd do it again if I tried to go somewhere else.

That wasn't the only thing bothering me.

Working for Monk, I'd seen a lot of dead bodies, but I hadn't been in the room when the people were killed. The murders on the plane and in Toujours Nuit happened right next to me. There was a frightening, violent intimacy to those crimes that rattled me.

I didn't want to be that close to death.

And I held Monk responsible for putting me in that position, whether or not it was really his fault.

I might have been easier on him, and less irrational, if he'd been as upset about the murders as I was or showed the slightest sensitivity to how I was feeling.

But he actually welcomed the murders—there was something sick about that. And that only made me more adamant about refusing to help him investigate them. It would be a waste of a trip to Paris, for one thing.

At least for me.

This trip wasn't turning out the way I'd hoped at all. That point became abundantly clear a moment later, when I found myself standing at Place de la Concorde without any idea how I got there.

I'd been so caught up in my thoughts that I hadn't paid any attention to the walk itself. I couldn't tell you what there was between Place de l'Alma and where I stood.

What a waste.

And it was Monk's fault. Again.

When I returned to our room, Monk was finishing up his telephone appointment with Dr. Kroger. It must have lasted more than an hour, though I hadn't kept track of the time. I guessed that Dr. Kroger was being generous in light of how things ended up in Germany.

Monk sat on the edge of his unruffled bed and held the phone out to me.

"Dr. Kroger would like to talk to you," he said.

I took the phone. "Good morning, Doctor. How are you doing?"

"Better and better," he said. "I'm concerned about Adrian."

If that was true, he wouldn't have fled Europe on the first flight out of Frankfurt the instant Monk solved those murders in Lohr. But I was too polite and respectful to say that.

"It's your job to be," I said.

"It's yours, too, and I'm worried that you aren't doing it."

I stepped out into the hall and closed the door. I didn't want Monk to hear me tear Dr. Kroger's head off.

"Then you can hop on the next flight to Paris and take over for me," I said.

"You manipulated Adrian into taking you to Paris when he didn't want to go," Dr. Kroger said. "And now that you're there, you are using emotional blackmail to force him into being someone that he's not."

That was all true, but it didn't matter. Dr. Kroger had personal reasons for supporting Monk on this.

"You're just mad at me because I didn't stop Mr. Monk from stalking you all the way to Germany," I said. "And because I punched you in the face."

"It's true that I wasn't very pleased about that," Dr. Kroger said. "But I'm over it."

"If you were, we wouldn't be having this conversation."

"Adrian is very upset, Natalie. I'm only reacting to what he's told me."

"What did he tell you?"

"That he discovered one murder and witnessed another and that you won't assist him in investigating those homicides. You know he can't do it without you, especially in a place far from home."

Okay, that was true, too. But I had a valid excuse.

"We're on vacation," I said. It came out sounding like a childish whine.

"You want to be. But you aren't."

"That's only because he won't take a week off from investigating murders."

"He can't."

"He could try."

"You might as well ask him not to breathe. Adrian is a detective. That's all he knows how to be. It's how he defines himself and how he interacts with the world. It's who he is. You can't expect him to shut it off."

"He's also obsessive-compulsive but you expect him to change."

"No, I don't. He will always be that way. I am helping him learn how to control his anxieties, phobias, and compulsive needs so he can function on his own."

"Maybe the need to detect all the time is something else he should learn to control."

"Why? So you can have a vacation?"

"Yes," I said. "What's wrong with that?"

"You created this situation, Natalie, when you essentially forced him to go with you to Paris. You can't blame him now for being exactly the person he's always been. You're suffering the consequences of your actions, and so is he. You're going to have to find a compromise or you will both be miserable."

"You're loving this," I said and disconnected the call.

The Brigade Criminelle of the Police Judiciare was located in the sprawling Prefecture du Police building directly across the plaza from Notre Dame Cathedral on the Île de la Cité.

The imposing nineteenth-century edifice had a tower at each of its four corners; they were ringed by pairs of faceless, helmeted stone centurions, law-abiding gargoyles that weren't going to be intimidated by the snarling, winged beasts perched on every corner of Notre Dame.

It didn't look like any police station I'd ever seen before. Monk seemed impressed by it, too, nodding his head in silent approval as we walked up.

But once we were inside, the grandeur was gone. It looked like any government office. Gunmetal desks, fluorescent lights, and white walls that had been scuffed, sun-blasted, and aged until they looked like the yellowed pages of an old paperback.

As far as I was concerned, if Le Roux wanted Monk's help on the investigation, then the chief inspector would have to assign a detective to be Monk's assistant because I was on vacation.

But they could give me a call anytime if they needed my advice on how to deal with Monk's Monkishness.

I thought that was a fair compromise. I didn't know

what Monk thought of it because I hadn't talked with him about it yet. I was waiting to see if Le Roux would accept Monk's offer to consult on the case.

We were given visitors' badges and escorted by an officer to Chief Inspector Le Roux's office, a glass-walled corner of a busy squad room full of detectives talking on their phones or typing at their computers.

It wasn't all that different from the homicide squad room in San Francisco—a similarity made even more evident by the surprising sight of Captain Leland Stottlemeyer standing with Le Roux at the coffee machine, filling their mugs from the pot.

Stottlemeyer's clothes were rumpled, and his hair was sticking up in spots. He'd obviously slept in his clothes and hadn't had a chance to change. Le Roux didn't look so hot, either. He was wearing the same clothes he was in last night.

"*Bienvenue à Paris*, Captain," I said.

Stottlemeyer turned and looked at us with bloodshot eyes that were underscored with dark shadows. He was unshaven and his mustache looked even bushier than usual.

"*Bonjour*, Natalie," he said wearily. "You, too, Monk."

I hadn't seen Monk with a smile that big since Lysol came out with pocket-sized cans of disinfectant spray. Le Roux waved away our escort.

"What a wonderful surprise," Monk said. "What are you doing here?"

"I wish I could say I'm here on vacation," Stottlemeyer said and dropped a couple of sugar cubes in his coffee.

"Me, too," I muttered.

I didn't know his story yet, but I knew that I might as well admit defeat. Any hope of a vacation was gone.

"I'm here because of you and that skull you found," Stottlemeyer said to Monk. "We got in an hour ago on the red-eye and took a taxi straight here."

"We?" I said.

Stottlemeyer took another sip of coffee and gestured into Le Roux's office. Monk and I both peeked inside and saw Lieutenant Randy Disher splayed across the vinyl couch, snoring away.

"Why are you interested in a skull Mr. Monk found in the Paris catacombs?" I asked.

"It's quite simple," Le Roux replied. "We ran the victim's dental work through our international databases and got a match. The dead man is Nathan Chalmers, an American from San Francisco."

"So you're here to assist with the investigation," Monk said to Stottlemeyer.

"More or less," Stottlemeyer said.

"It's going to be just like home," Monk said and began rearranging the coffee mugs on the counter by size.

"Is this your first trip to Paris, Captain?" Le Roux said.

"It's my first trip outside of the U.S. of A.," Stottlemeyer said. "Cops in America don't have a lot of discretionary income, especially if they are divorced and paying alimony and child support."

"The salaries aren't any better here," Le Roux lamented. "I can barely afford a wife and mistress."

Stottlemeyer raised an eyebrow. "Mistress?"

"Of course! Monogamy is monotony, Captain, and Frenchmen believe that must be avoided at all costs."

Stottlemeyer smiled. "My friends call me Leland. There's no need to be so formal."

"I'm afraid there is," Le Roux said. "We aren't quite so casual in France. I want to be certain that you are treated with the respect you deserve while you are working with us. I have to set the example for my men to follow."

I still didn't understand what Stottlemeyer and Disher were doing there.

"Is it common procedure for police departments in the United States to send detectives to Europe whenever an American citizen is murdered here?"

"Nope," Stottlemeyer said.

"Then Nathan Chalmers must have been a very important missing person," I said.

"He wasn't missing," Stottlemeyer said. "He was dead."

"We know that now," said Monk, who was carefully stacking the sugar cubes into a large square in the center of the bowl.

"We knew that ten years ago," Stottlemeyer said.

"You mean you assumed it," Monk said.

"No, we knew it. Nathan Chalmers threw himself into a tree mulcher in Golden Gate Park," Stottlemeyer said. "There was just enough left of him to make a positive ID."

"But the skull that I found was from a man who was killed within the last few months," Monk said. "It can't be the same person."

"The dental records are a perfect match," Le Roux said. "There's no question that the skull you found belongs to Nathan Chalmers."

"It's impossible," Monk said, finishing his square of sugar cubes.

Stottlemeyer took one of the cubes off the top and dropped it into his coffee. "Now you know why I'm here."

17

Mr. Monk Is on the Case

"Why did Chalmers throw himself into a tree mulcher?"
Le Roux asked.

"He was about to go on trial for swindling a lot of
very rich people out of twenty million dollars," Stottlemeyer said.

The captain went on to explain that Chalmers was
well educated, charismatic, and an impeccable dresser
who exuded the aura of wealth and success when, in
fact, it was all a sham.

Even so, Chalmers managed to convince a lot of
wealthy and influential people, particularly women, to
invest in his garment factory in India, where he was
making underwear and T-shirts at a cut rate for major
designer labels.

Stottlemeyer told us that Chalmers made generous
donations to candidates in gubernatorial and senato-
rial campaigns and helped raise money for charities and
popular ballot initiatives. Those activities got his picture
in the papers with his arm around politicians and movie

stars, which burnished his stature, established his legitimacy, and lured even more investors into his fold.

He used the money from the new investors to pay off the old ones, who raved about their success and invested even more with him, adding to his wealth and credibility and drawing still more well-heeled investors.

But there was no garment factory in India. In fact, Chalmers didn't have any businesses, just dozens of fictitious business names in the U.S. and abroad.

All the money Chalmers raised was used to support his increasingly high-flying lifestyle. His only source of income was from his investors, and since he kept taking more and more of them on, he couldn't possibly give them all a return on their money. It was a classic pyramid scheme, and at some point, it had to collapse.

By the time it did, the Mayor of San Francisco, the governor of California, a U.S. senator, and a bevy of Hollywood producers, actors, and studio heads all considered Chalmers one of their closest friends and top fund-raisers for their pet political and social causes.

His criminal trial promised to be politically devastating and socially embarrassing for a lot of people.

"He did everybody a favor by throwing himself into that tree mulcher," Stottlemeyer said. "All that was left of him was a shredded handmade Italian suit, a lot of bloody pulp, a finger, and a tooth."

"His upper-left second premolar," Monk said. He was busy restacking the sugar cubes again.

"That's right," Stottlemeyer said. "How did you know?"

"It was the only tooth missing from his skull."

"We were able to positively ID Chalmers from the tooth, which we matched to his dental records, and from a print taken from the severed finger. Case closed."

"He faked his suicide," Monk said. "He amputated his finger, pulled his own tooth, and shoved a homeless person into the mulcher, which is why nobody was ever reported missing at the time of his supposed death."

"That's what it looks like now," Stottlemeyer said.

"Did he do it so he could get away with the money?" Le Roux asked.

"No, he'd burned through it all before his arrest. That's how he got caught," Stottlemeyer said. "But he was facing a long stretch in prison. He'd swindled a lot of very powerful people who were less concerned about the money they'd lost than the embarrassment he'd caused them. They were going to make him pay dearly for it."

"So he fled to Paris," Le Roux said, "where he managed to live undetected by law enforcement until Monsieur Monk found his skull."

"Maybe I'm slow," I said. "I know his murderer has to be found and prosecuted for his crime, but what difference does it make to the San Francisco Police?"

"We wouldn't care, except someone in the department leaked the news to a *Chronicle* reporter that Chalmers had been alive all these years," Stottlemeyer said. "It was going to be a front-page story today. The police commissioner had to do some quick damage control. So he sent me and Randy here to assist Monk in his investigation."

"But Monk isn't investigating," I said.

Stottlemeyer grimaced a little, as if he had a bad taste in his mouth. "That's not what the commissioner disclosed at the press conference. He said that we always suspected Chalmers might be alive and never officially closed the case, which is why he sent Monk to Paris to investigate when some new leads came to light. And that's how the skull was found."

"That's a lie," I said.

"That's politics," Le Roux said. "Something we understand very well in France."

"The commissioner doesn't want people to think we bungled the investigation ten years ago," Stottlemeyer said. "This way, it looks like we weren't fooled and we never gave up the chase."

"So I'm finally on the case," Monk said, glancing at me for my reaction.

I'd already accepted the fact that my vacation wasn't going to happen and that we were back at work, but I wasn't ready to concede the point to Stottlemeyer just yet.

"If the commissioner wants to make his fiction a reality," I said, "then the department is picking up our airfare to Europe and back, all of our lodging costs, and all of our expenses, and they are paying Mr. Monk's consulting fee, retroactive to the day we left San Francisco."

"Done," Stottlemeyer said.

He replied so fast, and without any hesitation, that I wondered if I'd settled too cheap. After all, we had the commissioner over a barrel. On the other hand, Stottlemeyer knew Monk would investigate the case for nothing.

"Congratulations, Mr. Monk," I said. "Our vacation is over."

"Thank God," Monk said. "I don't know how much more of that I could take."

Stottlemeyer turned to Le Roux. "What have you got on the case so far?"

"Nothing beyond the identity of the victim," he said. "However, we may have made some progress going at it from another angle, assuming Monsieur Monk's theory about last night's murder is correct."

"What murder?" Stottlemeyer asked.

"In the restaurant where we had dinner last night," I said. "The woman sitting next to Mr. Monk was stabbed in the chest."

"You saw someone get killed?"

"Thankfully no," I said. "The dining room was completely dark, and we were served by blind waiters. The novelty of the place is that you can't see what you are eating."

"Or who is killed at your table," Le Roux said.

"Or the horse manure all over the floors," Monk said.

"It was a speck that was barely visible to the naked eye," I said. "It could be anything."

"Mr. Monk was right. The lab confirmed that it is horse manure," Le Roux said. "The sample was particularly rich in ammonia, nitrogen, and phosphates, more so than average manure. They found some more traces of it elsewhere on the floor as well."

"That's the last time I eat at a place where I can't see the food," Monk said. "Or the floors."

Stottlemeyer rubbed his temples. "What does any of this have to do with Nathan Chalmers?"

"The victim wanted to give me information about the skull," Monk said. "She said *I know who you found.*"

"How did she know who you were or that you had anything to do with the discovery of the skull?" Stottlemeyer asked.

"There were a lot of camera-toting tourists in the catacombs when Mr. Monk found it," I said. "Pictures of him holding the skull were in all the French newspapers this morning."

"Nice of them to give the killer a heads-up," Stottlemeyer said. "So he could eliminate any loose ends."

"We spent the night interviewing the other diners and

the service staff on the chance that one of them is the killer or his accomplice," Le Roux said. "We've only just begun that aspect of the investigation. That's not where we made our interesting discovery."

Le Roux motioned us to follow him down the hall to a cramped, windowless room, where we found an exhausted Inspector Gadois sitting amid several computer screens that showed surveillance footage from various streets.

The room was so small we had to leave the door open for all of us to fit inside. We also needed the air. It smelled like an armpit in there. Monk pinched his nose.

Le Roux made the necessary introductions and informed Gadois that Stottlemeyer, Monk, and I were now participating in the investigation.

"Cool," Gadois said, shaking Stottlemeyer's hand.

"What is all this?" Stottlemeyer asked, gesturing to the screens.

"Live video feeds from the city's security and traffic cameras," Gadois said.

"We assumed that you and Monsieur Monk took the Métro to the restaurant last night," Le Roux said, "so we pulled the security camera footage from the station at the time of your arrival. Look at what we found."

Gadois clicked his mouse a few times and one of the screens divided into quarters, each section showing a different angle on the subway tracks as a train pulled in. A crowd of people spilled out of the train, including Monk and me. That wasn't the only face I recognized in the crowd. The woman who was murdered at our table followed a few steps behind us.

Le Roux tapped the screen and looked at Stottlemeyer. "That is Aimee Dupon, the victim."

"Just because she got off the same subway train as we

did doesn't necessarily mean she was tailing us," I said. "It could be a coincidence."

"That's right," Le Roux said. "You told me that you'd visited Montmartre and Rue Saint-Honoré yesterday, so we looked at footage from our cameras there as well."

Gadois clicked his mouse again, and we got a split-screen image of two very different views. One side of the screen showed the terrace around the Sacré-Coeur Cathedral atop Montmartre; the other had a high angle on the swank storefronts along a portion of Rue Saint-Honoré.

On each screen, Monk and I could be seen strolling past the camera, trailed a few moments later by Aimee Dupon.

"She was following us all day," Monk said.

Le Roux nodded. "She probably picked you up when you left your hotel and was waiting for the right opportunity to approach you and still maintain her anonymity."

"When she saw us go into Toujours Nuit, she must have thought it was too good to be true," I said.

"I'm sure the killer thought the same thing," Stottlemeyer said. "Have you spotted any other familiar faces?"

Gadois shook his head. "Monsieur Monk, Mademoiselle Teeger, and Dupon are the only people who have shown up on camera at all three locations at the same time—at least that we can see."

"The killer must have been following us or Dupon," Monk said. "How else could he have known that the three of us were all in that restaurant at the same time?"

"Maybe he knew about our reservation and assumed she'd contact us there," I said.

"But how did he get in and out of the restaurant with-

out being seen?" Le Roux asked, absentmindedly strok-
ing his goatee. "And how did he find his way around a
crowded dining room in total darkness?"

"It's definitely a case for Monk," Stottlemeyer said.
"What do we know about this woman Aimee Dupon?"

"She's been arrested several times on minor charges
related to acts of civil disobedience," Le Roux said,
"most of the incidents arising from her illegal occupation of empty buildings against the wishes of the property owners."

"She's a squatter," Stottlemeyer said. "We used to get
'em a lot in San Francisco, too, back before everything
was gentrified. Have you tracked down where she's been
living lately?"

"Yes, but we haven't had the chance to follow up yet,"
Le Roux said. "It's taken us all night just to get this far.
We've barely scratched the surface checking out every-
body in the restaurant."

"If you don't mind, I'd like to check out Dupon's place
with Monk," Stottlemeyer said. "Lieutenant Disher can
stick around and help out your guys."

"Disher?" Gadois said, spinning around in his seat.
"As in Randy Disher? He's here in Paris?"

"Yeah, he's asleep on the chief inspector's couch,"
Stottlemeyer said. "Do you know him?"

"Like the brother I have never met." Gadois stood up
and scrutinized Stottlemeyer as if seeing him for the first
time. "You're *that* captain. I should have known from
your huge mustache."

"Qu'est-ce que vous racontez?" Le Roux demanded
angrily.

"Il est légendaire." Gadois pushed past us and hurried
out of the room.

Disher was a legend? Gadois had to be mistaken.

He couldn't have been talking about the same Randy Disher that we knew.

"I'm sorry, Captain," Le Roux said. "I have no idea why he is behaving this way. It must be the lack of sleep."

"There's no need for any apologies. You've done great work," Stottlemeyer said. "Once your men have had some rest, you might have them look into any unsolved major swindles you've got on your books. The only way Chalmers ever made money was to trick people out of it. I doubt he changed his ways when he came here."

"That's a good idea, Captain," Le Roux said. "What about you? Don't you need some sleep after your long flight?"

"I want to try to stay up until dark," Stottlemeyer said. "I hear that's the best way to beat jet lag."

We followed Le Roux back into the squad room, but even before we got there, we could hear a guitar and some familiar strains of music coming from inside.

"Oh, hell," Stottlemeyer said, wincing.

Gadois was sitting on the edge of Le Roux's desk, strumming on a guitar and singing along with Disher, who was standing on the couch, doing an enthusiastic air-guitar riff.

They were singing Disher's original tune "I Don't Need a Badge"—the one and only song produced by his garage band, the Randy Disher Project.

We were just in time to hear them sing the chorus:

I don't need a gun to make me feel strong.
I don't need a captain shootin' me down all day long.
I don't need your mustache. Don't you condescend to me.
I don't need nobody 'cause, baby, I am free. . . .

Gadois knew the words and music by heart (except he said *goatee* instead of mustache), which I found pretty astonishing considering that Randy distributed the song on CDs that he'd burned on his laptop and labeled himself. How had one of them made it all the way to France?

Le Roux looked at us with a pained expression on his face. "I'll take you to Dupon's place myself."

"Thank you," Stottlemeyer said, looking as pained as Le Roux. "Can we go now?"

"Absolutely," Le Roux said and abruptly headed for the stairs. He and the captain both seemed to be in a big hurry to get out of the building.

"I don't know what their problem is," Monk said to me. "I think it's a catchy tune."

"This from a man who considers 'A Hundred Bottles of Beer on the Wall' the best song ever written."

"Second only to 'Route 66,' " Monk said. "I also like '867-5309.' "

"Not because the song is any good but because the phone number adds up to thirty-eight."

"That's what makes it so good," he said.

18

Mr. Monk Is Disgusted

When Julie was a baby, the only way Mitch and I could get her to take a nap was to put her in the car and go for a drive. The problem was that she'd wake up the instant we stopped, so we had to keep moving. We either drove around San Francisco for a few hours or ended up in another town, which is why we kept a small gym bag with extra diapers and a change of clothes for the three of us in case we decided to get a room wherever we were.

I was reminded of that because two minutes after Le Roux started driving, Stottlemeyer fell asleep in the front seat, his cheek against the passenger-side window.

We didn't say a word for fear of waking him. The only sound in the car was from the police radio, which, since I didn't really speak French, was easy to tune out. I would have had to concentrate to make sense of the chatter, and even then I doubt I would have understood a word.

Instead, I just watched the city go by outside my window as if I was on a tourist bus. I recognized a few famous spots, like the Avenue de l'Opéra and the Galeries Lafayette department store, and I caught a brief glimpse of the Basilique du Sacré-Coeur, but after that, I completely lost my bearings.

The neighborhood around us seemed to decay the deeper we got into the maze of narrow, winding streets until we ended up in front of a nineteenth-century building that was covered in colorful graffiti over layers of peeling paint, rusted metal, and rotted wood. The street-level storefront was boarded up, but above there was laundry strung out to dry on the balconies and music wafted out the open windows with the aroma of hot grease and sizzling bacon. It gave the place a heartbeat.

Stottlemeyer jerked awake, startled and disoriented, the instant we stopped. He blinked hard and ran a hand through his wild hair. His right cheek was red where it had been pressed like a suction cup to the glass.

"We're here," Le Roux said.

"Did you enjoy your nap?" I asked Stottlemeyer.

"I wasn't asleep," he said. "I was just resting my eyes."

It amused me that so many men I knew wouldn't admit to taking naps. I didn't see how acknowledging a little siesta would threaten their masculinity. I asked Mitch about it once, after he'd nodded off on the couch while watching a football game on TV.

"You never see Dirty Harry, James Bond, Superman, or Captain Kirk take a snooze," he said. "Men of action don't need naps."

"Most men aren't action heroes," I said.

"But they think they are," he said, "or that they can be."

"What about you?"

"I'm a fighter pilot," he said. "So I'm definitely a man of action."

"Prove it to me," I said. And he did.

I got out of the car and saw Monk studying me.

"Thinking about Mitch?" he asked.

I felt my face flush with embarrassment. "How did you know?"

"You had that smile," he said.

I motioned to the building. "Don't you have some detecting to do?"

"Didn't I just do some?"

Le Roux stopped outside the front door and faced us like a tour guide about to present an exhibit to his group.

"For years, this building has been at the center of a complicated legal dispute. It was sold and the tenants evicted so the building could be completely gutted. The tenants sued. In the midst of that, the owner had financial difficulties. The bank took over the building and then sold it to someone else, but the previous owner is disputing the legality of the sale. While all of that has been going on, the building has been vacant and illegally occupied by homeless people. We run them out, but they keep returning."

"What harm are they doing?" I asked.

"It's private property," Stottlemeyer said. "And they are obviously trashing the place."

"Trashing is a very serious crime," Monk said.

"But the owner is planning to gut the building anyway," I said. "So what difference does it make?"

"There is never a justification for trashing," Monk said. "It's unforgivable."

"What if the owner changes his mind about renovating and wants to rent out the apartments?" Le Roux said. "Now he can't. They have damaged his property."

"More so than if the building had been left vacant and rotting?" I said.

"They also tap into the electrical and phone lines to get the services for free," Le Roux said, "which is a form of theft."

"And let's not forget the trashing part," Monk said.

Le Roux led us inside, where we were greeted in the lobby with resentful glares from the young couple who were coming down the stairs.

They didn't look like homeless people to me, despite their ragged clothing and long hair. They were too clean, healthy, and happy. Their grunginess struck me as more of a style choice than the result of unfortunate circumstances. They were a little too proud and self-conscious in the way they carried themselves.

Le Roux asked them in French if they knew which apartment Aimee Dupon occupied. I noticed he didn't say the equivalent of "lived in." He was refusing to acknowledge any legal right for them to be there.

The couple said some expletive-laced things about not helping the police harass her or anyone else who lived there. Le Roux bluntly told them that Dupon had been murdered. The news obviously shook them up, which was probably his intent. The girl started to cry. Le Roux said if they wanted Dupon's killer punished, they would answer his question.

The guy comforted the girl and gave Le Roux directions to Dupon's room. Le Roux thanked them and headed up the winding staircase past them.

I looked at Stottlemeyer and Monk before we followed. "Would you like me to translate any of that for you?"

"I think I got the gist of it," Stottlemeyer said and started up the stairs.

Monk held out his hand and motioned to me urgently. "Wipes, wipes."

"What did you touch?" I asked, reaching into my purse and handing him a package of disinfectant tissues.

"Nothing if I can help it," he said. "I need to be prepared for the worst. Hippies live here."

The couple scowled at him as we went up the stairs.

Aimee Dupon's apartment was on the fourth floor and the door was unlocked.

We walked into a very narrow hallway with a bedroom on one end and a living room on the other. In between were the kitchen and a bathroom. The white wainscoting on the yellowed walls was chipped and peeling. The ceiling was waterstained.

The place was sparsely and eclectically furnished, with no two pieces of furniture matching in style or color. Even the drapes didn't match. From the looks of it, Aimee Dupon was doing most of her shopping at thrift shops and garage sales.

"I don't know where she's spending the money she saves on rent," Stottlemeyer said. "But it isn't on decor."

Monk winced and held his arm in front of his face as if protecting himself from a painfully harsh glare. With his other arm, he did his zen thing, using the index finger and thumb on his free hand as an edge to frame his view of things.

We moved together through the apartment, our footsteps heavy on the creaking hardwood floors. I don't know what we expected to find, except maybe some trace of Aimee Dupon herself: who she was, who her friends were, and who might have wanted her dead.

We stepped into the kitchen. There were no doors on the cupboards, and the dishes didn't match. Neither did the glasses. Monk examined some of the canned and packaged goods.

"All this food is expired," Monk said. "The murderer could have saved himself the trouble of killing her by simply letting her eat another meal at home."

Le Roux opened the refrigerator, which was filled with packaged meats and bags from restaurants.

"The meat is expired, too," Le Roux said. "But she was eating at some very expensive restaurants in the seventh arrondissement."

"I guess that's where she spent her money," Stottlemeyer said.

"If she had such a refined palate, why would she let the food in her kitchen go bad?" Monk asked.

"I can relate to her. You should see my kitchen," Stottlemeyer said. "Then again, maybe you shouldn't."

We drifted into the bedroom. Her bed was unmade, which already was a big no-no for Monk. The pillowcases didn't match each other nor did the top and bottom sheets.

"My God," Monk said, "this is barbaric."

Her clothes were ironed and neatly folded in an open trunk. Most of it was thrift-shop chic but nothing I wouldn't have been happy to wear.

There was a stack of magazines on the nightstand beside the bed. Stottlemeyer picked up a couple of magazines and flipped through them, frowning.

"These all have subscription labels but with different names and addresses on them," Stottlemeyer said. "And they're all at least a month or two old."

Le Roux took some of the magazines from Stottlemeyer and examined the subscription labels.

"Quai Branly, Quai d'Orsay. These are all addresses in the seventh arrondissement," Le Roux said, "a very exclusive area along the Seine."

Right above the more than six million corpses in *les*

catacombes, but I guess that the wealthy people who lived there were too enamored of the view of the Seine to think about what was under their feet.

"And where are we?" Stottlemeyer asked.

"A much poorer area, the northeastern corner of the eighteenth," Le Roux said.

"Maybe she was working as someone's cleaning lady," Stottlemeyer said.

"And living like this?" Monk said. "Maybe she wasn't murdered. Maybe she killed herself."

"I don't think so," Le Roux said.

"I didn't either until I saw how she lived," Monk said. "If I had to sleep in a bed with mismatched sheets, I'd be suicidal, too."

We walked down the hall to the living room. There was an old stereo set, an old TV, and an old computer. The electronics were only a few years out-of-date but they already looked as if they should have been in a museum.

There was a newspaper on the kitchen table beside a magnifying glass and a stale loaf of half-eaten bread. Monk's picture was on the front page, holding the skull.

He cocked his head, regarding the picture from an angle.

"Admiring yourself?" Stottlemeyer asked.

Monk pointed to the skull he was holding in the photo. "You can see the gap where the victim's upper-left premolar is missing. I think that's how she recognized that the victim was Nathan Chalmers."

"But what was her relationship with him?" Stottlemeyer asked rhetorically. "Did she know him before his faked death? And if not, how did she meet him here and under what name?"

I glanced at the books on her shelves. There were

literary novels, art and photography books, and some biographies of politicians. The books were yellowed, water-damaged, and coffee-stained. Some of the paperbacks were missing their covers.

"For someone who seems to love books, she didn't take very good care of them," I said. "It's like she fished them out of the sewer."

Monk suddenly straightened up and rolled his shoulders. He'd figured something out.

"She probably did," Monk declared. "She's living in a trash Dumpster."

"It's not that bad," I said.

"No, that's exactly what this place is: a huge trash can," he said. "That's why her food is expired, nothing matches, and all her electronics are so out-of-date. She scavenged all of this from the trash. It's disgusting."

"Bien sûr!" Le Roux exclaimed. "It's so obvious. Why couldn't I see what was right in front of my face?"

"I know the feeling," Stottlemeyer said.

Monk's conclusion explained why everything in the apartment looked like it came from a thrift shop, from her clothes to the furniture. It also meant that the food in her refrigerator came from whatever the restaurants threw out at the end of the night. Yuck.

"So she's squatting in an empty building in the eighteenth and Dumpster-diving in the seventh," Stottlemeyer said. "She's choosy about her garbage."

"This doesn't make sense," I said. "Her clothes are washed, ironed, and neatly folded. She's well-read. She was clean and presentable. Perfect hair, skin, and nails." I looked at Monk and Le Roux. "You both saw her. Did she look like a street person to you?"

"Look at how she lived," Monk said, revolted.

"That's what I mean," I said. "Why wasn't she going

through trash cans closer to home? Why was she being so choosy? You know the old saying *Beggars can't be choosers.*"

"Maybe she didn't know the saying," Stottlemeyer said.

"Or perhaps was making the best out of her poverty," Le Roux said. "She was French, after all."

"It's not about poverty or being French," I said.

"Then what is it?" Le Roux asked.

"Disgusting," Monk said.

"I don't know," I said. "But she's not a beggar. We're missing something."

"Gas masks," Monk said, holding a wipe over his nose and mouth.

Le Roux shrugged. "You may be right, Mademoiselle Teeger. I suggest we go to the seventh arrondissement later and see if there are other scavengers there who might have known her."

"Why can't we go there now?" Stottlemeyer said.

"I want to secure the scene until an officer can come to take my place. He'll stay until a forensics unit can get here."

"What for?" I said.

"I don't want any of the squatters helping themselves to her things, particularly her computer. There might be files on it that can shed some light on her activities and her relationship to Monsieur Chalmers."

"We'll wait outside," Monk said. "We can't breathe any more of this garbage air."

Monk didn't wait for us. He bolted.

I turned and saw Stottlemeyer looking at me.

"Something's missing?" he said.

"I think there is," I said defensively.

"Until a couple of hours ago, you wanted nothing to do with this murder investigation."

"That's true, but the circumstances have changed."

"Is that so?" Stottlemeyer said.

"Mr. Monk is committed to the case, so I am, too," I said. "That's how it goes."

He gave me a cold look. "You know what you're becoming?"

"An enormous pain in the butt?"

He walked past me. "A half-decent detective."

19

Mr. Monk Cleans Up

It wasn't the first time Stottlemeyer had said something like that to me. And I wasn't sure whether to be flattered or not.

When I had first started working as Monk's assistant, I tried to be as unobtrusive as possible at crime scenes and not get any more involved in his interviews than I had to be in order to make sure things went smoothly for him.

That changed as time went on.

I don't know if it was because I got bored or more comfortable in my role, or if it was the result of visiting all those crime scenes and hanging out with cops, forensics experts, medical examiners, and murderers. But I started asking questions of my own, whether anyone asked me my opinion or not.

I suppose it was inevitable that I would begin to start thinking more like a detective, if only to be a more productive and helpful assistant to Monk.

Besides, once I got involved in an investigation with

Monk, my natural curiosity took over, and I couldn't help getting personally involved. Monk didn't get called into a case unless the mystery was particularly puzzling, which made it interesting for me, too.

Thinking like a detective, of course, didn't mean that I had any illusions about actually *being* one. Or that I wanted to be, which I didn't. It just gave me something else to do besides stand there handing Monk disinfectant wipes and making excuses for his behavior.

I wasn't quite sure how Stottlemeyer, Disher, and other law enforcement professionals like Chief Inspector Le Roux felt about my involvement, especially when I started asking questions.

Monk was an ex-cop and a brilliant detective. He'd earned their respect and his place at a crime scene. But me? I was simply a civilian with a big mouth.

Captain Stottlemeyer and Lieutenant Disher never pulled me aside and told me to butt out, so I guess I took that as tacit approval.

Or maybe they were just being polite, out of respect for Monk.

I don't think Monk cared one way or the other. He was in his own world. Unless something was filthy, out of place, asymmetrical, or uneven, he didn't notice it.

And I was none of those things.

The couple we'd met in the lobby was sitting on the stairs, watching through the open front doors as Monk cleaned the windshield of Le Roux's car with his disinfectant wipes.

Stottlemeyer took a photo out of his coat pocket and held it in front of the couple. It was a picture of a good-looking man with nice teeth, nice hair, a nice tan, and not an ounce of sincerity. It had to be Nathan Chalmers. How could anyone have been fooled by that guy? Or maybe I was just reading into his face what I already knew about him.

"Have you ever seen this man before?" Stottlemeyer asked the couple. They didn't say anything.

"Reconnaissez-vous cet homme—" I began, but Stottlemeyer interrupted me.

"Don't bother, Natalie. They understand what I'm saying," Stottlemeyer said.

"How do you know?" I asked.

"I saw the look on their faces when Monk made the remark about hippies living here," Stottlemeyer said. "They were ticked off."

"We aren't animals," the man said. "We chose to free ourselves from the forced addiction to consumerism that made us slaves to the corporations and the banks. That doesn't make us subhuman. We're more human than you are."

Stottlemeyer gave me a look, then shifted his gaze back to them. "Is that why you're living here? To teach the corporations a lesson?"

"You're ridiculing us," he said. "It's a mask to cover your jealousy."

"You think I want to live like this?" Stottlemeyer said, gesturing to the decaying building around us.

"You wish you had the courage and the strength to be free, like we are," the man said. "We don't have credit cards, mortgages, car leases, or a thousand other chains of debt shackling us in perpetual servitude to corporate masters. We don't suck the tainted milk from the corporate teat."

I was glad Monk wasn't there to hear that. Just the mention of milk was enough to give him the shivers. Add to that the image of a calf feeding at a cow's teat and he might have fainted.

"What about him?" Stottlemeyer said, waving the picture in front of them.

"Bob Smith would never hurt Aimee, if that's what you're thinking," the girl said. "He's a sweet, gentle man. A pacifist."

"I know *Bob* didn't kill Aimee," Stottlemeyer said.

"Then why are you looking for him?" the man asked.

"I'm not," Stottlemeyer said. "I know where he is."

"If that's true," the girl said, "why are you here asking us about him instead of talking to him yourself in New York?"

Stottlemeyer raised an eyebrow. "Is that where you think he is?"

"He went there to foster the movement in America," the man said. "That's why he left Aimee."

"The movement?" I said.

"They're Freegans," the man said. "They don't believe in the religion of consumerism. They live entirely off the goods that society wastes."

"Trash," Stottlemeyer said.

"Is it trash just because it isn't stylish anymore? Is it trash just because not all the food that was made was served? Is it trash just because a newer model has come out?" the man asked. "Is it trash just because of an arbitrary expiration date intended to make you keep spending?"

"That sounds like Bob, all right," Stottlemeyer asked. "Did he live here, too?"

"He used to come around to see Aimee and then he just disappeared," the girl said. "Aimee found out later that he went to New York. He knew he could never leave her if he had to tell her good-bye."

"Who told her that?" Stottlemeyer asked.

The girl shrugged. "Aimee never told me. Why are you asking all these questions about Bob?"

"Because he never left Paris," Stottlemeyer said. "He was murdered months ago. I'm thinking that whoever killed him probably killed Aimee, too."

The couple looked like they'd both been slapped.

"Are you sure you don't know anything else?" Stottlemeyer prodded. They both nodded. "Thanks for your help. I didn't get your names."

"No, you didn't," the man said. He took his girlfriend's hand, and they walked out.

I couldn't blame them for wanting to put some distance between themselves and us. We'd brought death into their lives and right into their home. It wouldn't surprise me if they packed up their things and were squatting somewhere else tomorrow.

A police car pulled up outside and dropped off an officer, who hurried past us up the stairs while his partner found a parking spot.

Stottlemeyer nodded at me.

"What?" I said.

"You were right," he said. "Aimee wasn't a beggar. She's a Freegan, whatever the hell that is."

"And so was Chalmers," I said.

Stottlemeyer frowned. "Not unless there was money in it for him."

"Rooting around in the trash doesn't sound very lucrative to me," I said. "How much can you make recycling soft drink cans?"

Le Roux came down the stairs. "The forensics team will be here in an hour, and they will take her computer so we can examine her hard drive. But in the meantime, I did some looking around. I found a box of her business cards."

"She has a job?" Stottlemeyer asked.

"Or she used to," Le Roux replied. "She was an editor at a publishing company. Maybe we can learn more about her from her coworkers."

"We've learned a few things about her and Chalmers already from her neighbors," Stottlemeyer said. "He used to visit Aimee here. He was using the name Bob Smith. We'll tell you and Monk all about it on the way."

"Monsieur Monk wasn't involved in the interview?" Le Roux asked. "What was he doing that was more important than that?"

We motioned outside to Le Roux's car. Monk was shining the headlights.

Le Roux's jaw dropped open. "He's washing my car?"

"Pretend you don't notice," Stottlemeyer said.

"But why would he do such a thing?" Le Roux asked.

"He loves it," Stottlemeyer said. "He finds it very relaxing."

"Driving around with Mr. Monk saves me a fortune on car washes," I said. "Dirt never gets a chance to build up."

"But whatever you do, don't tip him," Stottlemeyer said. "He'll just get spoiled."

If you're atop the Arc de Triomphe and you look straight up Avenue Charles de Gaulle, which is what the Champs-Élysées becomes after it passes through l'Étoile, in the distance you will see La Grande Arche, an enormous cube of white marble with an opening in the middle that could easily fit the Notre Dame cathedral.

I'm surprised they didn't put a full-scale replica under there just to prove it. La Grande Arche was an obnoxious attempt to out-arc the Arc de Triomphe. They may have accomplished their goal in size but not in elegance or class.

I figured it was only a matter of time before they built a grand tower of glass, steel, and neon in the direct line of sight from the *Tour Eiffel*, too.

The Courte-Dell Publishing Company was in one of the new skyscrapers clustered around La Grande Arche, which dominated the view from senior editor Laura Boucher's small office.

Her furnishings were identical to the furnishings in all the other offices that we passed and in the warren of cubicles outside her door.

One wall of her office was lined with shelves stacked with manuscripts. The opposite wall was occupied by two bookshelves crammed with piles of hardcover and paperback books mixed together in no particular order.

That was about to change. Monk immediately made it his job to organize the books by author and binding. If we were there long enough, I knew he'd arrange the books by copyright date and genre, too.

Monk didn't ask permission to reorganize Boucher's books, of course. He assumed it was his moral right. But she didn't object. She was preoccupied with the news that her former colleague, Aimee Dupon, had been killed.

"I was afraid things wouldn't end well for her," Laura said, sitting down in her chair. "It was like her mind just snapped."

Le Roux and Stottlemeyer took the two guest chairs. I stood beside Monk.

"What do you mean?" Le Roux asked as he sat down.

It was an open-ended cop question inviting her to

talk. Cops liked it when people talked. The more they jabbered, the more they revealed.

"Aimee was so passionate about books. They were her love," Laura said. "That's why she got into the publishing business. She thought it was all about finding and supporting great literature."

"It's not?" I said.

"What she didn't understand is that it's a business first. The book has to be marketable, the author has to have a promotable hook of some kind, and you have to prove to the number crunchers that a book will sell."

"So if it's a choice between publishing a novel by a Hollywood stripper, the President's dog, or a promising author," I said, "you'll go with the stripper or the dog."

"We might hire the promising author to ghost the book for the dog," she said. "But yes, you're right. There's also a lot of internal politics involved. There are only so many books this company can publish each year. Every editor in the building is fighting to make sure their books are among the chosen few that are published. After that, it's a fight to get the best release date, to get the sales staff to push your title, and to get the publicists to flog your book more than the others. Ultimately, whether a book is good or not is the least important part of the equation."

Monk was making good progress with the books and didn't seem the least bit interested in what Laura had to say.

Neither did Stottlemeyer. His head lolled to one side as he fought a losing battle with sleep. I gave his chair a nudge with the tip of my shoe. His head tipped up for a moment, then lolled to one side again.

"I assume the editors aren't just fighting for the books," Le Roux said. "They are fighting for their careers. There must be a lot of backstabbing going on."

"The more books you get published, the more likely you are to rise up in the company. Assuming your books succeed, which has as much to do with what happens in these halls as what happens in the stores," she said. "I had to step over a lot of bodies to get this office, in the metaphorical sense, of course."

"Of course," Le Roux said.

"Was Aimee's one of them?" I asked and gave Stottlemeyer's chair a good kick. He jerked awake.

"Aimee took herself down," Laura said.

"What does any of this have to do with her murder?" Stottlemeyer said, sounding surly. With his jet lag, he should never have taken a seat. It was asking for trouble.

"About two years ago, she fell in love with a graphic novel submission by artist Antoine Bisson about a young runaway who wanders into the catacombs of Paris and discovers a secret subterranean world that lives entirely off of society's trash."

"Freegans," I said.

"Lunatics," Monk said, not even looking up from his work. At least it proved he was listening.

"Aimee was totally captivated by it," Laura said. "And when Antoine told her that his work was more truth than fiction, she became immersed in that world and its ideals, which, of course, ran counter to everything this company stands for."

"Commerce over art," I said.

Laura gave me a cold look. "Nobody here believed there was a market for a comic book about homeless people living in the sewer. Does that sound like something you'd want to read?"

"It's disgusting," Monk said.

"See?" she said, gesturing to Monk. "That's the reaction we expected. And to be honest, Aimee wasn't the book's best advocate. Whenever she tried to argue for the book, she'd inevitably veer off into some emotional tirade against consumerism. When the project was killed, she was so disillusioned that she not only left the company—she dropped out of society to live underground in that idealized world."

Monk suddenly straightened up. "It really exists?"

I wondered why he was suddenly so interested.

"The tunnels do. There are immense sewers and catacombs under virtually every street in Paris, everybody knows that," Laura said. "And I suppose there are some homeless people who seek shelter down there. But I think the idea that there's some kind of utopian society under the streets is an urban myth."

"But Aimee bought into it," Le Roux said.

Laura shrugged. "She said Bisson showed it to her."

If it was there, I wanted to see it. There was something undeniably romantic about the idea, minus the sewage and the trash. But if it existed, she wasn't living there anymore. Something must have driven her out of the catacombs but not away from the Freegan movement. Did it have something to do with Nathan Chalmers? And was it what had gotten them both killed?

Le Roux shared a glance with me. I was pretty sure that he was thinking along the same lines as me. Stottlemeyer was falling asleep again, so I kicked his chair.

"So what?" Stottlemeyer grumbled, irritated. "How does this get us any closer to who killed her?"

"She was vulnerable and weak. Antoine Bisson filled her head with crap and led her to a life on the streets," Laura said. "And that's what got her killed."

"Or she got tired of the politics and greed here," I said, "so she chose a simpler and more sincere way of life."

"Living in a sewer and eating garbage?" Laura said.

I shrugged. "Maybe that's what she thought she was doing here."

"Now you sound like her," Laura said.

"You don't want to live in a sewer," Monk said to me. "You're just tired. All you really need is a vacation."

Ah, at last Monk was finally seeing the light. "Great, when do I get one?"

"You can begin tonight," he said. "You can clean our bathroom."

"That's your idea of a vacation?" I asked.

"It's a start," he replied.

Laura, Le Roux, and I all stared at Monk, who was admiring his neatly aligned rows of books. Stottlemeyer snored. I kicked his chair and he reached for his gun, which, thankfully, he didn't have.

"Do you know where we can find Antoine Bisson?" Le Roux asked Laura.

She did.

20

Mr. Monk and the Artist

Before we went to see Antoine Bisson, we stopped at a Starbucks across from the Courte-Dell building and got Captain Stottlemeyer a large coffee to wake him up. I tried to convince him to try the coffee at a small café next door instead, but he wasn't in the mood to experiment.

"Coffee is coffee," I said.

"Then what difference does it make whether I have a Starbucks or a cup from a French place?"

"Because you're in Paris," I said. "You should experience what the city has to offer."

"They're offering me Starbucks." Stottlemeyer sipped his venti cinnamon dolce latte and glanced at Le Roux, who was picking up his tall coffee from the barista. "What do you think of this coffee?"

"Very good," Le Roux said.

"How does it compare to the French stuff?" he asked.

Le Roux shrugged. "It's coffee."

Stottlemeyer returned his gaze to me. "I rest my case."

"So where would you like to have lunch?" I asked. "McDonald's?"

"Only if we can't find a Burger King," Stottlemeyer said.

I couldn't tell if he was joking or not. But to make a statement, I didn't get a cup of coffee at Starbucks. I held out for the French experience.

"You should try a croque monsieur for lunch," Monk said. "It's tasty."

Monk was eating a brownie with a knife and fork. I think he ordered it simply because it was square.

Stottlemeyer raised an eyebrow. "You tried something new?"

"I like to live on the edge," Monk said.

Le Roux stepped outside to make a phone call while the three of us sat inside at a table. I picked up a fork and stole a bite from Monk's brownie.

"What do you think of Paris so far?" I asked Stottlemeyer.

"I'm glad I've got a homicide to work on," he said.

"Me, too," Monk said.

"You both have to learn to relax," I said.

"I couldn't relax here," Stottlemeyer said. "The language, the look of the place, everything is different. I don't know my way."

"That's what makes the experience fresh and exciting," I said. "It's a journey of discovery."

"Investigating a crime, solving a mystery, and catching the bad guy—those are the kinds of discoveries I like to make."

"Me, too," Monk said.

"Investigating a new place is like solving a mystery,"

I said. "You're uncovering a different culture, learning how other people live. It's about finding yourself, not a perpetrator."

Stottlemeyer said, "I can't relax if I can't take care of myself, if I don't know the rules of the game."

"You mean when you aren't in control of your environment," I said.

"Everything here is strange and unfamiliar. It makes me uncomfortable," he said. "But I know how to investigate a homicide. I can find my bearings. I know what I've got to do and how to do it. That makes me comfortable."

"Me, too," Monk said.

"Comfortable is relaxing," Stottlemeyer said.

"I agree," Monk said.

"Did you hear that, Captain?" I said. "Mr. Monk agrees with you."

"Of course he does," Stottlemeyer said.

"You know why? Because you sound just like him. Neither one of you can leave your safe, orderly environments. You're the same."

Stottlemeyer looked at Monk for a long moment. I could almost hear him replaying our conversation in his mind.

"Oh, my God," he said, "we are."

"Do you have an uncontrollable desire to count the coffee beans on display at the counter?" I asked the captain. "Maybe you'd like to bus a few of the tables before we go."

Monk smiled at Stottlemeyer. "I knew you'd come around eventually. I never lost faith in you. Now we can begin working on the bigger issues."

"What bigger issues?" Stottlemeyer said.

"You have foam on your mustache," Monk said.

Stottlemeyer dabbed at his mustache with a napkin. "That wasn't so big. Issue resolved."

"Not quite," Monk said. "You have to shave it off."

"I am not shaving my mustache," Stottlemeyer said.

"It will prevent you from getting foam on it," Monk said. "Or anything else."

"I like my mustache," he said.

"It's unsanitary," Monk said.

"There's nothing unsanitary about a mustache," Stottlemeyer said.

"You get all kinds of food and dirt stuck in it," Monk said.

"I do not," Stottlemeyer said.

"And nasal discharge," Monk said.

"Stop," Stottlemeyer said sternly, pointing a finger at him.

"It's like holding a handful of garbage up to your nose all day," Monk said. "You are poisoning yourself every time you inhale."

"The mustache is staying," Stottlemeyer said. "End of discussion."

"At least breathe through your mouth," Monk said. "You'll thank me later."

Le Roux came back inside and slipped his phone into his pocket.

"Antoine Bisson is available to see us," he said. "Shall we go?"

Stottlemeyer couldn't get up fast enough. But Monk wasn't ready to leave just yet.

He had some tables to clean first. And some coffee beans to count.

Antoine Bisson's loft was in the first arrondissement near the Centre Pompidou art museum, where Chief Inspector Le Roux parked in a spot reserved for official vehicles. I guess it was one of the perks of being a police officer in Paris.

Monk was mortified by the Pompidou and started complaining about it the instant he caught sight of the colorful, utterly distinctive building.

"It's inside out," he said.

That was true.

The infrastructure of the Pompidou—the steel beams, the escalators, and the multicolored pipes, ducts, and ventilation shafts—was all on the outside of the building instead of hidden within its walls. I thought there was something fanciful about its colorful industrial look. It could have been a jelly-bean factory in Candyland.

"That's what makes it special," I said.

"All of that should be inside the walls." Monk turned to Le Roux. "You should do something about it."

"I'm a police officer," Le Roux said, "not an architecture critic."

It was the first time I'd heard an irritable edge in Le Roux's voice while he was talking to Monk. Stottlemeyer caught it, too, and it made him smile. It meant that Le Roux was one more person who could sympathize with the captain's plight.

"What if someone walked by with his guts hanging out?" Monk asked. "Would you do something about that?"

"I would call an ambulance," Le Roux said.

"That building needs an ambulance," Monk said, "or a wrecking ball."

"I'm sorry you don't like it, Monsieur Monk," Le Roux said. "But it's outside of my authority."

"This is all going in my report," Monk said.

"What report?" Le Roux asked.

"To the authorities," Monk said. "There's a lot in Paris that needs straightening out."

"He means that literally," Stottlemeyer said to Le Roux.

We got out of the car and Le Roux led us across the plaza in front of the museum.

Monk shielded his eyes from the sight of the Pompidou until we made our way onto Rue Denis, a narrow side street lined with walk-up take-out places offering crepes, sandwiches, falafel, and pizzas.

At the corner of Rue Denis and Rue des Lombards, there was a door squeezed between two take-out places. I would never have noticed the door if Le Roux hadn't walked up to it. He leaned on a bell and announced us and we were buzzed in.

Once again, we had to go up a winding staircase. A stained and faded rug ran down the middle of the steps, which were bowed from centuries of use.

Antoine Bisson was waiting for us in an open doorway on the third floor. He was lanky, with a day's growth of beard on his face, his long hair pulled back into a ponytail. He wore an untucked shirt over another untucked shirt, and his hands were flecked with paint.

He introduced himself in French, offering Le Roux and Stottlemeyer his hand. They shook. Monk hid behind me, hoping to avoid the handshake ritual altogether. I shook hands with Bisson twice.

"La première poignée de main est pour moi. La seconde est pour Monsieur Monk," I said, explaining that I was shaking for me and Monk.

Bisson gave Monk an amused once-over. *"A-t-il peur d'attraper quelque chose?"*

He wondered if Monk was afraid of catching something.

More like everything, and that was what I told him. *"Il a peur d'attraper tous les choses."*

Bisson smiled and ushered us inside, the wood floor creaking under our feet as we followed him.

"Welcome to my home," Bisson said in an accent so heavy, it made his English sound like French.

The bathroom was to our immediate left, the kitchen was to our right, and in front of us was an open space that doubled as the bedroom, living room, and studio.

There was a large easel, a stool, and a palette of fresh paint in front of one of the windows that overlooked the Rue Denis. Bisson was working on a painting of a woman in black spandex holding a crossbow. It looked to me like an illustration for a book cover, minus the title and author.

It was amazing that Bisson was so thin. The smell of hot bread, sizzling fat, and bubbling cheese that wafted in the open windows from the street would have made me hungry all day.

There were shelves lined with books, but unlike Laura Boucher's office, these appeared to be neatly and meticulously organized. It was probably the only aspect of the place that met with Monk's approval.

Instead of hanging artwork and photos to decorate his loft, Bisson had painted pictures of framed paintings and photos directly onto his walls, complete with illustrated crooked nails and hanging wires.

The paintings of paintings included a windswept beach, a topless Mona Lisa, a still life of a fish skeleton on a chipped plate, an overtly clichéd Paris street scene, and a wall of femurs and skulls like the ones in *les catacombes*.

I took a second look at the Mona Lisa. There was something about her that seemed familiar. And then it hit me with a jolt.

It was Aimee Dupon—but with the Mona Lisa's hair, high forehead, and the same hauntingly ambiguous expression.

The painting was equally ambiguous to me. What did it mean? Was it a joke? Was it a tribute? Why was she nude? Bisson was making some kind of comment about Aimee and about how he perceived a great work of art, but I had no idea what it was.

He caught me admiring his walls. "I am an artist who can't afford any art but his own. *Il est triste.*"

"I like it," I said. "It tells me more about your personality than I could ever learn from what you've chosen of other people's work."

Bisson offered me a beguiling smile. "You wish to learn about me?"

Stottlemeyer spoke up. "*We* wish to learn about Aimee Dupon."

I wondered if Stottlemeyer recognized the model for Antoine's Mona Lisa. He hadn't had a good look at Aimee, but Le Roux and Monk had. I doubted Monk was paying much attention to the Mona Lisa, not with the nudity. Monk could study a dead body, even a naked one on a morgue slab, but he couldn't bear nudity in any other context. It embarrassed him and offended his sense of decency.

Bisson's smile faded. "I was heartbroken to hear about her death."

"It was a murder," Monk said. "We understand you convinced her to live in trash."

"That's not what happened," Bisson said.

"I find that hard to believe, coming from a man with not one but *two* untucked shirts."

"All I did was submit a graphic novel to her that she liked," Bisson said. "As far as I know, that's not a crime."

"Tell us about that book," Le Roux said.

"I can do better than that," he said. "I can show it to you."

Bisson went to his kitchen table, where he had a portfolio of artwork open and waiting for us. The panels on display showed a group of young people wearing overalls, backpacks, and night-vision goggles, entering a huge underground cavern, every inch of it decorated with all kinds of art. The walls and ceilings were covered with graffiti, paintings, sketches, frescoes, and elaborate mosaics. Statues, fluted columns, gargoyles, and castles were sculpted in the rock.

"Is there really a chamber like this in the catacombs?" I asked.

"There are thousands," Bisson said. "The graphic novel was inspired by my explorations of the greatest art gallery on earth, the Paris netherworld."

He'd obviously been inspired by that world when he painted his loft. I could understand that. But I didn't see the point of toiling for weeks in the dank caverns on a sculpture or mosaic that only the rats would enjoy.

"Why would anyone waste their time doing artwork in the catacombs instead of working on stuff in their own studios that has a chance to earn them some notice or a paycheck?"

"There is a human need to leave one's mark on the world, to say *Yes, I was there,*" Bisson said. "The catacomb walls are more than art. They are the record of three centuries of French history by those who witnessed it: miners, fugitives, students, resistance fighters, whores, soldiers, revolutionaries, vagrants, and artists. There's artwork from the riots of the nineteen sixties, the storming of the Bastille, the German occupation during World War II, the Franco-Prussian war, the Reign of Terror—

every significant and notorious event that shaped this city, all mixed together in various forms of expression. It's exhilarating in a way no museum could ever be."

His eyes sparkled with excitement as he spoke. He made the catacombs sound magical, at least to me. I wanted to see it for myself.

"There's no order to it," Monk said. "It's just a big mess."

"It is a reflection of life," Bisson said. "It is art in its purest sense."

"Pure art would be clean rocks," Monk said. "The earth as it was meant to be."

"If that were true, we would not be here soiling the earth with our existence, and we would not have been blessed with imagination and creativity," Bisson said. "Even prehistoric man drew on the walls of his cave."

"And a civilized man cleaned it off," Monk said.

"How did you find this cavern?" Stottlemeyer said.

Bisson went to a backpack that was propped against the wall along with some dirt-caked hiking boots, a pair of night-vision goggles, and a walking stick carved to look like a snake was curled around it. He opened a zipper on the backpack and pulled out a map, which he brought to the table and spread out over his portfolio. The original printed map was covered with hand-scrawled additions, deletions, and scribbled notes.

"Some of the abandoned quarries under the city began to collapse in the late seventeen hundreds and swallow entire streets," Bisson explained. "So the government sent inspectors to map the catacombs and shore up crumbling chambers. But they had to build even more passages to get around and repair everything. There are two hundred miles of tunnels down there. The original map has been revised by generations of Cataphiles like me. It's ever-changing."

"Anyone can go down there?" I asked.

"It's illegal and very dangerous," Le Roux said. "But there is little we can do to stop it. The network of tunnels is simply too vast."

I imagined the catacombs also presented a terrorism threat, but that was hardly new, considering how long the tunnels had existed under Paris and how often they had been used over the centuries by enemies of the government and fugitives from the law as a hideout and a base of operations.

"I am just one of thousands of Cataphiles who use the tunnels as a canvas or a stone to chisel." Bisson glanced at me. "Unfortunately, as you correctly observed, mademoiselle, I can't make any money on that."

"So you created the Freegans and made a comic book out of it," Stottlemeyer said.

"I didn't create the Freegans. They're real. But I am not one of them. I fictionalized them, made them more noble and romantic than they really are."

"Which is what?" Le Roux asked.

"Vagrants. They don't work, unless you count the time they spend in trash Dumpsters. They refuse to take part in what Lucien Barlier calls the *corrupt, wasteful, environment-killing consumer society*."

Le Roux took out a notebook and began making some notations. "Who is Lucien Barlier?"

"He's the leader of the Freegans. The King Rat. Supposedly, Lucien became so disgusted by the economic and social injustices of capitalism that he quit his high-paying job, gave away all of his nonessential possessions, and decided to *opt out*, to stop earning and spending money. That's how he found inner peace and so have his followers."

"In other words," Stottlemeyer said, "the Freegans mooch off everybody else. They're bums."

"Just because they don't buy stuff?" I said. "From what we've heard, they aren't asking for anything from anybody. It seems to me that they are making something positive out of what we discard as useless. What's the harm in that?"

"Whatever they may be," Bisson said, "Aimee didn't see them for who they are. She saw the mythical version I created in my book: an egalitarian society of poets, artists, philosophers, and dreamers seeking shelter from the greed, avarice, and cruelty of the world above."

"And they aren't?" I said.

"They don't want to work, which is about more than capitalism. It's about giving something back to society, whether it's cutting somebody's hair, inventing a new computer chip, or writing a song. What are they doing?"

"Showing us another, perhaps more reasonable way of living that isn't wasteful," I said.

"You sound like Aimee," he said.

"Don't worry," I said. "I'm not ready to give up my apartment and live in a cave, even if it is in Paris."

I was sure a Paris cave was much nicer than a cave anywhere else. Everything in Paris was better.

"I told Aimee that she didn't have to, either. But Lucien Barlier is smoother than I am," Bisson said, folding up the map. "After Courte-Dell rejected my book, Aimee wanted out of the whole corporate, consumer-driven world. She joined the Freegans."

"What about you?" Le Roux asked.

"The Cataphiles and the Freegans try to stay out of one another's way. I love the catacombs, but I'm not interested in eating someone's garbage or giving up all of my decadent luxuries."

"That must have put a strain on your relationship with Mademoiselle Dupon," Le Roux said.

"For a while, I was Aimee's lover and her guide to the underground realm. But once she found the Freegans, she didn't need me anymore. I was tossed onto the bone heap like one of those skeletons in the ossuaries."

"Speaking of which." Stottlemeyer held up a photo of Nathan Chalmers. "Have you ever run into him?"

Bisson nodded. "That's Bob Smith. He was Aimee's new lover. She met him underground. From what I hear, Bob showed up out of nowhere a few years ago and developed some radical ideas that really shook up the Freegans."

"Like what?" Stottlemeyer prodded.

"Bob felt if you really wanted to make a difference, you weren't going to do it living in caves and eating what people scraped off their plates. You had to make the corporations and the worst abusers of society feel it, or they'd never instigate change."

"How did *Bob* intend to do that?"

"I don't know, but whatever it was, Bob and Lucien clashed bitterly over it."

"Knowing *Bob*, I'm sure it involved money," Stottlemeyer said.

"Then it's no wonder Lucien was against it. But by then, Aimee was aligned with Bob and so were some of the Freegans. She and their faction moved aboveground. But I guess Bob still wasn't happy. I heard he went back to America."

"He didn't," Stottlemeyer said. "He's in the morgue."

"Only his skull, at this point," Le Roux said. "We are still looking for the rest of him."

"That's the skull that was found in the catacombs?" Bisson said in surprise.

"A day before Aimee Dupon was murdered at Toujours Nuit," Le Roux said.

I wasn't a detective, but even I could see the outlines of a motive for murder taking shape.

Had Nathan Chalmers, aka Bob Smith, been killed in a Freegan turf battle with Lucien Barlier? Was Aimee Dupon killed because she figured it out and had some kind of evidence to prove whodunit?

It was while I was pondering those questions that I realized that Monk hadn't said a word for a half hour. In fact, he wasn't even standing at the table with us.

He was gone.

"Mr. Monk?" I turned to look for him and, in doing so, inadvertently drew everyone else's attention to me.

Monk was standing on the other side of the room, holding a palette and paintbrush. He was dabbing the brush on the wall, but his head was turned away and his eyes were closed.

"What are you doing?" Bisson yelled, as if chastising a dog for peeing on the rug. He hurried over.

"Some little touch-ups," Monk said, his eyes still closed. "You'll thank me later."

"You've covered up everything," Bisson said, more shocked than angry. We walked over to see for ourselves.

"Then I'm done." Monk opened his eyes and regarded his work with pride. *"Magnifique."*

He'd painted two big black squares over the Mona Lisa's formerly exposed breasts.

Le Roux looked at the painting. "You painted those perfect squares with your eyes closed?"

"Of course," Monk said. "Otherwise I would have had to look."

"He doodles in straight lines, too," Stottlemeyer said.

I couldn't believe that Monk had actually vandalized a painting in someone's home. Of course I understood, in the context of his psychological disorder, why he felt compelled to do it, but that didn't mean he had to act on his impulses. Didn't he have any social graces whatsoever?

I turned to Bisson. "I am so sorry."

He held up his hand. "It's all right. At least he didn't damage the face."

Le Roux was still looking at the Mona Lisa. "That's Aimee Dupon."

"It is?" Stottlemeyer said, regarding the painting anew.

"She was a work of art," Bisson said. "That's how I want to remember her. Are you done here?"

"Not quite," Monk said, moving toward the still life. "I need to fix the chip on that fish plate."

Bisson snatched the paintbrush from Monk's hand. "You're done."

"One more question," Le Roux said. "Do you know where we can find Lucien Barlier?"

"Most mornings he's usually scavenging in the Dumpsters behind the patisseries, fromageries, boulangeries, bistros, and markets along Rue Cler," Bisson said, then handed me the map to the underground. "Or you can drop in on him at home."

21

Mr. Monk and the Rock Star

Captain Stottlemeyer was ready to crash, despite his goal of staying up until nightfall.

Le Roux had thoughtfully booked Stottlemeyer and Disher into the same hotel as us. We swung by the hotel after the interview with Bisson so Stottlemeyer could take a short nap before we all gathered again at eight p.m. for dinner.

Le Roux dropped us off before returning to his office to catch up on his paperwork. He said he would return at seven thirty to give us a ride to the restaurant.

Lieutenant Randy Disher was standing at the front desk when we arrived at the hotel. He was wearing a PARIS baseball cap and dark sunglasses, and the collar of his jacket was turned up. He looked like a movie star trying to go incognito, which, of course, only made them stand out more since nobody except stars trying to go incognito ever dressed that way.

"Hey, Randy, how are you holding up?" I said.

"Sshhhhh, you'll draw a crowd," Disher said and ushered me around to the cocktail bar side of the front desk. Stottlemeyer and Monk followed us.

"It's not that unusual for friends to greet one another in a hotel lobby," I said. "Even in France."

"You don't understand." Disher lowered his voice. "I'm a rock star over here."

I laughed. "Your jet lag has made you delusional."

"It's the truth," Disher said.

I turned to the desk clerk, who was the ghostly female apparition who'd checked us in two days before. "Have you ever heard of Randy Disher?"

She looked perplexed. "I believe he is the man you are speaking to."

"But had you ever heard of him until this moment?"

"No," she said.

I turned back to Disher. "Your disguise must have fooled her."

"I'm a cult sensation," Disher said, "among the intelligentsia."

"Where did you get that idea?" Stottlemeyer asked.

"Inspector Guy Gadois," Disher said.

"He's the intelligentsia?"

"He's the lead singer in one of my tribute bands."

"There's more than one?" Stottlemeyer said.

"In cities all over France," Disher said. "Guy calls his the Guy Gadois Project."

"But you only have one song," I said.

"And it's barely that," Stottlemeyer added.

"It's like 'Stairway to Heaven,'" Disher said, "for the Now Generation."

"What is the *Now* Generation?" Monk asked.

"Not the *Then* Generation," Disher said, waving his arm behind him at the past. "You can see for yourself tonight. We're all meeting for dinner at this hip Paris nightclub. You can be my entourage."

"Did you and Gadois squeeze in some work between songs today?" Stottlemeyer said.

"We cleared the customers and staff at Toujours Nuit. None of them has a connection to either victim," Disher said. "I checked out the U.S. end while Guy handled Europe."

"Did the crime scene techs come up with anything?"

"They found Chalmers' fingerprints all over Aimee Dupon's apartment and her computer keyboard."

I couldn't imagine what Chalmers had been using the computer for. My clock radio probably had more computing power than that old thing.

"Was there anything useful on the computer?" Stottlemeyer asked.

"There was inside," Disher said.

"You know what I mean," Stottlemeyer said sharply.

"I don't mean what you mean," Disher said. "I really mean inside. The computer is a five-year-old junker on the outside but it's state-of-the-art inside. Five gigabytes of RAM, five hundred gig hard drive, top-of-the-line graphics, and a wireless card, which he was using to hijack the signal from an unsecured router in the building next door. We also found an external hard drive hidden in the apartment. He was probably using it to back up his data."

"I can believe he found that old computer in the trash, but not the state-of-the-art components," Stottlemeyer said. "Where did he get the money for all of that and what was he using all that power for?"

"We don't know," Disher said. "The files on the hard drive are encrypted, but Inspector Gadois has their tech guys working overtime on it."

Stottlemeyer, Monk, and I quickly filled Disher in on what we'd learned from Boucher and Bisson, though Monk's contribution to the discussion mostly concerned Boucher's bookshelf and Bisson's two untucked shirts.

All we knew was that Aimee Dupon had left her publishing company and joined the Freegans, where she met Nathan Chalmers, aka Bob Smith, who was living in the Paris catacombs with them and had some ideas for changing the movement that put him at odds with Lucien Barlier, the group's leader.

"I get why Chalmers joined the Freegans and moved underground," Stottlemeyer said. "What better way is there to avoid being noticed in our highly computerized society than living underground and existing on trash?"

"He would have been better off throwing himself into that tree mulcher," Monk said.

"By following the Freegans and rejecting the consumer culture, he didn't need a job or have to fill out any employment documents," Stottlemeyer said. "He also stayed away from credit cards, rental agreements, utility bills—basically any activity that might have put his name, even a false one, into a database."

"It was a smart move," Disher said.

"I want to know what his big plans were for the Freegans," Stottlemeyer said. "And how they made him money."

"Whatever they were," Disher said, "they got him killed."

"After living on trash," Monk said, "he was probably thankful to be put out of his misery."

"Chalmers was desperate and on the run," I said. "He was doing what he had to do to survive and avoid capture."

"He was running from a prison sentence," Monk said.

"But I think a cell would have been preferable to living in a cave and eating spoiled food."

"Monk has got a point," Disher said.

"That's why I know Chalmers was working a scam," Stottlemeyer said. "He was living like a rat because he thought it would somehow make him rich. If we can figure out what his scheme was, it will lead us to his killer."

"Do you really care who killed him?" I asked.

"Not really. I'm just doing my job," Stottlemeyer said. "But if somebody helped him fake his death and flee to France, I'm taking that guy back to San Francisco with me in handcuffs."

"I'm sure Lucien Barlier will tell us tomorrow what Chalmers was up to," I said, "or at least what his grand vision for the Freegans was."

"It feels like it's already tomorrow to me and I missed last night," Stottlemeyer said and glanced at his watch. "I need a nap. Wake me for dinner."

He trudged to the elevators. That left me alone with Monk and Disher.

"Anyone up for a little sightseeing?"

Disher practically jumped in the air. "Let's do it. But I don't want to get mobbed by a throng of fans. So while we are in public, you can call me Derek."

I glanced at Monk. "Are you going to join me and Derek?"

"I suppose so," he said, with all the enthusiasm of someone on their way to a root canal.

So off we went. For Disher's sake, we headed up to the Arc de Triomphe, took a few pictures of him standing in front of it, and then strolled down the Champs-Élysées.

"I can't believe I am here," Disher said.

He was wired. I could almost feel the energy crackling

off of him. Paris does that to people the first time they see it. It did for me.

I suddenly wished Julie was there to see it with me, too. I made a promise to myself to bring her back there sometime to show her the places that her father and I had visited. I might even show her the places I went to with Monk. She'd probably get a macabre kick out of *les catacombes*.

A few yards ahead of us, some city garbagemen wearing jumpsuits similar to what Monk had worn the other day were taking a break at a bench. Parked beside the bench was a strange green vehicle that was a hybrid of a ride-on lawn mower and a street-cleaning truck.

Monk stopped to admire the vehicle, ogling it as if it was a Ferrari sports car.

The vehicle had the crouching posture of a puppy that was eager to play. The front end was low, with a vacuum underneath and two long arms outstretched in front with swirling round brushes for its paws. Its rear end was high, with a tractor seat, motorcycle handlebars, and a lawn mower–like collection bag. There was also an extendable tube, resembling an elephant's trunk, on one side of the vehicle and a broom and a dustpan on the other to get to those hard-to-reach messes that the *motocrotte*'s assortment of features could not.

Monk turned to a garbageman who was eating a baguette with some cheese, which he'd sliced off a round that he'd laid out on the bench on a napkin and was sharing with his coworkers.

"Excusez-moi, monsieur," Monk said. "What is this splendid machine and what does it do?"

Monk naturally assumed that everybody spoke English simply because he did. I knew how this offended the French. But before I could make apologies and translate Monk's question, the garbageman spoke up, answering in English.

"It's a *motocrotte*," he said. "It sweeps, vacuums, and washes the sidewalks. It even sprays air freshener."

I didn't translate the name of the vehicle for Monk. I decided it was best if he didn't know it was referred to disdainfully as a *poop motorcycle*.

"And you get to drive this?" Monk asked in awe.

"All day, every day, up and down the streets," he said. "I am a *motocrotteur*."

"You are a very lucky man," Monk said.

"You think so?" the garbageman asked.

"You are doing God's work."

"So that's why I don't get laid," he said, eliciting guffaws from his friends. "It's because women think I'm a man of God. I always thought it was because I pick up shit."

"I have enormous respect for what you do. You are protecting the city from disease. You are the true descendants of the original Paris police force," Monk said. "Would it be okay if I sat on the *motocrotte*?"

The garbageman consented with a grandiose wave of his arm. "Be my guest. Take it for a ride if you want."

Monk got on it reverently. It didn't take an expert to figure out how to start the ignition or drive the thing. He turned the key, pressed on the gas, and drove forward a few feet. He looked back at the garbageman.

"Could I clean something?" Monk asked.

"You can do the whole block," the guy replied jokingly. "You can take over my shift if you want while I sit here and enjoy a coffee."

Monk looked up, wide-eyed. "Could I? That would be wonderful."

"Are you serious?" the garbageman asked.

"Are you?" I replied.

The garbageman looked at his friends, who shrugged. He turned back to me.

"Is he some kind of nut?"

"You can trust him," Disher said and flashed his SFPD badge. "He's one of us."

The garbageman squinted at the badge. Disher shut it quickly and shoved it into his pocket.

"You probably noticed that my name is Randy Disher, but I'm not *that* Randy Disher. It's like somebody named James Bond. There are lots of them but they aren't *that* James Bond. They are just regular James Bonds. I'm a regular Randy Disher."

The garbageman looked at Disher for a long moment. I was afraid that Disher had just talked the garbageman out of letting Monk drive the sidewalk sweeper.

The garbageman motioned to Monk. "He can drive the *motocrotte* all he wants." He pointed to Disher. "But you can't."

Monk grinned. "*Merci beaucoup, monsieur.* I won't let you down." He shifted his gaze to us. "You can go. I'll be fine. More than fine. Super fine. *Au revoir.*"

He turned on the brushes and chortled away. I don't think I'd ever seen him so happy.

So we left Monk to beautify the Paris streets while we went off to see whatever sights we could cram into the few hours we had before dinner.

Inspector Gadois had already taken Disher to see Notre Dame, so we went to the Louvre, the Eiffel Tower, and the Jardin des Tuileries. Disher was a great touring companion, easygoing and enthusiastic. Anywhere I wanted to go was fine with him.

I found myself noticing every manhole cover and sub-way station we passed and imagining the world below our feet. I'll admit the picture in my mind was closer to Antoine Bisson's mythical take than the reality that I'd seen in the sewers and catacombs. I guess I was a hopeless romantic at heart. Or maybe Paris just has that effect on people.

When we got back to the Champs-Élysées, it was nightfall, but the sidewalks were gleaming.

Monk was still astride his *motocrotte* when he caught sight of us and sadly brought the vehicle to a stop beside the garbagemen, who were sitting at an outdoor café, several empty bottles of wine on the table indicating how they'd enjoyed their free time.

"How did it go, Monk?" Disher asked.

"It was awesome. I cleaned the Champs-Élysées," Monk said, getting off the vehicle. "It's something most Americans can only dream of."

"I bet now you're glad that we came to Paris," I said.

"I'm miserable," Monk said.

"But you just said that this experience was a dream come true. How can you possibly be miserable?"

"Because it's over." Monk dropped the keys to the sidewalk sweeper on the table in front of the garbageman he'd spoken to before. "This has been one of the best days of my life, Pierre. I wish it didn't have to end."

"Me, too, Adrian," Pierre said, his words slightly slurred from a bit too much wine. "You can do our jobs anytime."

Monk put a hand to his heart. "I'm honored."

"Wait," Pierre said. "There's something we want you to have."

The garbageman got up, took the broom off the sidewalk sweeper, and presented it to Monk.

"This is new," Pierre said. "We haven't had a chance to use it yet."

Monk held it as if it was made of gold. "I can't take this," he stammered.

"We insist," Pierre said and looked at his friends. "Don't we?" They all raised their glasses and cheered. "You are now an unofficial *Agent de Sanitation de Paris.*"

Monk bowed his head. "Thank you. I promise I will uphold the principles this broom represents and never shame it."

He held the broom to his side like a soldier's rifle.

Disher snapped a few photos of Monk with the garbagemen posing beside the *motocrotte*, and then the three of us headed back to the hotel.

"How many Americans get to bring home an authentic Paris department of sanitation broom?" Monk asked.

"I think it's safe to say you are among the select few," I said.

"This is a special day," he said, "perhaps even historic."

"It certainly is," I said.

"I ought to contact the Smithsonian," Monk said.

"Why?" Disher said.

"They'll want this for their collection," Monk said. "It was given to me, but it really belongs to our country."

"I think it should belong to you for a little while first," I said.

"Maybe you're right," Monk said.

"I know I am," I said. "You'll thank me later."

He smiled. I'd told him what he wanted to hear and that made him happy, which was one of the few ways that Adrian Monk was just like any other man.

22

Mr. Monk Goes to a Club

Captain Stottlemeyer was rested but I wouldn't say he was refreshed when we met him in the hotel lobby. His eyes were bloodshot, and he looked a little dazed despite having napped, showered, and changed.

"Nice broom," he said to Monk. "A souvenir?"

"It's an official cleaning implement from the department of sanitation," Monk said.

"It looks like an ordinary broom to me," Stottlemeyer said.

"Perhaps to the untrained eye," Monk said, then looked at me. "Do you think this will fit in the room safe?"

"You don't have a room safe," I said. "But I'm sure the hotel staff would be glad to hold it for you."

Monk took the broom up to the desk clerk. "Could you secure this somewhere for me until I get back from dinner?"

"Of course," she said and propped the broom up against the wall behind her.

"Is that your idea of securing it? It's in plain sight, an open invitation to thieves," Monk said.

"Why would anyone want to steal a broom?" she asked.

"It's no ordinary broom," Stottlemeyer said.

"Does it fly?" she said.

"Could you please lock it up somewhere?" Monk asked.

"I'll put it in your room," she said.

Chief Inspector Le Roux arrived at that moment and drove the four of us to the nightclub, which was located in the basement of a building somewhere on the Left Bank. It was a neighborhood filled with bookstores, cafés, and college students lugging backpacks and carrying books.

The club was a throwback to another era. There were beaded curtains in the entranceway, and the walls were plastered with vintage concert posters of Serge Gainsbourg, Jane Birkin, Johnny Hallyday, Françoise Hardy, Jacques Dutronc, Sylvie Vartan, Joe Dassin, Claude François, and other sixties and seventies French music icons.

There were about two dozen people in the small club, not counting the waitresses and bartender. We were escorted to two tiny tables near the stage.

As we sat down, I noticed that every man there, with the exception of Stottlemeyer and Le Roux, looked vaguely like Disher.

That was also when I realized that Monk was still back at the beaded curtain, counting the beads.

I got up and dragged Monk to the table.

"Do you notice anything odd about the men in this place?" I asked.

Before Monk could answer, Disher spoke up. "They're all powerful examples of raw male masculinity."

"That's funny," Stottlemeyer said, "because I thought they all looked kinda like you."

"That's what I just said," Disher responded.

"They all have the same haircut, same build, same kind of clothes," I said, then added with a smile, "It's like a convention of Brad Pitt impersonators."

"Closer to Tom Cruise," Disher said, "in *Risky Business.*"

He was serious.

Le Roux opened a menu and scowled. "I don't understand why Gadois picked this club. There are much better places in Paris for food and entertainment."

"He didn't tell you?" I said.

"Tell me what?"

"You're going to love this," Stottlemeyer said.

As if on cue, the curtain opened and revealed a three-man band fronted by Guy Gadois, guitarist and lead singer. Without introduction, Gadois immediately launched into a driving French version of Randy's song, "Don't Need a Badge." The only significant changes in translation were the substitutions of the words *captain* with *Inspector* and *mustache* with *goatee* in the chorus.

Chief Inspector Le Roux and Captain Stottlemeyer grimaced through the whole performance, though I think Stottlemeyer was more amused than irritated. I'm pretty sure that I saw a smile tugging at the edges of his forced grimace.

When the performance was over, everyone applauded, except Le Roux and Stottlemeyer.

Gadois held up his hand to silence the crowd and then, in French, announced that he had a very special surprise for the audience.

"Randy Disher est dans la maison!"

There was a collective gasp in the audience. The band started playing the song again.

Disher stood up, whipped off his cap, sunglasses, and jacket as if he was Clark Kent changing into Superman.

There were gasps in the audience as they spotted him, and several women shrieked with lusty glee.

I wasn't one of them.

Disher jumped up on the stage, took a guitar that was waiting for him on a stand, and began belting out his song in English, picking it up from one of the later stanzas over enthusiastic applause.

> *It's been a long, long time cleanin' up the streets.*
> *Now Papa's got a new gig. He's got a brand-new*
> *   beat.*
> *It's called rock 'n' roll, and, baby, I hold the key.*
> *This guitar here's my badge, and music set me*
> *   free. . . .*

Women rushed up to the stage and threw their panties at Disher. He caught one pair and wiped his brow.

Monk bolted out of his seat and demanded that everyone keep their undergarments on and in their possession at all times, but his words were drowned out by the music and the whooping of the women.

Disher was having the time of his life, but it seemed surreal to me, like a truly awful episode of *The Twilight Zone,* though I think Rod Serling would have written a better song. He probably could have sung it better, too.

Stottlemeyer covered his face with his hands, more out of shame than anything else.

My guess was that Disher's performance didn't exactly reflect how the captain wanted the French to view the San Francisco Police Department.

Chief Inspector Le Roux looked equally mortified. I don't think the show was his idea of how to impress foreign law enforcement officials with his department's professionalism.

But Disher and Gadois were cheerfully oblivious to the impact their performance was having on their superiors. They sang with gusto, snarling and growling the lyrics.

> *I don't need a gun to make me feel strong.*
> *I don't need a captain shootin' me down all day*
>   *long.*
> *I don't need your mustache. Don't you condescend*
>   *to me.*
> *I don't need nobody, 'cause, baby, I am free. . . .*

Disher tore off his shirt and flung it into the crowd.

That was more than Monk could take.

Me, too.

It was a good thing we hadn't eaten yet or I might have seen my dinner again.

Monk fled the club, and I went after him. He was waiting for me on the street when I got out.

"I'm sorry," he said. "But I can't eat in a strip club."

"It's not a strip club, Mr. Monk."

"Then why were they stripping?"

"Because they're nuts," I said.

"Maybe it's a French thing," Monk said. "Maybe it's how they clap."

"I don't think so."

"I'm disgusted but I'm still hungry."

"So am I," I said.

"Could I treat you to a croque monsieur someplace?"

"Sure," I said. "I'd like that."

"Preferably at a restaurant where they keep their underwear on."

"I think we can manage that," I said.

There were a half a dozen cafés right across the street, and all of them served croque monsieurs. We took a window table at one of them and ordered our meals.

As we dined in comfortable silence, I noticed that Monk seemed content for the first time since Dr. Kroger went on his vacation and we followed him to Germany.

Granted, we hadn't arrived in Europe under the best of circumstances. Monk was in the midst of a nervous breakdown, and as if that wasn't enough, he spotted the man he thought was responsible for his wife's death.

And as soon as we'd worked out those problems, and solved some murders and survived a near-death experience, I blackmailed him into going to yet another strange foreign country against his will.

No wonder he'd been in a lousy mood.

Only now, after embarking on a new murder investigation, reuniting with his friends from home, and cleaning the Paris streets, did he finally seem to me to be truly centered and happy.

Well, at least as centered and happy as he was capable of being.

Monk was in his comfort zone, doing what he did best, surrounded by familiar faces in an unfamiliar place. There was no better way for him to experience a new country (except, perhaps, if Dr. Kroger was there, too, and Monk had his own bedding and dishes).

I thought that maybe now he would begin to truly enjoy Paris.

And maybe, just maybe, so would I.

After dinner, we rode the subway from the Saint-Michel station to Charles de Gaulle Étoile, which was only a block away from our hotel.

He sat in his seat and, with his sleeves down over his hands, clutched the bar and gritted his teeth as if he was riding a roller coaster. From the look on his face, and his stifled screams, you'd think we were doing loops and dropping from enormous heights instead of cruising smoothly along with nary a curve.

Luckily, we had the train car pretty much to ourselves. The few people who were on board kept their distance from Monk, which was fine with him.

It was a short trip. At Charles de Gaulle Étoile, we climbed the steps up to the street to face the Champs-Élysées. We walked around the Arc de Triomphe toward Avenue Carnot.

"We can't let Captain Stottlemeyer and Lieutenant Disher know our shame," Monk said.

"Remind me," I said. "Which shame are we talking about?"

"That we're cohabitating in a hotel room."

"Don't worry. They know us. More important, they know you. They won't think anything illicit is going on. It wouldn't even occur to them."

"We can't be seen going into the same room together," Monk said. "You take the elevator and I will take the stairs, and never at the same time. Before you emerge from our room, make sure there's no one in the hall. Try to avoid any mention whatsoever of our room number in front of others."

"I don't think that's a good idea, Mr. Monk. If we start acting suspiciously, we'll create suspicion. They'll start thinking something is going on when there isn't."

"You don't want people thinking you're a loose woman," Monk said, "or that you took advantage of me."

"Thanks for your concern," I said. "It's heartwarming."

As we turned the corner onto Avenue Carnot, we could see a bright green *motocrotte* parked under a streetlamp on the sidewalk in front of our hotel.

When we got closer, I could see that the *motocrotte* had been washed, waxed, and buffed.

"What a beautiful machine," Monk said. "It's like a work of art."

"Maybe I should trade in my car for one," I said.

"That's a great idea," Monk said.

"There's only one seat," I said.

"That's okay," Monk said. "If I had one of these, I wouldn't need a driver. We'd each have our own. We'd ride in tandem down the wide-open road. Like in *Easy Rider*."

I doubted that he'd ever seen the movie. He only knew that they rode motorcycles on the highway.

"Except we'd be riding down the wide-open sidewalk," I said.

"Cleaning as we go, the sweet smell of disinfectant in the air," Monk said. "Imagine the freedom."

"I don't think they are available in the U.S.," I said.

"Don't step on the dream," he said.

"Sorry," I said and we went inside.

The desk clerk waved us over. She presented an envelope and a large box to Monk.

He opened the envelope first. There were a card and a set of keys inside.

Monk read the card. "It's from Pierre. He's letting me have the *motocrotte* to use during my stay in Paris. For free. All he's asking in return is that I drive it up and down the Champs-Élysées once or twice each day."

In other words, he wanted Monk to do his job for him.

"But you have two murders to investigate," I said.

"I know that," Monk said. "But I still need to get around, don't I? And this is much better than a car. Or a limousine."

He opened the box and pulled out a brand-new sanitation department jumpsuit. Pierre had it all figured out.

"Wow," Monk said.

"Mr. Monk, he's taking advantage of you."

"Au contraire," Monk said.

23

Mr. Monk and the
Dumpster Divers

Before we went to bed, Monk asked me to show him
on the map where the seventh arrondissement was,
and the general area where we intended to begin our
search for Lucien Barlier so he could meet us there in
the morning.

Monk intended to get up early, make one pass over
the Champs-Élysées with his *motocrotte*, and then find
his way to the neighborhood on his own.

I could only guess where we'd be going since we
hadn't had a chance to make any plans with Le Roux
or Stottlemeyer about when and where we'd start our
search for the Freegans.

But I picked a spot and I figured I'd tell the others
about it in the morning. That would be where we started
whether they liked it or not.

Monk went to sleep with his official broom propped
beside his bed, a smile on his face. At least he didn't
sleep with the broom, clutching it like a teddy bear.

True to his word, Monk was gone when I woke up

at seven the next morning. I showered, got dressed, and headed out for some breakfast. I figured I'd return to the hotel at about nine and hang around the lobby until Stottlemeyer either showed up or gave me a call.

But when I got to the lobby, Stottlemeyer was already there, sitting in a chair, reading the international edition of *USA Today* and sipping a cup of coffee.

"Good morning, Captain. Did you sleep well?"

"I did," he said. "I went to bed at about midnight and woke up at four."

"What have you been doing for the last few hours?"

"I took a long walk," he said. "I had the streets pretty much to myself, if you don't include Monk."

"You saw him?"

"He was hard to miss," Stottlemeyer said. "Are you two sharing a room?"

"Yes," I said. "But don't tell him you know. He's ashamed."

"Of what? I know nothing is going on. He's Monk, and you're not interested."

"Not remotely," I said, perhaps too forcefully, considering I was stating the obvious.

"So how's it working out?"

"Have you ever shared a room with Mr. Monk?"

He held up a hand. "Say no more. You have my heartfelt sympathy."

I invited the captain to join me for breakfast, and I led him to the café that I'd been to the day before. On the way, I asked him how things had gone at the club after we left.

"The band did a few encores," Stottlemeyer said.

"But they only have one song."

"That's why Le Roux and I didn't stick around. He took me to a restaurant in the neighborhood. We had a couple of steaks and wine and talked shop until I started to fall asleep in my french fries. I like Le Roux. He's pretty sharp."

"Can you believe that the Randy Disher Project actually has a cult following here?"

Stottlemeyer shrugged. "Stranger things have happened."

"Name one," I said.

"I saw Adrian Monk at dawn in Paris today. He was wearing a garbageman's uniform and cleaning the Champs-Élysées on a sidewalk sweeper."

"You win," I said.

Over croissants, pastries, and some coffee, I told him about the plans I'd made with Monk. In turn, Stottlemeyer told me about the plans he'd made with Le Roux.

The chief inspector and Gadois would remain at the office, checking the information we'd already gathered, and Disher would assist them. Stottlemeyer, Monk, and I would talk to Lucien Barlier and the Freegans on our own.

It was Le Roux's feeling we'd have better luck with the Freegans if we weren't accompanied by the police. Afterward, we'd all get together at Le Roux's office to compare notes and figure out our next move in the investigation.

It sounded good to me, as long as Monk was able to find us.

"Monk can read a map," Stottlemeyer said.

"He may not want to," I said. "He was so desperate to investigate these murders, but now that he can, he seems more interested in picking up garbage."

"Monk is always distracted by something," Stottlemeyer said. "But he's still catching all the details, whether it seems like it or not. It's involuntary for him. At some point, all of it is going to suddenly snap together in his head. He'll roll his shoulders, point to somebody, and say *That's the guy*. And he'll be right."

"So what's left for us to do?"

"We can help ourselves to another croissant," he said.

"I can do that," I said.

It's a good thing we ate before heading off to Rue Cler, or we would have spent an hour or two of investigating time eating our way up and down the street.

Rue Cler was between Rue Saint-Dominique and Rue de Grenelle, walking distance for the nannies, cooks, and butlers to do their daily shopping for their wealthy and powerful employers.

The cobblestone street was lined on both sides with the swankiest cafés, cheese shops, butchers, markets, and bakeries in Paris.

Stottlemeyer and I strolled down the center of the street, which was closed off to automobile traffic, and absorbed the sights and smells.

The fruits and vegetables on display outside one of the markets were so perfect, so clean, and so neatly arranged in rows that Monk would have been proud. The vendors wore aprons that were stain-free and finely pressed.

The baguettes in the bakeries were golden, crusty, and arranged like flowers in big baskets. I could have taken them all.

There was an Italian deli with a huge assortment of pastas, meats, olives, and olive oils. They even had a couple of olive trees out front. I wanted to try everything— and I hate olives.

We passed a *fromagerie*, something I'd never seen in

San Francisco. The display of wheels, wedges, and balls of assorted cheese was pretty to look at, but the stench of it all was worse than a decomposing corpse. But the worst-smelling wedges seemed to draw the most attention from the customers, who leaned in and sniffed some more with delight.

Next door to the cheese shop was a gourmet food store that served elaborate take-out meals that included steaks, quail stuffed with fois gras, lobsters, caviar, and bottles of fine wine. I guess that was the French idea of a Happy Meal. It would be mine, too, if only I could afford it.

The fish at the *poissonnerie* looked like they'd been sculpted by the same artist who'd done the fruit and vegetables we'd seen earlier. They were so beautiful, such perfect examples of the variety of marine life, that I thought that people should buy them not to eat but to display in their homes.

The pastries, tarts, and cakes in the window at Lenôtre, one of the finest patisseries in France, also looked like works of art, but I found them impossible to resist. I had to stop and eat one.

Okay, two.

The women who served me were dressed in white, wore gloves, and handled the sweets with tremendous care and concentration, as if they were holding fragile china or nitroglycerin.

I made Stottlemeyer take a picture of the sliver of chocolate opera cake and the strawberry tart for posterity before I devoured them (one scrumptious dessert was not enough). I offered him a taste, but he showed enormous willpower and declined. It made no sense to me.

"Don't tell me you'd prefer a Twinkie."

"No, those look great."

"So have one," I said. "You're in Paris. Indulge."

That should be the city's motto.

He shook his head. "I don't like interviewing people with sticky fingers and chocolate on my face. Besides, I'm watching my weight."

"Why?" I asked. "You're not fat."

"I'm single. It's bad enough that I'm on the wrong side of forty and I've got more hair under my nose than on my head. If I get a gut, too, I might as well forget all about women."

"Women look at more than a man's waistline."

"Not if that's what they see first," he said.

"Looks aren't the most important factor," I said. "Sensitivity and a sense of humor mean a lot more. Women aren't as superficial as men."

"Uh-huh," Stottlemeyer said. "So tell me about the last fat, bald guy you dated who was sensitive and funny and wasn't a millionaire."

I hadn't dated a millionaire of any shape or size. But I'd dated a leper once. Granted, he was a very successful leper. He ended up dumping me for a Hawaiian Tropics swimsuit model.

"You think women don't care how a man looks as long as he's rich," I said.

"I do. But you won't find many guys who'll go for an unattractive woman, no matter how loaded she is."

"I don't look at a man's wallet," I said.

"What do you look at?"

"His heart," I said.

Stottlemeyer laughed. "Men may be superficial, but at least we're honest about it."

Amid all the places selling food and drink, there were shops selling dishware, cutlery, and other household goods. There was even a flower shop with astonishing bouquets and floral arrangements that each cost more than all the landscaping in my backyard.

Once we made our tour of the storefronts, we rounded the corner and went up the alley behind them.

It was, perhaps, the cleanest alley I'd ever been in, befitting, I suppose, the street on the other side. But it was still an alley, lined with Dumpsters.

Midway down the alley, there was a crew of a dozen people foraging in the trash. The Freegans were evenly split between men and women, each wearing gloves, work boots, and protective goggles, all of them working together with what appeared to be choreographed efficiency.

There were two people in each Dumpster, waist deep in the trash. One person sorted through everything, while the other collected the rejected items in plastic bags, which were then cinched closed.

A third person stood on a stepladder beside the bin, holding a milk crate lined with a plastic bag for the found items. When the crates were full, they were loaded up in shopping carts.

There was almost a musical rhythm to their work, as if they were choreographed and dancing to the same beat.

It wouldn't have surprised me if they'd suddenly broken into a chorus of "Whistle While You Work" and been joined in their labors by joyful birds and adorable animals.

Judging by the Dumpsters the Freegans hadn't hit yet, the crew was leaving the alley cleaner, and the trash more organized, than they had found them.

The crates of found goods were loaded with fruits and vegetables as well as canned and packaged items. It looked as if the Freegans had been shopping in a gourmet grocery store rather than foraging through trash.

Although we didn't know what Lucien Barlier looked like, it was obvious who the leader of the group was. He had an aura that illuminated him as if he was under a spotlight. I'm sure that the effect was all in my mind and that I was instinctively interpreting the subliminal signals, like the body language and facial expressions, of the Freegans.

But it wasn't just me. I could see that Stottlemeyer's gaze was fixed on the same thirtyish man who was standing in the Dumpster to my right, a broad smile on his face and a certain loose, devil-may-care attitude to his actions.

I'd imagined that the Freegans looked like hobbits and that their leader would be someone who had a long beard and matted hair and wore either filthy clothes or long robes.

But my preconceptions were way off. The Freegans looked like an Ivy League debate team that took time out from their studies to clean up the alleys.

"Lucien Barlier?" Stottlemeyer said to the man we'd both homed in on.

"That's me. You must be Adrian Monk," Barlier said, taking off his goggles to reveal his startlingly blue eyes. "I wondered when you would get around to me."

"If you knew anything about Monk, you'd never mistake me for him. He'll be here soon," Stottlemeyer said, flashing his badge. "I'm Captain Leland Stottlemeyer of the San Francisco Police Department, and this is Monk's assistant, Natalie Teeger. How did you know we'd be coming?"

Barlier didn't interrupt his sorting, and the others kept working, too, though they were obviously listening to the conversation.

"I heard that the Paris police and some officials from the U.S. were investigating Aimee Dupon's murder," Barlier said. "What I don't understand is why her murder concerns you."

"I'm only interested in how it connects to Bob Smith," Stottlemeyer said.

"What has Bob done?" Barlier asked.

"He got himself killed," Stottlemeyer said.

That bit of news got everyone's attention.

Barlier climbed out of the trash bin, took off his gloves, and joined us. Another Freegan took his place in the Dumpster to sort the trash.

"In San Francisco?" Barlier asked.

"Here," I said. "Mr. Monk found his skull in the catacombs."

"And since that's where you live," Stottlemeyer said, "and both Smith and Dupon were part of your movement, we thought you might be able to help us."

"It's not a movement," Barlier began.

"Yeah, yeah, I know," Stottlemeyer said. "It's a way of life."

Barlier smiled. "You already understand us better than Bob ever did."

"How did you meet Bob?"

"He was homeless and seeking shelter in the catacombs. We took him in and showed him our ways."

"You didn't think it was odd to run into a homeless American in the tunnels?"

"We live there by choice but many do not. The homeless come from all nationalities. Poverty and misfortune don't respect national boundaries. For three hundred years, the catacombs have offered sanctuary to the lost and to the desperate, to resistance fighters and—"

"Fugitives from justice," Stottlemeyer interrupted.

"Them, too," Barlier conceded. "Though one man's criminal is another man's hero."

"Which was Bob?"

"I don't know. How Bob ended up in the tunnels was none of my business, and he didn't share his story with me," Barlier said. "We helped him develop the skills to survive comfortably and happily. I was pleased that Bob not only came to accept his circumstances but ultimately to see the benefits of no longer participating in a consumer society."

"So you're saying you didn't know him before," Stottlemeyer said.

"Before what?"

"When he was Nathan Chalmers," Stottlemeyer said.

"You've lost me," Barlier said.

"He had another life before you met him," I said.

"We all had other lives," Barlier said, motioning to the other Freegans around him and then locking his gaze on me. "Haven't you?"

To answer that question, all I had to do was compare who I was the last time I'd visited Paris with the woman I was that day.

I felt as if I'd lived three lives—before Mitch, with Mitch, and after Mitch. And in each one, I was a person the other Natalies would hardly recognize.

Barlier studied my face in a curious, caring way and found the answer to his question. He nodded slightly to himself.

"Bob was a crook," Stottlemeyer said. "He stole a lot of money and got caught at it. So he faked his death and fled to Paris, where he hid out with you."

"We didn't hide him," Barlier said.

"How did you become a Freegan?" I asked.

"I was once an active player of the consumer game,"

Barlier said. "I worked hard at a job I didn't like to earn enormous amounts of money that I spent on things I didn't need and then discarded when something more stylish or trendy came along. I existed only to buy things, not for necessity, but because I had to. How many millions of people live that way? It's empty. I had no relationships, nothing of value besides my possessions. And then one sleepless night, I had an epiphany. The days were passing too fast, all of my time was being wasted mindlessly making money. I wasn't living. God didn't put me on earth simply to earn money and to spend it. I was missing the peace, beauty, and joy the world has to offer."

Stottlemeyer tipped his head in the direction of the trash bins. "And this is it?"

Barlier smiled. "I am not cold, hungry, and destitute. I spend a couple of hours gathering the things I need to survive, and I devote the rest of my time to appreciating what life has to offer, enjoying art, music, nature, and the company of others."

He glanced at me when he said that, and I felt myself blush, which embarrassed me, which made me blush even more. It was only then that I realized I was attracted to him.

"I am clean, healthy, and happy," Barlier said. "What more do I need? An iPhone perhaps? Would that make me complete, Captain?"

"Maybe a home that isn't in the sewer?"

"I could show you parts of this city that are worse than sewers, and they aren't underground," Barlier said. "The sewers and subway tunnels are only part of the catacombs. It is a city beneath the city. It is an art gallery of the ages. It is solitude and peace."

"It's a hole in the ground," Stottlemeyer said.

"It sounds amazing," I said.

"Would you like to see it?" Barlier asked me, a twinkle in his eye.

Before I could answer, Stottlemeyer spoke up. "We heard that you and Bob had a big fight."

"We had a difference of opinion. Bob felt that what we were doing would never make an impact, that we'd never change society by our example," Barlier said. "He wanted us to take action against those who waste resources and exploit others."

"What kind of action?" I asked.

"We never got into specifics because it didn't matter to me. I was fundamentally and philosophically opposed to his point of view. Being a Freegan is a lifestyle, an ethical and moral choice, not a political movement. He felt differently."

"So you threw him out," Stottlemeyer said.

"He decided to go," Barlier said.

"There wasn't room in the hundreds of miles of tunnels and chambers down there for the both of you?"

"Of course there is. The tunnels don't belong to me. They belong to everyone. Besides, not all the Freegans live underground," Barlier said. "Some own property. Many others live in unoccupied buildings."

"You mean they take other people's property," Stottlemeyer said.

"Everyone has a right to shelter," Barlier said. "An empty building is a wasted resource. That's the real crime."

"We know that Bob took a bunch of Freegans with him," Stottlemeyer said, "and left your group bitterly divided."

We didn't know that. Stottlemeyer was embellishing what we'd heard from Antoine Bisson and the couple in Aimee's building.

Barlier didn't argue the point, he simply shrugged. Either it didn't matter to him or that was what he wanted us to think. But Stottlemeyer had scored a small point—he'd learned that Bob's departure had caused a deep rift in the Freegans.

"People are free to believe what they like. This isn't a cult. I don't have or want followers. But I welcome friends. Bob had his way and I had mine. I wished him the best."

"Did that include taking your girlfriend?" Stottlemeyer said.

Barlier's face got a little pinched. "Aimee and I were lovers, but we weren't in love."

"How very French," Stottlemeyer said.

I thought that was a snotty thing to say. I didn't see any reason to treat Lucien Barlier in such a hostile manner simply because Stottlemeyer didn't approve of the way he lived. And as far as I knew, there was no evidence pointing to Barlier as the killer of either Nathan Chalmers or Aimee Dupon.

Maybe that was it, I thought. Maybe the captain was intentionally baiting him, hoping that if Barlier got angry, he'd say something incriminating without realizing it and we'd finally have a credible suspect.

That was when we heard the low rumble of an engine behind us.

We turned to see Monk arriving on his *motocrotte*. He came to a stop beside us and dismounted the vehicle like a frontier sheriff getting off a horse.

"You're all under arrest," Monk said.

24

Mr. Monk and the Mean Streets

"What are the charges?" Lucien Barlier asked with amusement.

"Endangering public health, not to mention your own," Monk said. "You'll have to be quarantined."

"On whose authority?"

"I'm Adrian Monk, an honorary *agent de sanitation* and a consultant to the San Francisco police."

"In other words," Barlier said, "you have no authority at all to make arrests, here or anywhere else."

"I have moral authority," Monk said, and took his broom from the *motocrotte* and held it firmly at his side as if that somehow proved his point.

"We haven't done anything immoral," Barlier said. "People throw away fifty million pounds of food each year, not because it has gone bad, but because we buy more than we can consume and we produce more than can be bought. *That's* immoral. What we are doing is living off what others have wasted and thoughtlessly discarded. Take a look at this."

Barlier led us over to his basket of items that he'd taken from the Dumpster.

He'd collected apples, oranges, peaches, bananas, lettuce, and corn. There were bagged salads, loaves of bread, and boxes of cereal, cake, and cookie mix. There were even fully cooked meals of pasta and chicken in hard plastic containers.

The food looked a lot better than what was on the shelves at my local grocery store and the Freegans got it all for nothing.

Even the trash was better in Paris than it was at home.

"These fruits and vegetable were thrown out simply because they are bruised or scratched," Barlier said.

"And it's a good thing, too," Monk said. "They're ruined."

"A bruise doesn't make them inedible," Barlier said.

"Yes, it does," Monk said. "Whoever threw them out should be congratulated."

Barlier looked at Monk with disbelief, then turned to Stottlemeyer and me for support, but he wasn't going to get any from us. In fact, the captain seemed to enjoy Barlier's frustration.

"A bruised apple never hurt anyone." Barlier took an apple from the basket and held it up for Monk to see.

"You're right," Monk said. "It killed them."

Barlier rubbed the apple on his shirt and took a bite out of it.

Monk let out a squeal and took a big step away from him.

"Everyone stand back," he yelled.

"He's not going to explode, Monk," Stottlemeyer said.

"He's probably contagious," Monk said.

"With what?" I said.

"The man eats rotten food and wallows in garbage," Monk said. "He's a walking cesspool of disease. It's a miracle he's still standing."

"This apple is crunchy and delicious." Barlier gestured to other items in his basket. "This bread is only a day old. These rotisserie chickens were cooked yesterday but were thrown out because they weren't sold. These canned and boxed goods are a day or two past their expiration dates."

"That's exactly why they should be thrown out."

"This is all good, nutritious food," Barlier said. "But wasted food is only a fraction of what is unnecessarily and thoughtlessly discarded. I have found computers, suits, rugs, furniture, paintings, blankets, CDs, and books in the trash. There was nothing wrong with any of it. Just because something is thrown away doesn't mean it's rotten, broken, or obsolete."

"Of course it does," Monk said. "Or it wouldn't be in the trash."

"The people who owned those things were bored with them, or thought they weren't stylish anymore, or wanted to make room for more things they don't need."

"Even if what you say is true," Monk said, "and any sane person knows it's not, the instant anything lands in a Dumpster, or within ten yards of one, it has been contaminated. You can't use it and you certainly can't eat it."

"Most of this food is bagged or canned and whatever isn't can be washed. There's nothing on these fruits and vegetables that's any worse than the dirt they were grown in."

Monk cringed. Just the mention of dirt was enough to give him the creeps. He once told me that there is nothing dirtier than dirt—that's why they call it dirt.

"I can make a gourmet meal from this tonight," Barlier said and shifted his gaze to me. "For two. Anything less would be wasteful."

"Is that an invitation?" I asked.

"It's a threat," Monk said.

"Let me show you my world," Barlier said, ignoring Monk. "I can guarantee it's a side of Paris you've never seen before."

"She's already visited the sewer," Monk said. "She just doesn't want to eat from it, too."

"I'd be glad to have dinner with you," I said to Barlier. "When and where shall we meet?"

I don't know whether I accepted his invitation because I didn't like Stottlemeyer's hostility toward him, or because I was tired of Monk's judgmental attitude, or because I just liked being contrary where Monk was concerned.

Or maybe it was because I found the idea of a secret world under Paris irresistibly romantic and Lucien Barlier's eyes a particularly enchanting shade of blue.

"Are you insane?" Monk shrieked.

I pretended he wasn't there, and so did Barlier, who smiled at me.

"Let's meet at the Musée d'Orsay Métro station at seven p.m."

"How shall I dress?"

"Wear whatever you like," he said. "I'm sure you would be radiant in anything."

It was a corny thing to say, but I felt myself blush anyway. Was I really that easy to flatter? And when did I become such a blusher?

"I'll see you then," I said.

Barlier gave me a little bow, lowered his goggles, and climbed back into his Dumpster.

Monk narrowed his eyes and watched him go. Stottle-meyer was eyeing Barlier warily, too.

"You're taking your life in your hands," Monk said to me.

"I appreciate your concern for me, Mr. Monk. But I think you're being overly dramatic."

Whatever Barlier served me for dinner couldn't be worse than some of the food I kept in my refrigerator.

"He's the guy," Monk said.

"What guy?" Stottlemeyer asked.

"*The* guy," Monk said. "He's the one who killed Nathan Chalmers and Aimee Dupon."

"Can you prove it?" Stottlemeyer said.

"Not yet," Monk said. "But he's the guy."

"You're just saying that because he lives off what other people throw away," I said, not bothering to disguise my irritation.

"That's right," Monk said.

"That doesn't make him a murderer," I said.

"It proves he's capable of unspeakable depravity," Monk said. "If he hasn't murdered anybody yet, he will."

"I was hoping for something a bit more conclusive than that," Stottlemeyer said.

"What more could you want?"

"Oh, I don't know," Stottlemeyer said. "How about physical evidence that ties him directly and irrefutably to both murders?"

"He eats trash and lives in the sewers," Monk said. "That's enough reason to lock him up."

"Think of my dinner with him as part of the investigation," I said. "I'll keep my eyes open for clues."

"You won't have to look far," Monk said. "It will be on your plate, with a nice garnish of maggots."

"The Freegans seem clean and healthy to me," I said.

Monk gestured to the Dumpster. "They're standing in Dumpsters. It's not safe for you to eat with him."

"You know where I'm going and who I'll be with," I said. "Lucien won't hurt me."

"He's Lucien now?" Stottlemeyer said. I ignored the remark.

"He'll poison you," Monk said. "But you're probably right—it won't hurt. You'll die instantly."

I glanced at my watch. "Shouldn't we be going to police headquarters to see Chief Inspector Le Roux? Maybe he has made some progress in the investigation."

"That would be nice," Stottlemeyer said, "because we certainly haven't made any."

"Speak for yourself. I've spent the morning cleaning up the mean streets." Monk put his broom back in its special harness, climbed onto his *motocrotte*, and started the engine. "I'll meet you at headquarters."

"Are you sure you can find it?" I said.

"I'm a detective. Finding things is what I do," Monk said and scooted off, the brushes on the front of his vehicle sweeping the sidewalk.

We watched him go; then Stottlemeyer looked at me and asked, "Did you accept Barlier's invitation just to piss Monk off?"

I looked over at Lucien Barlier, who was back in the Dumpster, busily and happily sorting through the trash, and then I met Stottlemeyer's gaze.

"I'm not sure," I said.

"Are you having second thoughts yet?"

"Nope," I said.

"If we were in San Francisco, would you have accepted a dinner date with a homeless man who lives in the sewers and eats trash?"

When he put it that way, I actually began to have second thoughts, but I quickly shrugged them off.

"But we aren't in San Francisco, Captain. We're in Paris."

"And that makes a difference?"

"Vive la différence," I said. "That's what Paris is all about."

"Then to hell with watching my weight," Stottlemeyer said. "We're going back to Lenôtre."

25

Mr. Monk Reviews the Evidence

When we walked into the squad room, we found Disher at the coffee machine, filling his cup. His hair was a mess, his clothes were wrinkled, and his eyes were bloodshot. There were scratches on his neck and his lips were chapped.

"Morning, Randy," Stottlemeyer said. "How did it go after we left?"

"I didn't sleep at all last night," he said. His voice sounded raw.

"Did the jet lag catch up with you?" I asked.

"No, my groupies did," Disher said. "Hordes of lusty, insatiable Frenchwomen."

"Aren't they all?" Stottlemeyer said.

"They wanted to sample the Dish."

"Excuse me. I'm going to check my e-mail before I vomit," Stottlemeyer said and walked over to one of the empty desks.

"The Dish?" I said.

"That's what they call me," Disher said. "I was the main dish in a feast of love. You can't imagine it."

"I'm trying not to," I said. "God, how I am trying."

Disher took me by the arm and led me into the hall-way, glancing over his shoulder to check on Stottlemeyer, who was sitting in front of a computer, not paying any attention to us at all.

"I'm thinking of staying," Disher whispered.

"You mean extending your Paris visit into a vacation?"

"I mean staying for good and following my muse," Disher said.

"So far, your muse has only led you to one song," I said.

"There's more music in me," Disher said. "Much, much more. I can feel it."

It's probably gas, I thought.

"Maybe you should wait until those songs are out there, and you've developed a body of work, before you make any big decisions. Do you really want to risk ev-erything on one song that's a cult hit in France?"

"But I have groupies," Disher said. "I have their un-derwear to prove it."

And there was another image I didn't want in my head.

"How long will they stick with you if your next song is a flop?" I said. "You could be another Bertie Higgins. Or Joey Scarbury. Or Van McCoy."

"Who are they?"

"That's what I mean," I said. "They had groupies, too."

"Lusty, insatiable, French ones?"

"Probably," I said.

"But I don't have groupies in San Francisco," Disher said. "Nobody calls me the Dish."

"Maybe that will change when you've got more songs."

"Until then, will you call me the Dish?"

"No," I said.

"Do I sense a little wiggle room?"

"No," I said.

"I'm pretty sure that I did," he said.

"You didn't," I said. "And don't even think about asking me to throw my panties at you."

Naturally, that was the moment that Monk walked up, no longer wearing his sanitation uniform. He looked at me with dismay.

"What has gotten into you?" Monk said. "First you accept a date with a homeless person and now you're soliciting a police officer."

"I wasn't soliciting him, Mr. Monk. I was drawing a line."

"With your underwear," Monk said.

"Yes," I said. "It's an important line."

He walked past us into the squad room, where Stottlemeyer was talking with Chief Inspector Le Roux and Inspector Gadois.

"Ah, perfect timing," Le Roux said. "Captain Stottlemeyer was just filling us in on your interview with Lucien Barlier."

"He's the guy," Monk said.

Le Roux shared a confused look with Gadois. Stottlemeyer noticed.

"What Monk means is that he believes Barlier is the killer," Stottlemeyer said.

"Based on what?" Gadois asked.

"He eats garbage," Monk said. "He's a sicko."

"I don't know the finer points of the American justice system," Le Roux said, "but in France, that isn't enough to secure a conviction."

"All the evidence points to him," Monk said.

"I wasn't aware that we had any evidence," Stottlemeyer said.

"We have some new leads that, unfortunately, don't immediately point to a suspect," Le Roux said. "Actually, Captain, we have you to thank for the discoveries."

"What did I do?" Stottlemeyer asked.

"You kept saying that Nathan Chalmers, otherwise known as Bob Smith, wouldn't be involved with the Freegans unless there was money to be made at it. So I did some checking. Since the time that Chalmers presumably arrived in France, the cases of major identity theft and credit card fraud in the seventh arrondissement have tripled."

"Aren't identity thefts increasing everywhere these days?" Disher said.

"That's true, Lieutenant," Le Roux said. "But the percentage in that neighborhood remains significantly higher than other comparable neighborhoods in the same socioeconomic class."

Stottlemeyer chewed his lower lip for a moment, mulling over what he'd heard.

"So Chalmers was going through the trash looking for financial documents, utility bills, credit card statements, and anything else he could use to steal people's identities and empty their bank accounts."

"That's our guess, Captain," Gadois said. "He'd taken at least a million euros, perhaps much more. We're hoping to know more after we crack the encryption on Aimee Dupon's computer."

"Why wait until then?" Monk said. "Let's go arrest Barlier, preferably before dinner."

"You still don't have any proof that he killed Nathan Chalmers or Aimee Dupon," I said.

"I saw him eat a bruised apple," Monk said, "without washing it first."

"Sadly, that has nothing to do with the murders," Le Roux said. "All we have are Chalmers' skull and some of his bones that we recovered from *les catacombes*. We don't even know where he was actually killed or what the murder weapon was."

"It's the opposite with Aimee Dupon's murder," Gadois said. "We know where and when it happened, and we even have the murder weapon and dozens of witnesses, but we don't know how it was done or who did it."

"It was Lucien Barlier," Monk said. "Here's what happened."

Monk began his explanation by recapping what we already knew: Chalmers amputated a finger, pulled a tooth, and pushed a transient into a tree mulcher in order to fake his own death and avoid what was likely to be a long prison sentence.

Chalmers escaped to France and joined the Freegans, adopting their anticonsumerism philosophy to avoid getting a job, paying rent, or any other activities that might put his face, fingerprints, or fake name in a database somewhere.

Monk believed that either Barlier was already using the anticonsumerism lifestyle as a front for rummaging through the trash for financial documents or Chalmers gave him the idea. Either way, Chalmers probably got greedy. He wanted more money and Barlier's lover, too.

Barlier wasn't willing to lose the money and Dupon, so he killed Chalmers and convinced everyone that the American went to New York.

Everything went smoothly until Monk found the skull, and Dupon somehow figured out that the victim was Chalmers. She sought out Monk to tell him what she knew.

"Barlier couldn't let that happen," Monk said. "He had to kill her before she could talk. He barely managed it in time."

There was a long moment of silence as everyone pondered Monk's theory.

"You've described a possible motive for the murders," Le Roux said. "But it's all conjecture. There's no evidence to support any of it. Chalmers could just as easily have been killed by someone he bilked."

"He wasn't," Monk said.

"You haven't explained how Barlier tracked you and Aimee Dupon to Toujours Nuit or how he slipped into the restaurant without being seen," Le Roux said. "You also haven't explained how he found Dupon in total darkness, stabbed her to death, and escaped without detection."

"I will," Monk said.

"In France, you need to do that *before* we can make an arrest," Le Roux said.

"Monk is usually right about this stuff," Disher said.

Monk smiled appreciatively at Disher for jumping to his defense, which is usually my job, but today I couldn't do it in good conscience.

"That's true, but Mr. Monk usually isn't distracted by an intense personal bias," I said and faced Monk. "You can't see past Lucien Barlier's alternative lifestyle. I think it's tainting your judgment."

"Don't talk to me about good judgment," Monk said. "You're going on a date in the sewer tonight with a filthy hobo."

"She is?" Gadois said.

"It's not a date. I'm investigating," I said. "He'll be

on his home turf. He'll be relaxed and comfortable. In a casual setting, he's likely to reveal more to me than he would to you in a police interrogation. It would be foolish for me to turn down his invitation. We might not get a break like this again."

Even as I was offering my defense, it sounded like a lame rationalization at best, or a lie at worst, for why I accepted the date. I braced myself for the ridicule and incredulity that was about to come.

"I agree," Le Roux said, much to my surprise. "If Monsieur Monk is right about Barlier's guilt, then this could be a valuable opportunity to learn more about him and his activities."

I wanted to look at the expression on Le Roux's face to determine whether he really agreed with me or was doing me a favor, but I was afraid what my own expression might reveal.

So I looked at my hands and found something fascinating about my cuticles instead.

"What do you know about him already?" Stottlemeyer asked Le Roux.

"He's a garbage-eating sicko who lives in a hole and kills people," Monk said.

"Not much more than he told you and Mademoiselle Teeger this morning," Le Roux said. "He's only had one arrest."

"Vagrancy? Burglary? Vandalism? Extortion?" Monk offered.

"Clock repair," Le Roux said.

"That's a crime in France?" I asked.

"It is when you break into a museum to do it," Le Roux said. "He and a retired horologist used the tunnels to visit the Musée de l'Art Néoclassique every night for a year to fix the three-hundred-year-old clock that towers over the main lobby. It's an elaborate neoclassical masterpiece, which, sadly, had rusted and fallen into disrepair after decades of neglect."

"He did it without being noticed by the guards or tripping the alarms?" Monk asked.

Le Roux nodded. "They set up a workshop behind the clock and tapped into the building's electrical and communications grid. They used a laptop to monitor the security cameras and to contact expert clockmakers over the Internet for advice. They even had a coffee machine."

"So how did you catch him?" Disher asked.

"We didn't," Le Roux said. "Barlier notified museum officials that the clock had been repaired, and they filed charges against him."

"He sounds like a very scary man to me," I said.

"Finally, you're seeing reason," Monk said. "When did he get out of prison?"

"He was never jailed," Le Roux said. "Barlier was ordered to perform two hundred hours of community service."

"Picking up trash, no doubt," I said.

"Let's just say everything worked out for the best for all concerned," Le Roux said.

"You mean that he learned he could break the law and get away with it," Monk said.

"I don't see it quite that way, Monsieur Monk."

Stottlemeyer sighed. "So what now?"

"We should arrest Barlier before he kills again," Monk said.

"Who is he going to kill?" Gadois asked.

"Natalie," Monk said. "Tonight."

"We all know where she is going to be and with whom," Le Roux said. "He has nothing to gain and everything to lose by harming her. He'd have to be insane."

"We're talking about a man who chose to give up everything so he could eat garbage," Monk protested. "If that isn't crazy, what is?"

I thought of a few examples—cleaning your doorknobs each month in the dishwasher, campaigning for a Constitutional amendment to outlaw Neapolitan ice cream, and only using a bar of soap once—but I kept my mouth shut.

He could see that his arguments hadn't swayed any of us. Barlier wasn't going to be arrested, and I was keeping my date.

"My God, you've all lost your minds," he said.

And with that, he marched out of police headquarters and didn't return.

26

Mr. Monk's Assistant Goes Underground

Monk spent the rest of the day on his *motocrotte* cleaning the sidewalks in the eighth arrondissement.

I tagged along with Stottlemeyer, acting as his translator while he, armed with a list given to him by Le Roux, sought out victims of identity theft in the seventh arrondissement, where the Freegans did most of their foraging.

One of the identify-theft victims we talked to led us to a neighbor in his building who'd been blackmailed based on love letters and photographs to his business partner's wife that he'd torn up and thrown away. The man made three payments to his blackmailer, but when he refused to give him any more money, his secrets were exposed, and he lost his marriage and his business.

Stottlemeyer showed him a picture of Barlier and Chalmers. The man instantly recognized Chalmers as the man who'd been blackmailing him.

The captain managed to prove that Le Roux's theory about Barlier's scheme was right.

When we returned to headquarters, we learned that the encryption on Dupon's computer had finally been cracked.

Chalmers had been using the computer to deplete bank accounts, clone credit card numbers, and shift the funds to banks in Switzerland and the Cayman Islands. Le Roux passed that aspect of the case to a special division of the police department that focused on financial crimes.

All in all, I thought it was a busy and productive day. I left headquarters at four p.m. to give myself plenty of time to prepare for my dinner date.

On the way to the Métro station, I bought a small but powerful flashlight and some batteries. If I got separated from Barlier for any reason while we were underground, I wanted to be able to find my way out again.

I'd done a little research on the catacombs online at police headquarters, and a story I read gnawed at me a little. In November 1793 Philibert Aspairt, the gatekeeper at Val de Grâce hospital, decided to explore the underground quarries by candlelight for the fabled wine cellar of the Carthusian monks. He got lost and was never heard from again. Eleven years later, engineers mapping the catacombs stumbled on his skeleton, just a few feet away from an exit. They buried him where he was found.

Maybe the story was apocryphal, but I figured it was best to take precautions anyway.

I took the subway back to the hotel. As I emerged from the station at Charles de Gaulle Étoile, I spotted Monk scooting around on his *motocrotte*, but I didn't try to attract his attention. I wasn't interested in another lecture about how foolhardy he thought I was being.

I charged my cell phone, then showered and changed into fresh casual clothes. I put on a V-neck sweater, jeans, running shoes, and a light jacket, since I figured it was probably damp and at least ten degrees cooler underground than it was on the streets.

I tucked Antoine Bisson's map of the catacombs into my purse and grabbed my recharged cell phone, though it would be a miracle if I could get a signal a hundred feet below Paris in an abandoned limestone quarry.

The ride to the Musée d'Orsay Métro station was surprisingly fast, and I arrived a good fifteen minutes early. But when I got out of the train, Lucien Barlier was waiting for me on one of the benches, reading the newspaper.

He wore a suit-vest over a shirt that was open at the collar, and he flashed a smile with enough wattage to power a small village.

He folded the newspaper and left it on the seat beside him before striding over to greet me.

"It's good to see you," he said. "I was afraid you might not come."

"What made you think I'd stand you up?"

"Your boss," he said. "He really didn't want you to do this."

"He also doesn't want me eating tossed salads but I do it anyway. I make my own decisions, and I don't expect everyone to live their lives the same way that I do."

"You're a woman with an open mind."

"Does that mean you think you've got a shot at talking me into becoming a Freegan?"

"That's not my intention," he said.

"What are your intentions?"

I cringed all over the instant I spoke. I sounded like my dad talking to one of my high school boyfriends.

"I'd like to show you my world and learn something about yours."

"My world isn't that interesting," I said.

"I doubt that." He held out his hand to me. I took it and he led me down the long platform toward a railing at the mouth of the subway tunnel.

"This is the tricky part," he said. "The platform is monitored by closed-circuit cameras. We have to climb the rail, jump onto the track, and run into the subway tunnel before security can catch us and the next train goes through."

My heart started to race. There is something undeniably thrilling about breaking rules and taking risks.

"How much time do we have?"

"Two or three minutes," he said. "Oh, and try not to step on the electric rail."

"I'll keep that in mind," I said.

He vaulted over the railing and dropped onto the gravel beside the tracks. I did the same. He took my hand and we ran into the dark tunnels, which smelled of moisture and oil and urine.

I felt like I was in a scene in a movie and we were two tragic lovers on the run for a crime we didn't commit. The only thing we were guilty of was passion.

The reality and the fantasy were exhilarating.

I could feel a rumble under my feet and looked over my shoulder to see a train speeding into the station behind us. For a moment, I was afraid it wouldn't stop. But it did and I heard the hiss and hum of the train doors sliding open.

Barlier drew me away from the tracks and I was so close to the wall that my shoulder scraped the rough stone. It was a good thing I was wearing an old jacket.

"Hurry," he said.

It wasn't easy running on the gravel in the darkness. I didn't know where I was going. I tightened my grip on his hand. It was my lifeline.

I felt the rumble again. This time the train was definitely coming our way. Fast.

Barlier pulled me into a tiny alcove and held me tight against him as the train sped by inches away from us, creating a blast of wind that felt like it could sweep me onto the tracks.

But he held me firm. He smelled of soap and aftershave. It was a very masculine scent, with just a hint of mildewy dampness in it that probably came from his clothes, which he kept in his subterranean home.

I'd smelled that mildewy scent before, or something very much like it, in the darkness of Toujours Nuit. But not the aftershave. I clung to that difference as I clung to him.

The train seemed endless, shaking the ground, whipping us with wind. His arms were strong, his chest was warm, and I was tempted to rest my cheek against his shoulder, wrap my arms around his waist, and close my eyes.

When the train passed, I was almost sorry it had. It was easy to forget what it felt like to be held and how much I needed it.

That was when I heard the ticking from the pocket watch in his vest pocket. I remembered that Monk had heard ticking as the killer passed by him in the restaurant.

Maybe it wasn't the same ticking. Maybe I wasn't in a dark tunnel in the arms of a murderer.

Barlier reached behind him with one hand and opened the heavy metal door that he was leaning against.

The door led us into a narrow utility corridor lined with pipes and lit every few yards by a single lightbulb. It was only wide enough for us to move single file and bent nearly in half.

He took my hand and we hurried down the corridor until we reached a T intersection.

There were two miner helmets on the floor with flashlights mounted on them. He put one on and handed the other to me. He'd obviously left them there for us earlier.

"Now the fun starts," he said.

I thought it already had, but I didn't say anything. I strapped the helmet on my head and followed him down the corridor.

I could hear footsteps and voices closing in behind us, but Barlier didn't seem concerned.

We only went a short distance before he ducked under some pipes, swept aside a piece of corrugated metal, and revealed an opening just large enough to crawl through.

I was glad I'd decided not to wear my evening gown.

He gestured to me to go through it. Down the rabbit hole I went.

I scrambled through the hole into pitch-darkness on the other side. I remained on my hands and feet, unsure how low the ceiling might be.

Barlier came through the hole after me and, using a wire looped through the sheet of corrugated metal, closed the crawl space behind him.

A moment later we heard voices in the utility corridor and footsteps rushing past.

Once they were gone, Barlier flicked on the light on his helmet and so did I, illuminating a tunnel that was carved into the rocks. It was high enough for us to stand up straight and wide enough for us to walk side by side.

"Do you have to do this every time you come home?" I whispered.

He shook his head. "There are thousands of ways into the catacombs—manholes, basements, abandoned Métro stations, parking garages, even a few aboveground entrances hidden by brush in parks and vacant lots."

"So why didn't we use one of those?"

"I thought this would be a more memorable experience for you," he said. "Besides, this will take us along the scenic route."

Once again, he led the way and I followed him, only this time he didn't offer me his hand.

The temperature was cooler here than in the Métro station but still comfortable. I could smell the moisture in the air, the dirt, and the rocks.

We made several turns and switchbacks and then the tunnel opened into a large chamber. In the beams of his light and mine, I could see graffiti everywhere, paintings of people and animals, and crude sketches of people doing crude things.

On one wall, someone had carved a huge dinosaur skeleton into the rock. In another corner, someone had carved a series of faces that seemed to push against the rock as if it was a bedsheet.

Whoever had done those carvings had had to lug their tools down there, not to mention food, water, and light. Then they had spent weeks picking at the rock with a hammer and chisel, alone in the dank darkness.

Why had they done it? What did they hope to accomplish? Did they think their work would have a better chance of lasting there rather than in the world above? Was it a bid for immortality? Or was it something else entirely?

There were tiny nooks and crannies everywhere, thick

with hardened streaks of dripped wax where candles had once burned. Empty wine bottles were lined up on the floor against one wall.

We walked across the gallery into one of the many tunnels that branched off of it like spokes on a wheel. The artwork continued into the tunnel which was lined, wall and ceiling, with frescoes, carvings, paintings, cartoons, and sketches.

There were notes, initials, and dates on the walls, too. Lots of dates: 1870, 1942, 1768, 2002, 1790, 1961. I was running backward and forward and sideways through time.

This wasn't just a labyrinth—it was a time machine.

Far from being a dark hole, these tunnels were a kaleidoscope of color, images, and words, caught in fleeting bursts of light by our headlamps.

It was far too much for me to absorb, but in trying to, I realized I'd lost all sense of direction. I was grateful for the map in my purse and, every so often, the glimpse of a street sign or building address on the wall amid the art.

I noticed a feculent odor that was getting stronger the deeper we got into the tunnel. If this was what the catacombs smelled like, I wouldn't be eating much dinner, even if Gordon Ramsey was there to prepare it.

I wasn't any kind of expert on effluent, but as the odor got stronger, it smelled less like sewage and more like a barn.

"Do you keep farm animals down here?" I asked.

"No, of course not," he said. "What you're smelling is the manure we use for fertilizer."

We turned a corner and walked into a long chamber lit by electric lamps. It was like *les catacombes*, only instead of bones, there were mushroom beds stretching as far as my eye could see.

The rows were ridged, like a Ruffles potato chip, with narrow pathways in between them where a half dozen people in dirty overalls were spreading manure with their bare hands and packing it with their knees. It was a sight I hoped Monk never had to see.

"These abandoned quarries are ideal for growing mushrooms," Barlier said. "The air is moist, the temperatures are perfect, and the powdered dirt is rich in salt."

"What kind of manure are you using?"

"Horse," he said. "The best fertilizer on earth. It's natural, abundant, and rich in ammonia, nitrogen, phosphates, and potassium. But we're very particular about where we get ours."

"You don't sweep it off the streets?"

"There aren't enough horses in Paris to meet our needs. We use two thousand tons of manure a year for our mushroom beds, and it has to be pure and chemical-free. So we buy our manure directly from farms outside of Paris, where the horses are more likely to be worked hard, kept with other animals, and fed a steady diet of good, dry straw."

"You buy it? With money? Doesn't that violate your Freegan ethos?"

"I didn't say that we never use money," he said. "We only buy what others haven't discarded or that we can't legally obtain through barter or donation. Prescription drugs and medical care, for instance. Growing mushrooms and selling them is the one thing we do to generate cash."

Identity theft might be another thing they did for money, but I didn't ask him about that.

"Is there really a demand for mushrooms grown down here?"

"These are Paris white mushrooms," he said. "They

are considered a delicacy. In the nineteenth century, thousands of tons of mushrooms were harvested from these caves and tunnels each year. We're the last still doing it here, the old-fashioned way. You'll find our gourmet mushrooms on the menus of some of the finest restaurants in Paris."

I wondered if that included Toujours Nuit, and if that would explain the specks of horse manure recovered from the floors the night of Aimee Dupon's murder.

There was, of course, another more unsettling explanation that I didn't want to think about. Even so, I intentionally stepped in some of the manure so Le Roux's forensics experts could scrape my shoes later to see if the poop matched the sample they'd recovered, though I was willing to bet that it did.

"I assume there will be mushrooms on our menu tonight," I said.

"Of course," he said. "Young, plump, and farm fresh."

We continued across the mushroom beds and into another richly decorated tunnel. We passed through more chambers, braced with stone pillars to prevent cave-ins and covered with three centuries' worth of art by transients, fugitives, revolutionaries, and artists and *official* signage and notations left by engineers, quarry workers, mushroom growers, and soldiers.

But this wasn't just an immense art gallery or a historical landmark. It was also a place for parties and illicit encounters. There were lots of empty bottles, cans, and fast-food containers littering the chambers, as well as soiled mattresses, sleeping bags, and used contraceptives.

The odor of the mushroom bed had long since disappeared and now I could smell moisture again, carried on a light breeze of cool air.

After a few more twists and turns, we walked down a set of winding stone steps that looked as if they'd been carved ages ago and then worn smooth by the feet that had trodden upon them for centuries.

The steps led to a lancet archway that opened into what I assumed was another chamber. Dim, flickering light spilled out, and I could hear what sounded like water gently lapping against a shore.

Barlier stood beside the archway and beckoned me to walk through.

"Welcome to my home," he said.

I stepped past him and what I saw took my breath away.

27

Mr. Monk's Assistant Has Dinner

One of my favorite movies from my childhood is *Willy Wonka and the Chocolate Factory*. There's this great scene where the kids discover a massive, edible candy garden with a chocolate river flowing through it, and Gene Wilder starts singing about living in a world of pure imagination.

Now I knew how those kids felt.

I stepped into a huge, vaulted chamber carved out of the limestone, supported by elegant columns and lit by dozens of table lamps and hundreds of candles, the flickering light reflecting off the shimmering surface of the underground lake to my right.

There was a rowboat moored to the sandy shore and, to my left, an Astroturf putting green stretched deep into a wide tunnel. The expanse was lit by an assortment of discarded table lamps, set in carved-out niches, their power cords attached to the bundles of utility lines that ran along the tunnel walls.

In front of me, at the end of a stone path that crossed

the putting green, was Barlier's open living area, decorated in a style that I'll call Swiss Family Robinson Thrift Shop Chic.

The kitchen was built into a shallow cavern, the wooden shelves neatly filled with dishes and silverware, paper plates and plastic utensils, pots and pans, bottled water and canned foods. There were a wine rack filled with bottles and several appliances, including a small refrigerator, a hot plate, a microwave, and even an espresso machine.

The dinner table was a collection of wooden and plastic chairs organized around a piece of cloth-covered plywood laid upon stacked-stone legs. The settings for our candlelight dinner were already laid out.

Outside of the kitchen, shelves were carved into the stone and stuffed with books, DVDs, and CDs. There were several televisions, a DVD player, and an old desktop computer perched on crates.

I could see several curtained caverns, which I assumed he used as closets, since I saw some clothes hanging behind a half-closed curtain.

He'd hung two hammocks between pillars and aligned several folding beach chairs and a chaise longue around a fire pit.

For decoration, there were area rugs, potted fake flowers, and plastic trees, and the walls of the living area were adorned with framed posters and paintings.

Barlier was clearly delighted by my slack-jawed reaction to his subterranean home.

"It's amazing," I said.

"I always wanted to have a lakefront home on a golf course," he said. "I just never thought it would be underground."

"It's like something out of *Phantom of the Opera*, only you aren't wearing a mask."

"We all wear masks," he said.

Barlier sauntered past me to the first hole of his putting green, where he had a bag of clubs. He extracted an odd-shaped high-tech putter with a face like a warped waffle iron.

"Would you like to play a few holes before dinner?"

He tapped a golf ball and sent it rolling into the first hole.

"Miniature golf has never been my game," I said and gestured to the lake. "Is that freshwater?"

"It is, from a natural spring, though I still wouldn't drink it. But it's safe to bathe in, pretty to look at, and great for hitting a bucket of golf balls by."

I walked across the stone path to his living area. "Everything you have is so out in the open. Aren't you afraid some *Cataphiles* might come here and steal all of this?"

He shrugged. "I'm not really attached to material things and it was all scavenged from the trash anyway. There's nothing here that can't be easily replaced. Besides, I usually know when someone is in the tunnels. Those TVs are hooked up to the city's closed-circuit public surveillance system."

I suddenly remembered Inspector Gadois showing us the surveillance-camera footage of Aimee Dupon following Monk and me as we were sightseeing in Paris. We didn't see anyone else but her trailing us on the footage. But it never occurred to us that someone might have used those same cameras to follow us from afar.

Barlier could have followed us without leaving the comfort of his hammock. Of course if he could do it, so could someone else. The same utility lines he'd tapped in to for the video feed ran throughout the caverns under the city.

Barlier went to the table and pulled out a seat for me. "Please sit down while I prepare our dinner."

I sat down and he went into the kitchen, bringing out a basket of bread, some cheese, and a bottle of wine.

While I noshed on hors d'oeuvres and sipped my wine, Barlier put on a CD, the classical music echoing off the walls. The acoustics were perfect. Being there that night was unlike any experience I'd ever had before. Unforgettable, in fact. And I had Monk to thank for it.

I hated to admit it, even to myself, but he was right that taking on a homicide investigation would show me a side of Paris I would never have seen otherwise. And to have an experience that was unique and entirely different from the one I'd had with Mitch.

I was pondering the pros and cons of sharing that realization with Monk when Barlier served me a garden salad of lettuce, carrots, cucumbers, and white mushrooms with a light vinaigrette dressing.

"All of this came from the trash?" I said as he set the salad down in front of me.

"Except for the mushrooms," he said, taking his seat across from me. "I picked them fresh this morning."

I hesitated for a moment and then took a bite. The salad tasted fresh and delicious. If he hadn't told me these were vegetables that had been thrown out, I never would have known from the look, the texture, or the taste.

"It's great," I said.

"You sound surprised."

"I saw where you did your shopping," I said and took another bite.

"It takes a little while to get past your aversion to anything that comes out of the Dumpster," he said. "But once you discover that something isn't inherently garbage just because someone decided to throw it out, the negative feelings disappear. All it takes is a day or two in the Dumpsters and seeing for yourself how many things are thrown away that aren't broken or rotten. Everyone should have to do it."

"For a guy who says he doesn't want followers, you do a lot of proselytizing."

"Forgive me," he said. "It's just something I am passionate about."

"I'm still not entirely clear how that passion developed," I said. "All you said is that one day you had an epiphany. Something must have prompted it. I can't believe you just woke up one day and decided to resign from society."

"I'm still part of our society," he said. "I just stopped devoting my life to earning money and spending it."

"You're dodging my question," I said.

"I am," he said.

"Then the answer must be something embarrassing," I said, "or painful."

He sighed and set down his fork.

"I was in love with a woman. She was a rising executive at a big corporation, just like I was, though in a different field. She was talented, ambitious, and competitive. We both were. Part of the game is looking like a winner: wearing the right clothes, driving the right cars, living in the right neighborhood. We made time for each other whenever we could, but they were stolen moments— work always came first. For both of us. Then one day, she was crossing the street and got hit by a truck. She was killed."

"I'm sorry," I said.

"She was talking on her cell phone and wasn't paying attention," he said.

"That could happen to anybody," I said.

"She was talking to me when she crossed the street,"

he said. "BMW had just redesigned the five series and I was leasing the previous model. I'd been driving it for less than six months. She was telling me to back out of the lease because it wouldn't look good for me to be seen in that car."

"You can't beat yourself up over what happened," I said. "She could have been talking to anybody about anything. It wasn't your fault that she got killed."

He cleared our salad plates and went to the kitchen to prepare the next main course. As he spoke, he took something out of the refrigerator and stuck it in the microwave.

"I know that. It was an accident. But the fact remains that she died worrying about leasing a car we didn't need simply because of how it looked to others. It made me realize how pointless and superficial our lives were, how much time we lost together, and how much joy we'd missed out on because we were so caught up in earning money and showing off our status, which was measured by what we bought. There had to be more to life. There had to be another way to live. That's when I had my epiphany."

Now the drastic changes he made in his life made a lot more sense to me. He was motivated by grief, anger, and guilt. I'm not implying that he didn't believe wholeheartedly in the Freegan philosophy, but there was more behind it than concern for our society, our environment, and his fellow man. He was doing penance.

That was my amateur-psychologist take on it, anyway.

"So you've tried to make something good come from the tragedy."

"I wasn't trying to change the way other people thought or behaved," he said. "I was only trying to change myself. That's still true. But I would be dishonest if I said I wasn't pleased that others have chosen to follow my example."

"But Bob Smith went in a different direction," I said.

"He did," Barlier said. The microwave dinged. He took out a platter and, with his back to me, began putting whatever it was on our plates.

"He took material from the trash he could use for identity theft and blackmail," I said. "Was that his new direction, or were you doing that, too?"

Barlier brought me my dinner plate and, to his credit, didn't dump it in my lap for accusing him of being a crook in his own home.

"That's game hen stuffed with wild rice, brussels sprouts, and mashed potatoes," he said, went back to the kitchen for his own plate, then sat down across from me.

I hadn't started eating yet. He looked at me and sighed.

"That was Bob's idea. He thought we should punish the rich, the industry barons, and CEOs who not only benefit the most from our consumer society but, on a personal level, indulge in more waste. He felt they deserved to lose some cash. The production and distribution of products create untold social injustices and inequities, not to mention enormous waste of natural resources. They profit from that. We could use the money to support conservation causes, help those victimized by our consumer society, and promote our cause."

"You had a problem with that?" I asked and started eating my game hen. It was excellent.

"It's illegal," he said.

"So is living down here," I said, "and tapping into the utility lines to get electricity, cable television, and phone service, and using the city's closed-circuit cameras."

"What Bob was doing was a different degree of illegal, at least for me," he said. "It went against what I believed in, and if he was caught, it could destroy the Freegan culture. So he left."

"And took a lot of others with him," I said, "including Aimee Dupon."

"She was very angry with corporations," he said. "Her father devoted his life to one, and just before he retired, it turned out the greedy execs had pillaged the pension fund to finance their excessive lifestyles. Her dad was left with nothing. She wanted to get back at them, and Bob offered her a way to do it."

"You took an ethical stand," I said.

"My whole life now is about living ethically," he said.

"A more cynical person, even if he believed you weren't involved in the identity theft and blackmail, could view what Bob did, and the threat he posed to you, as a strong motive for murder."

"Are you that cynical?"

Before I had a chance to answer, Adrian Monk did it for me.

"It has nothing to do with cynicism," Monk said, "and everything to do with the evidence."

We turned and saw Monk in his sanitation uniform coming through the archway, followed by Stottlemeyer, Le Roux, and Antoine Bisson, a pair of night-vision goggles around his neck.

"You're under arrest," Monk said.

28

Mr. Monk Solves Two Murders

I got up and faced Monk as he crossed the putting green. "What are you doing here?"

I was angry and I didn't try to hide it.

"I thought I just explained that," he said.

Chief Inspector Le Roux stepped forward and bowed apologetically. "I'm sorry that we intruded on your evening, but Monsieur Monk was adamant."

"He's always adamant," I said.

"Monk was going to have Bisson bring him down here with or without us," Stottlemeyer said, looking around in amazement. "I thought it would be better for everyone if we came along. Is this place for real?"

"As long as you're here, pull up a chair," Barlier said. "Have something to eat with us."

"We didn't come here on a suicide mission," Monk said. "We came to solve the murders of Nathan Chalmers and Aimee Dupon."

"I sincerely hope that you succeed," Barlier said. "But you won't find your answers here."

"Only the missing murder weapon." Monk motioned to the putter that Barlier left lying on the green. "The pattern on that putter matches the wound on Chalmers' skull."

"Incroyable," Le Roux said and squatted beside the putter, staring at it closely. "I believe it does."

And now that I thought about it, I realized that I did, too.

Damn.

Monk was right all along, not that it was a surprise. He was always right when it came to murder.

All the clues were in front of me, and I saw them this time, so why did I keep giving Barlier the benefit of the doubt?

Was I so caught up in my pathetic romantic fantasies that I willingly deluded myself?

I was angrier at myself than I was at Monk for showing up or at Barlier for being a killer.

"If I killed Bob," Barlier said, "do you really think I would keep the murder weapon in my home?"

"You can't throw anything out," Monk said. "Your ethos is also your undoing."

"There are probably thousands of identical putters on the market," Barlier said. "Anyone could have killed Bob with one of those."

"Seeing how and where you live, I'm sure you didn't clean this putter thoroughly enough," Monk said. "The forensics unit will find traces of his blood and skin on it and that will be that."

"Even if they do, it proves nothing," Barlier said, his voice tinged with anger now. "You can see how easy it is to come in here. Anybody could have used that putter to kill him and then put it back in my bag."

"Perhaps a judge would believe that," Monk said,

striding to the kitchen area, "if not for all the evidence that proves you murdered Aimee Dupon."

"You bastard," Bisson said, glaring at Barlier. "How could you?"

"I didn't kill her," Barlier said to Bisson. "I loved her."

"That's not what you told us this morning," Stottlemeyer said.

"I may not have been entirely honest about my feelings," he said. "But that was only to avoid casting suspicion on myself. You can't blame me for that."

"We can arrest you for it," Le Roux said.

"Not without proof that I had something to do with her death and I didn't."

"You brainwashed her," Bisson said. "You made her think that this was how people should live. And when she left you the way she left me, you killed her."

"That isn't true," Barlier said.

"The evidence says otherwise," Monk said. "Here's what happened—"

"Allow me," I interrupted and faced Barlier, who looked at me with disappointment, as if I'd betrayed him. "You followed us and Aimee Dupon to Toujours Nuit using the city's own surveillance system. You told me there are thousands of ways into the tunnels, including basements. You used the tunnels to get to Toujours Nuit and entered through the basement, which is why no one saw you enter or leave the restaurant."

"That's because I wasn't there," Barlier said.

"You made a mistake," I said. "You tracked horse manure from the mushroom garden onto the restaurant carpet."

"The horse manure proves nothing," he said. "Anyone could have done what you just described. It doesn't mean that it was me."

"He's got a point," Le Roux said.

"We smelled your musty clothes in the darkness," I said. "We heard the ticking of your pocket watch."

"I would recognize the ticking anywhere," Monk said.

"That's not proof," Barlier said. "You have nothing that puts me in the restaurant that night."

"We don't," Monk said. "But you do."

"What are you talking about?" Barlier said.

"After the murder, I noticed that the garbage can outside of the dining room was empty," Monk said. "There wasn't even a bag inside. That's because you took the bag with you."

"That's absurd," he said. "I wasn't in the restaurant. And while I may forage through Dumpsters, I don't take all the trash from every garbage can that I see."

"Before we were served, I asked the waitress to bring us new plates because ours were chipped," Monk said. "She argued that the plates were perfectly good, but I insisted that she throw them out for public safety. So she did. You overheard the conversation."

Monk picked up a napkin and used it to take a plate off the shelf in the kitchen. He held it up for all of us to see.

"This was my plate," he said. "But you thought it was just fine to use. You couldn't stand the idea of it going in the trash."

"You were eating in pitch-blackness," Le Roux said. "How could you possibly recognize the plates?"

"I felt them," Monk said.

"But you didn't see them," Le Roux said.

"No two chipped plates are the same," Monk said. "And if you examine the manufacturer's mark underneath, you will see they are the same plates used by Toujours Nuit. If that's not enough, I am certain you will find my fingerprints, as well as those of the waitress and other restaurant staff, on the plate."

Barlier shook his head. "You honestly believe I murdered Aimee and then brought your plate home because I couldn't bear it being thrown out?"

"Not just my plate," Monk said. "But Natalie's, too."

"I would have to be insane to do that," Barlier said.

"Look how you are living," Monk said. "Case closed."

"Indeed," Le Roux said. "Monsieur Barlier, you are under arrest for the murders of Nathan Chalmers and Aimee Dupon. Stand up and put your hands behind your back."

Barlier did as he was told, staring at me as Le Roux handcuffed him.

"I'm not guilty," he said.

Le Roux looked at Monk. "*Incroyable, Monsieur.* You are the greatest detective I have ever known."

Stottlemeyer groaned. "Did you have to say that, Inspector?"

"But it is true," Le Roux said.

"He's right, Captain," Monk said. "It is."

Monk was probably the most immodest detective Le Roux had ever known, too.

"Monsieur Bisson," Le Roux said, "would you be so kind as to lead us back to the street?"

"My pleasure," Bisson said, slipped the night-vision goggles on, and headed for the archway.

I remained in my seat for a moment, thinking about what had transpired. There was still one question that hadn't been answered.

I was about to say something about it when Monk, as if reading my mind, did the most extraordinary thing.

He put a finger to his lips and winked at me.

*   *   *

Lieutenant Disher and Inspector Gadois and two uniformed police officers were waiting for us outside of the Musée d'Orsay Métro station when we emerged onto the street. There were two police cars parked at the curb.

Monk still held the two plates and Stottlemeyer had the putter.

Chief Inspector Le Roux led Barlier over to Gadois. "Take this man to headquarters and charge him with the murders of Nathan Chalmers and Aimee Dupon."

"Yes, sir," Gadois said and guided Barlier into the backseat of one of the cars.

Disher dismissed Barlier with a glance. "So that's Natalie's Phantom of the Opera. Big deal. I don't see the appeal. He looks like an ordinary perp to me."

"It must be the French accent," Stottlemeyer said. "Women can't resist it."

"That's why I've been working on mine," Disher said.

I had to turn my back before I either punched one of them or got sick to my stomach or both.

"Thank you, Monsieur Monk, for seeing that justice was done," Antoine Bisson said. "That scum might never have been caught if not for you."

"The cruel irony is that prison will be a step up from the way he's been living," Monk said.

Le Roux opened the trunk of his car, took out some large evidence bags, and brought them over to Monk, who carefully placed the two plates into them.

"I hope Lucien's conservation philosophy can survive this," I said.

Bisson looked at me. "What is there to preserve? It was corrupt from the start. They were stealing money."

Stottlemeyer bagged the putter and laid it in the trunk.

Monk joined the two detectives at the car and had a few words with Le Roux that I didn't hear.

"Chalmers was stealing it," I said, "not Barlier."

"How do you know?" Bisson asked.

"It violated his ethics," I said.

"But murder didn't," Bisson said. "What a bizarre set of ethics he has."

Le Roux approached Bisson. "We'll take you home and take your statement there. It will be more comfortable for you than going down to headquarters."

"Merci," Bisson said.

We all got into the car. Monk and Le Roux in the front, Stottlemeyer, Bisson, and me in the back.

We were silent during the ride, each lost in his own thoughts. The only voices came from the police-band radio. But I did notice something odd in the rearview mirror.

Gadois and Disher weren't on the way to headquarters with Barlier. They were right behind us.

29

Mr. Monk and the Work of Art

By the time we reached Bisson's building, Gadois had gone in another direction. I guess Bisson's place was on the way to headquarters after all. The five of us got out of the car and trooped upstairs to the apartment.

Bisson turned to Monk as he unlocked his door. "Do you promise not to vandalize my artwork?"

"I wouldn't touch it," Monk said.

We walked inside. Nothing seemed to have changed. He hadn't even made any progress on the work on his easel.

"How come you didn't have that self-control last time you were here?" Bisson asked Monk. "I had to stop you from *fixing* my other work."

"You mean your confession," Monk said, standing in front of the painting that Bisson had prevented him from retouching.

The painting was a still life of a finished meal, a fish skeleton on a chipped plate.

And then I realized what I was looking at. So did everyone else except, perhaps, Antoine Bisson. Or maybe he just didn't want to acknowledge it. I could understand why.

"I haven't named the piece yet," Bisson said.

"Then I've just saved you the trouble," Monk said. "That's my dinner plate from Toujours Nuit."

"That's just a chipped plate. You're projecting yourself and your own experiences into the work," Bisson said. "That's the emotional power of great art. Don't worry. I take it as a compliment."

As if on cue, Disher, Gadois, and Barlier entered the apartment. I immediately noticed two things: Barlier wasn't handcuffed anymore and Gadois held the evidence bag containing the chipped plate.

Monk took the bag from Gadois and held the plate up to the wall alongside the painting.

It was an exact match.

"You even got the appetizer right," Monk said. "Smoked fish, though we never got a chance to eat it."

"I hope you took it back in a doggie bag," Disher said. "Smoked fish is very tasty."

"Barlier killed Aimee," Bisson said. "You proved it."

Monk shook his head. "Barlier's insane but he's not stupid. Here's what happened. You killed Chalmers with Barlier's putter, then disposed of the body somewhere in the tunnels, hoping it would be found by some Cataphiles and Barlier would go down. But my guess is that Barlier stumbled on the body first. He didn't know how Chalmers was killed, or who did it, but he knew he'd be the prime suspect anyway. So he scattered the bones in the one place he thought they'd never be found."

"I'm still amazed that they were," Barlier said, nodding his head in confirmation of Monk's remarks.

"But once I found them, everything began to unravel,"

Monk said, shifting his gaze back to Bisson. "You knew Aimee would realize the victim was Chalmers and, since she knew Barlier would never resort to violence, that you were probably the culprit. You didn't want to kill her, but you had to and you blamed Barlier for it, because he seduced her into the Freegan world to begin with. So you framed him."

Monk went on to say that it all went down the way he'd explained it before, only with Bisson in the villain role, watching us on surveillance cameras and using the tunnels to get into, and out of, the restaurant.

When Bisson heard Monk demand that the waitress throw out our plates, he saw a concrete way to implicate Barlier in the murder. He was also careful to stand close enough to us for us to smell the mildew on his clothes and to hear the ticking.

"Except that the ticking of Barlier's pocket watch is not the same ticking I heard in the restaurant," Monk said. "You were using a stopwatch."

"You can tell the difference between two ticking watches?" Gadois said in astonishment. "And remember it?"

"It's no different from distinguishing between two voices," Monk said.

"Only for someone who can separate peanuts from their shells, mix them up, and then reconstruct them again," Stottlemeyer said.

"That's impossible," Le Roux said.

"I've seen him do it," I said, "for fun."

It was how he'd passed the time in Hawaii when he wasn't solving murders.

"It's a popular game in America," Monk said. "You should try it."

"You're crazier than Barlier," Bisson said.

"You were so eager for us to find him and the evidence you'd planted that you literally gave us a map showing us how to get there," Monk said. "I asked you to guide us to his pit tonight because I wanted to be certain you knew the way. You even led us through the mushroom garden to be sure we made the connection to the horse doo-doo. But that's when you made your big mistake."

"Bigger than painting something on his wall that only the murderer could have seen?" Stottlemeyer said.

"The mistake was *how* he saw what he painted," Monk said. "The night of the murder, he was wearing infrared goggles. That's how he moved freely around the pitch-black restaurant without using a light and it's how he led us to Barlier tonight."

Monk had just answered the question that was bothering me earlier—how had Barlier seen everything in the restaurant without turning on his flashlight? Now I knew why Monk hushed me. He didn't want me tipping Bisson off that everything that had just happened was staged for his benefit. I don't think Le Roux was in on it either until Monk whispered in his ear at the trunk of the police car outside of the Musée d'Orsay Métro station.

"Barlier could have worn night-vision goggles," Bisson said.

"But everything he owns is scavenged from the trash," Monk said. "Nobody would throw out a working pair of infrared goggles."

"So he bought them," Bisson said.

"Except he doesn't buy things. It goes against what he believes in," Monk said. "And he doesn't have any night-vision goggles in his home."

"He obviously ditched them," Bisson said.

"Why would he keep the putter he murdered Chalmers with, and salvage plates from the trash where he murdered Aimee Dupon, but throw away an expensive and useful pair of goggles?" Monk said. "It doesn't make any sense, does it?"

"I loved her," Bisson said softly, "more than life itself."

"Then you should have taken yours," Barlier said, "not hers."

"You're right," Bisson said and bolted for the window.

Stottlemeyer moved quickly, but not quick enough.

Bisson dove into the glass, his arms out in front of him, his head down, his body straight, as if he was diving gracefully into a swimming pool instead of thin air.

By the time we all reached the shattered window, Bisson had already crashed headfirst through the awning of the falafel hut on the street below and fallen onto the grill, shards of glass raining down on him.

But Bisson was past feeling any more pain. He was past feeling anything at all.

I turned away, sickened, and Barlier held me. But the seasoned cops kept staring down at the gruesome sight as if they were regarding nothing more than a questionable stain.

"Now I understand why every French movie I've ever seen ends with a suicide," Disher said.

After Bisson was wheeled away in a body bag, and the crime scene techs had taken all their pictures, Monk began sweeping up the broken glass on the street with his official sanitation department broom, which had been stowed in the trunk of Le Roux's car.

I stepped up to him as he worked. "You don't have to do that, Mr. Monk."

"I like it," Monk said. "It helps me think."

"What's left to think about?" I asked. "You've already solved the murders."

"A day later than I should have," Monk said.

"I was going to ask you about that," I said. "You saw that painting in Bisson's apartment yesterday. Why didn't you make the connection then?"

"I think I was doubly distracted. I was shocked by the pornographic painting of Aimee Dupon and totally disgusted by everything I'd heard about Lucien Barlier's crazy and unsanitary lifestyle," Monk said. "You were right, Natalie. I wanted Barlier to be the guy so much that it tainted my perspective on everything."

"So what made you realize your mistake?"

"This," Monk said, tipping his head toward the broom. "I was on my *motocrotte*, going up and down the Champs-Élysées, and in a moment of startling clarity and peace that only comes from deep cleaning, it just hit me. I remembered the painting and realized that Bisson was the killer. Once I got past being ashamed of myself, I realized that I still had to prove it."

"But without the plate, you had nothing."

Monk nodded. "I thought all hope was lost."

"You always think that," I said.

"But then I remembered the empty trash can outside the dining room and I knew where I could find the plate," Monk said. "All I needed was to get Bisson to take me there and incriminate himself in his eagerness to bring down Barlier."

"What I don't get is why Bisson painted a picture on his wall that directly implicated himself in the murder."

"He's an artist. Their best work comes from their tortured souls," Monk said.

"And you know that because . . . ?"

"I am something of an artist myself," Monk said, "not with paint or clay, but with solving murders."

There was no doubt that Monk's psychological hang-ups were what made him such a good detective. It was also why he refused to take Dioxynl except when traveling. It stole his mojo.

"Besides," Monk continued, "Bisson thought he was the only one in the dining room who actually saw the plate."

"But Bisson was counting on you recognizing the plates at Barlier's."

"He was counting on me to *find* them," Monk said. "Bisson never expected me to positively identify them on sight after only touching them briefly in the dark."

Of course Bisson hadn't expected that. It was like a superpower, and as far as I knew, Adrian Monk was the only man on earth who possessed it.

"He obviously didn't know you very well," I said.

"But you do, maybe better than I know myself. You saw the mistake I was making and tried to warn me."

"It works both ways," I said. "That first night here, when I had my emotional breakdown on the street, you knew why before I did. I was glad you were there for me."

Monk looked up from his sweeping at me. "I helped you?"

"Yes," I said, "you did."

"In our relationship, isn't it supposed to be the other way around?"

"Sometimes things don't work out the way you plan, Mr. Monk." I gestured to the morgue wagon. "Just ask Antoine Bisson."

Monk and I stayed in Paris for two more days. We spent a day giving statements to the police so they could close the file on the two murder cases. And then we took one day off for ourselves.

I spent my free day with Lucien Barlier, who turned out to be a wonderful tour guide aboveground, too. Things remained chaste between us, except for a phenomenal good-bye kiss.

I returned to the hotel on our final night in a relaxed, slightly melancholy mood. I was eager to go home and yet, at the same time, a little sad to be leaving.

It turned out Monk was feeling the same way.

When I walked up, Monk was reluctantly handing over the keys to his *motocrotte* to Pierre, who was pretty depressed himself. The sanitation worker's paid vacation was coming to an end.

Pierre scooted off in the *motocrotte*, Monk looking after him forlornly.

"This was a great vacation," Monk said.

"Yes, it was," I said.

"I'm actually glad that you blackmailed me into it," he said.

"Thank you."

"But you will destroy those pictures now, right?"

"Absolutely," I lied.

I intended to keep the pictures of the two of us, singed and covered in muck, for sentimental reasons.

But I wouldn't embarrass Monk by showing the photos to anyone else, except perhaps Julie, and even then I would make her take a blood oath of secrecy.

Maybe, someday, when Monk conquered his phobias, I could show them to him again, too, and maybe he would appreciate that I'd captured our once-in-a-lifetime near-death moment in Germany for posterity.

"Now that you're a seasoned European traveler," I said, "maybe you'll come back someday."

"And solve more murders," he said.

"You might want to try enjoying a vacation without anyone getting killed."

"What would I do with myself?"

"You could wash sidewalks," I said. "Think about it. You could be the first American to clean streets in all the great capitals of Europe. But why stop there? Why not clean Asia, Africa, and the Middle East, too?"

Monk nodded. "It's something to dream about."

"We all need that," I said.

"But first, we have a scathing letter to write."

"A letter?" I said. "To whom?"

"The French government, of course, about all the things they need to fix. You have the list, don't you?"

"No," I said, "I thought you were keeping the list."

The truth was that I was hoping he'd forget about his grievances with French culture once we got into investigating the murders.

I should have known better.

"It's okay." Monk tapped his head. "Lucky for you, I've got an amazing memory."

"Oh, yes," I said, "lucky me."

Monk is called in to consult whenever there is a crime that totally stumps Stottlemeyer and his detectives. He inevitably solves the mystery so easily that the captain feels stupid for not seeing the clues himself. I know this because the captain has said so on many occasions.

That's one thing I really like about Stottlemeyer. He always expresses his gratitude and gives Monk all the credit he deserves. But I know it takes a toll on him. Relying on Monk implies that the captain and his men weren't good enough to solve the crime on their own . . . or at least not as quickly.

What's got to make it even worse is that even on the homicide cases that Stottlemeyer and his detectives *could* and undoubtedly *would* solve on their own, Monk often figures out the solution while they are still taking out their notebooks.

The fact is that every time Monk performs brilliantly at a crime scene, he's unintentionally demonstrating that Stottlemeyer isn't as good at the job as he is.

Monk is oblivious to that, of course. But I'm not.

It's been going on like that day after day, year after year, and it's got to be hard on the captain's self-esteem.

I know it's hard on mine and I don't even want to be a detective.

Witnessing Monk's natural ability and affinity for his work over and over again only reminds me that I've yet to demonstrate anything like that in my own life.

It's got to be much worse for Stottlemeyer, who is not only in the same profession, but in a leadership position.

All those conflicts were on my mind the morning we walked into the lecture hall in one of the newer buildings at the University of California San Francisco's law school.

We were supposed to meet Stottlemeyer at headquarters to pick up Monk's paycheck and, by extension, my own, but the captain and Disher got called away to investigate a shooting at the university. Since we were desperate for the money, and Monk couldn't resist visiting a crime scene, we went out there, too.

It was a big lecture hall with dry-erase boards and flat-screen monitors behind the lectern. Pretty soon, chalkboards and erasers will be as extinct as typewriters, vinyl records, and carbon paper.

All the seats in the room had power plugs and tables for laptop computers. I imagined that being a student here was like listening to lectures in the business-class section of a British Airways jet. The only thing missing was someone pushing a cart down the aisles serving beverages and snacks.

I did a rough head count of the students in the room. There were about a hundred of them and they were still in their seats, fidgeting nervously as a handful of detectives questioned them one by one.

The questions probably had to do with the dead guy.

The victim looked to me like one of the students, except that unlike the others he had a gunshot wound in his chest and he was dead.

His body was sprawled at the bottom of the aisle that ran down the left side of the room. There were streaks of blood on the floor that indicated he'd rolled halfway down the aisle before his foot snagged on one of those fancy seats.

I could see a gun lying in the blood. A numbered yellow evidence cone marked the spot in case nobody had noticed the weapon, the blood, or the body.

Lieutenant Disher was in front of the lecture hall, pencil poised over his notebook, interviewing a jowly man who had gray hair and wore a suit and tie.

The jowly man had a short beard that I figured he grew to give his first chin more definition and distract attention from his second one.

He held his chins high, his back straight, and stared down his long nose at Disher as if regarding a misbehaving child. I wondered if he'd had that posture before he became a professor, or if it had come with the job, or if it was a vain attempt to stretch his flabby neck taut.

Lieutenant Disher was in his midthirties, eager-to-please and surprisingly friendly for a homicide detective, which put most people at ease and got them to open up to him, revealing far more than they would to anybody else with a badge. But from what I could see I didn't think the man Disher was talking to then was one of those people.

There were a couple of crime scene technicians taking pictures and gathering forensic evidence and trying very hard to look as cool as David Caruso and Marg Helgenberger while they worked. They weren't succeeding.

They were too self-conscious about striking poses and they didn't have the wardrobe, the stylists, or the buff bodies to pull it off.

Stottlemeyer wasn't trying to impress anyone. In fact, he looked more haggard and weary than usual. His jacket and slacks were wrinkled and his bushy mustache needed trimming. He was standing with his hands on his hips, staring down at the body as we approached.

He acknowledged us with a quick glance and a nod.

"You didn't have to come all the way down here," Stottlemeyer said.

"We came for Mr. Monk's check," I said.

"It's back at the office," he said. "Stop by later this afternoon and I'll have it for you."

Monk crouched down to examine the body, holding his hands out in front of him like a movie director framing a shot with his thumbs.

"Mr. Monk thought if he helped you out here, we wouldn't have to wait until this afternoon."

He eyed me suspiciously. "It was Monk's idea."

"I might have given him some advice on the matter," I said. "The check is a week late as it is."

"The department keeps slashing my budget and I have to prioritize my spending," Stottlemeyer said. "I'm afraid consultants are at the bottom of the list."

"Then you can forget about getting any help from Mr. Monk today," I said. "He doesn't work for free."

"I don't need his help right now," Stottlemeyer said. "There's no mystery about what happened here."

"The guy on the floor burst into the room in the middle of class and pointed a gun at the professor," Monk said, standing up. "The gunman was about to shoot but the professor shot him first."

"That's exactly what happened," Stottlemeyer said.

"It was a clear case of self-defense and we've got a lecture hall full of eyewitnesses to back it up."

"What was the professor doing with a gun?" Monk asked.

"He's a former federal prosecutor who put a lot of scary people away in his day," Stottlemeyer said. "He's licensed to carry a concealed weapon."

Monk looked to the front of the room. "Is that Professor Jeremiah Cowan?"

"Yeah. You know him?" Stottlemeyer said.

"I took his Introduction to Criminal Law class when I was at Berkeley."

"That's the class he was teaching today," Stottlemeyer said. "But I don't think the lesson the students got was on the syllabus."

Monk rolled his head as if trying to work out a kink in his neck. But I knew it wasn't his neck that was bothering him. The kink was in his mind. There was some detail that wasn't fitting where it should and that worried me.

"You're not working today, Mr. Monk," I said. "You haven't been paid."

"I'm not working," he said.

"Then what was this?" I rolled my head the way he did.

"It was nothing," he said.

"Of course it was nothing," Stottlemeyer said. "This case was closed before you got here. There's nothing left to do now but the paperwork."

"Good," I said. "Then there's no reason you can't hurry back to the office to sign Mr. Monk's check."

Monk headed straight for Professor Cowan, who seemed to recoil at the sight of him approaching.

Stottlemeyer and I followed Monk, neither one of us too happy that he was getting himself involved in this.

"Oh my God," Cowan said. "It's Adrian Monk."

"You still remember me after all these years?" Monk said.

"Before each class, you drew lines on the chalkboard for me to write on," Cowan said. "You insisted that I use a fresh box of chalk. And you'd never let me erase the board. You had to do it yourself. It took you hours."

Monk looked at Stottlemeyer and me and shrugged with false modesty. "I was kind of a teacher's pet. The entire faculty loved me."

"You're fortunate I wasn't carrying a gun in those days," Cowan said.